HOLY
WATER

ALSO BY BRADLEY WRIGHT

Tom Walker

Killer Instinct

Holy Water

Blind Pass

Alexander King

THE SECRET WEAPON

COLD WAR

MOST WANTED

POWER MOVE

ENEMY LINES

SMOKE SCREEN

SPY RING

Alexander King Prequels

WHISKEY & ROSES

VANQUISH

KING'S RANSOM

KING'S REIGN

SCOURGE

Lawson Raines

WHEN THE MAN COMES AROUND

SHOOTING STAR

Saint Nick

SAINT NICK

SAINT NICK 2

HOLY WATER

For Tim, Chris, Abby, Tammy, and Chuck. From the moment I met all of you I've felt like part of the family. Thanks for all the great memories over the years. I love you like my own.

"Beauty is mysterious as well as terrible. God and devil are fighting there, and the battlefield is the heart of man."

— FYODOR DOSTOEVSKY

1

Tom Walker ran his fingers over the cassette tape cases filed in rows in his old Converse shoe box. He came to Otis Redding, thought about how he was literally going to be sitting on the dock of the bay—or lake, in his case—and removed it, pulled the cassette, and inserted it into the small, old-school boom box he'd ordered off Amazon. He'd ordered a lot of things from Amazon in the four weeks he'd been house-sitting on the lake for Chuck and Tammy Smith. Courtesy of a phone call from Alison Brookins to help Walker disappear for a while.

And disappear he had.

However, in a twist of irony, while getting lost—far away from the world of assassinations and violence he'd been living for so long—he felt as though he was actually finding himself. Walker wasn't big on psychobabble, but there was no denying he was a much different person since arriving at the lake. The thick ribeye steak cooking in the sous vide water bath beside the new boom box was a perfect example. A few weeks ago he didn't know what the hell a sous vide was. Now he'd spent more hours than he'd care to admit learning how it was the greatest way in the world to cook meat.

He pulled the steak from the water bath, and just like the videos said, he removed it from its air-sealed bag, patted it dry, and carried it out to the grill that he had going at full blast out on the deck. Otis was singing about being Mr. Pitiful. Walker thought some might see his time at the lake as such, seeing as how he was alone, experiencing Groundhog Day just about every day, but for the moment, it was really suiting him.

He reverse-seared the ribeye over the bright orange flame. The juices hissed at him as they released from the meat. One minute on both sides was plenty to get that nice char of crust that made each medium-rare bite so delicious. He turned off the propane, brought the steak inside, and placed it on the plate where he'd already air-fried (the air fryer another Amazon splurge) some asparagus. He knifed a big pat of homemade garlic-and-herb butter (another YouTube special) and placed it on top of the still sizzling steak to let it melt. On the tray he had some coarse sea salt, a glass, and a bottle of Angel's Envy rye whiskey. He'd given wine a couple of chances, but it just wasn't his thing.

Walker had picked up a local newspaper when he'd gone into town to get the steak from a local butcher, and he rolled it up and stuck it in his back pocket. He slid the handle of the boom box over his wrist, picked up the tray, and walked out of the kitchen. He turned right, navigating the stairs down to the basement. Walking past the ping-pong/pool table, he slid open the door and walked out, closed it, then walked down the lower deck's stairs onto the stone cuts that lined his way to the stairs leading to the dock, which was about a hundred feet down over the hill.

At that point, he probably could have made the trip with

his eyes closed, he'd walked it so many times, but then he'd miss the watercolor sky above from the sun that was setting on the side of the house opposite the lake. The stones gave way to the composite steps that led down to the dock. He walked across and over to the edge where he'd set up a little table and his one lonely "Mr. Pitiful" chair. He felt anything but pitiful, however, when he looked out over the rail, appreciating the expanse of Lake Chickamauga laid bare in front of him.

He set down his tray, and as he let his steak rest a couple more minutes, he took in the view. The day had been a scorcher, almost unbearable really, at a humid ninety-eight degrees. And though it had only cooled to eight-five at that point, the breeze rustling the surrounding oak and maple trees kept Walker from a full sweat. Lake Chickamauga was huge. It was a reservoir of the Tennessee river with over 810 miles of shoreline just outside Chattanooga, Tennessee. Supposedly it was also a killer bass fishing hub if one was into that sort of thing. Tom Walker was not.

He sat down at his table. Cut his steak into slices. Then cracked a very generous dusting of sea salt over top. He then poured himself a glass of whiskey and dug in. The cook was perfect. Crispy, salty crust that gave way to a burst of juicy, buttery, prime beefy flavor. A knock of the sweet rye whiskey paired perfectly. Otis Redding was still crooning as a fishing boat went trolling by. Walker had found that people on the lake loved to wave as they passed. He didn't mind reciprocating.

Halfway through his steak, and pour number two of the rye, Walker decided to pull out the paper. *The Chattanooga Times Free Press*. After one look at the very first story on the top of the front page, he really wished he'd never picked up that paper at all. The headline read DAUGHTER OF SODDY

DAISY MAYOR STILL MISSING. The headline was bad, but it was the picture beneath it of the twelve-year-old girl that ruined Walker's dinner. Not just because it was a sad story about an innocent girl, but because the girl in the picture looked almost identical to a girl Walker had shared a year with at one of his foster homes. His first kiss, no less, so Kelly Clark still held a special place in his heart, even though he hadn't seen her in over twenty years. Looking at the mayor's daughter was like seeing a ghost from his past, golden-blond curls and all.

It didn't help matters that the missing girl—Amy Turnberry—was taken from the town of Soddy Daisy, right where the lake house Walker was sitting for was located. Made it feel even closer to home. While Walker had absolutely no clue what it was like to have children, let alone have one go missing, he could only imagine how grief- and panic-stricken the girl's home must be. Did her parents live together? Did she have brothers and sisters? It was all just a really sad story. So much so that Walker put away the paper and focused on the lake and the whiskey in front of him.

Walker decided he was okay enough to finish the steak. Besides, it wasn't like he knew the girl or her family. He wasn't from Soddy Daisy. He had no connections. He supposed it was just the way Amy Turnberry reminded him of an old friend, one of the only producers of good memories he had from such a horrible upbringing.

He packed up his things and headed up the hill back to the house. The mosquitos would be arriving soon, and he wanted no part of that. As Kim, his foster mom, used to say, *"The skeeters really liked him 'cause he was so dang sweet."* Speaking of Kim, she'd called him the night before. She'd just watched a luau on the beach at her resort in Honolulu, Hawaii. She was all spun up. Walker was happy she was having fun. She'd said the name of the resort, Halekulani, or something like that. But it was either her hillbilly accent or a few too many Mai Tais that made it come out more like "Heylllleykyoulllaunee." Walker had laughed and wished her well.

It had been a busy day yesterday because Alison Brookins had also checked in (that's right, two phone calls was busy on the lake). Walker was happy to hear from her too. She had yet to be able to extract her money from her bank due to her being declared legally dead and all, but she was doing well. Staying with a friend in Miami. Trying to stay out of trouble. Walker didn't ask her to elaborate, so she didn't. But he was glad all was well.

Walker scraped his plate into the trash, rinsed it, then set it in the dishwasher. He thought for a minute about another whiskey, but he was going for a long run in the morning and didn't want it to drag him down. Instead, he grabbed his copy of *The Fireman* by Joe Hill, his boom box, the *Let's Stay Together* cassette by Al Green and headed out to the screened-in porch.

He flipped on the yellow porch light, because the evening's light had mostly gone. The lake was nearing blackness down the hill. He sat and enjoyed the novel for about an hour, then decided it was time to call it a night. He closed his book, shut off Al Green just as he was asking about how one can mend a broken heart, and headed upstairs to bed.

The master bedroom was on the main level. Just on the other side of the kitchen. But Walker didn't feel right about sleeping in another couple's bed, so he laid claim to one of the three spare bedrooms upstairs. Walker brushed his teeth, flossed, then hopped in the sack. About the same exact day as he'd had for the last thirty. And he hadn't grown tired of any one of them yet. But something was different that night. He felt . . . off. And when he reached over and shut off the lamp, the reason he felt off was the only thing he could see when he closed his eyes.

Amy Turnberry's innocent face.

It just didn't feel right to Walker that he was comfortable in that bed in Soddy Daisy, Tennessee, while she was torn away from the safety of her own. But what was right couldn't really matter to Walker. Who the hell was he? Just a stranger in a quiet corner of the earth, doing his best to keep his head down and his profile low. The article said the SDPD were all over it. She was the mayor's daughter after all. If anyone was going to get allocated resources in a missing persons case, it was going to be Amy.

That thought helped Walker relax, and he finally drifted off to sleep.

2

Walker woke up to the same amount of light coming through the windows as when he'd fallen asleep. Full dark. Just the way he liked it. If he ever woke up past six in the morning, he felt like the day was already shot. Luckily, it was only five a.m. Pretty much the same time he'd been waking up since his first trainer, John Sparks, drilled the habit into him, even after he'd had six straight fifteen-hour training days. "God took the seventh day off," John would say. "The enemy doesn't. So we don't have that luxury."

Old habits die hard.

Walker brushed his teeth, started a pot of coffee, then threw on his running gear. There was nothing he loved more than outworking everyone around him. In Soddy Daisy, it was easy. Most of these homes were where the owners would come for lazy weekends. They didn't know any better, but they were soft. Every last one of them. And the reason they could afford to be that way was because men like Walker got up and ate shit every day. Making sure they were protected. Walker never technically served in the military, but he went on many a mission piggybacking the best and the brightest.

Another good reason to get out early, especially on the most humid dog days of summer, was that it was cooler. But again, it was the darkness that Walker enjoyed. If there were people awake at that hour, he enjoyed the ability to stay incognito. On the way out the door, he grabbed his Spyderco Yojimbo 2 tactical knife and clipped it to the waistband of his running shorts. Always being prepared— another habit that would never die.

One hour, a bucket of sweat, six hundred tired muscles, and ten miles later, Walker made it back to the driveway. He kissed his fingers and placed them on his prized possession, his silver 1967 Shelby GT500 fastback, on his way to the front door. When he entered the house, the smell of freshly brewed coffee greeted him. The old Folger's jingle—*The best part of waking up*—traveled through his mind as he slipped off his shoes and his soaking-wet shirt.

The lake house he was keeping an eye on really was magnificent. The front door opened immediately to the stairs going up to his left, and on his right, a huge vaulted ceiling presided over an oversize living-room–dining-room combo. Windows for walls, the lake view could be seen all the way from the front door. Three-quarters of the way through the family room, past the stairs going up and the ones leading to the basement on his left, the wall opened up to a phenomenal kitchen. It was longer than it was wide, with a center island running the length of the entire kitchen. On the far right, the sink overlooked the wrap-around screened-in deck, then another little sitting nook with a second television. Beyond that corner of the kitchen was the master, which Walker hadn't even been in to look around. But he was sure it was nice.

Walker downed a glass of water, poured a cup of coffee, and then, as he'd done for the past thirty days, he enjoyed his coffee out on the deck as he watched the fishermen troll by. They were the only other people on the lake as dedicated as Walker. By afternoon, the fishing boats would turn into pleasure boats, hauling skiers and tubers behind them as they raced across the water. Walker checked his phone; it was Saturday, July 1st. There was a reason that day meant something to him, but he couldn't remember for the life of him why.

Then his phone dinged a text message. It was from the only other person who had Walker's cell phone number (aside from Chuck and Tammy, of course), and the only person he'd gotten to know even a little bit in Soddy Daisy. A man named Tim Lawson. Walker had only shared a couple of conversations with the man, but he liked him. Tim had been in California visiting his son's family the last couple of weeks but had kept in touch to make sure Walker had everything he needed.

Before Tim left, he'd told the story of why he was Walker's contact while Chuck and Tammy were away. It was a story for the ages, really. Tammy Smith, whom Walker was house-sitting for, had once been known as Tammy Lawson. Apparently, many years ago, after Tammy and Tim amicably split, Tammy went on to marry Chuck. One of Tim's friends. As if that weren't enough, they all remained friends, and to that very day they had dinners together, gathered when the kids were all in town, and made just about the best of their divorce that any two people could make, under any circumstances.

There were other reasons Walker liked Tim early on. Their senses of humor aligned, and Tim was great at telling stories—which Walker had always been a sucker for—and they both loved a good bite and a great drink. But more than that, Walker realized—on one of his thirty do-absolutely-nothing-days—Walker never had a father. Not even close. And though he'd only had a couple of kick-around conversations with Tim, Tim had a way of making Walker feel . . . special. It sounded weird to Walker when he'd first had the thought himself, but it was true. Tim cared about every word Walker said, and he really cared to get to know him. Very few people in the world had that wonderful trait auto-ingrained in them, but Tim Lawson was one of them. And he had it in spades.

Needless to say, Walker was happy to see the message from Tim. And even happier to see that Tim had made it back from California last night, and was wondering if Walker wanted some company that evening.

Tim's message read, "*I'll just be kicking around the farm if I don't come over there. I'll cook some burgers and we'll tell some stories. Get the boat out if you want.*"

Walker replied, "*Stories? Burgers? Boating? Sign me up.*"

Walker wasn't sure the way he texted was the way it worked. The only messages he'd ever really sent were work related, and all top secret, so he wasn't sure just how things translated in a civilian conversation. Tim was almost twice Walker's age, and Tim was better than he was at it. Walker chalked it up to having kids and grandkids that kept Tim young.

However bad Walker might have been at texting, Tim got the drift, and he would be coming over later that evening.

Walker set his phone down. The sunrise coming up over the trees across the lake was beautiful. However, it quickly became impossible to stare into, and it kicked up the morning heat at least five or six degrees. Walker laid his head back on the wicker chair and closed his eyes. At first, all he saw was a purple ball from where the sun imprinted, but that slowly gave way to that damn picture he saw in the paper yesterday. For whatever reason, he couldn't get away from Amy Turnberry. It was almost an eerie feeling at that point, enough to give his arms goose pimples.

He wasn't going to sit and wallow in something he had no part in, so he jumped up, went upstairs, and got in the shower. On his way through his room he clicked on the TV for some background noise.

Ten minutes later he was squeaky clean but shivering. Walker only took showers with the cold water on full. No heat. There were few things better for a human being than an ice bath, but since he had no access to those, cold showers would have to do. No matter how good or bad a day was going, a cold shower always made it better. It got the adrenaline pumping and the endorphins flowing.

Walker hopped out, toweled off, then stepped over to the mirror. Another benefit of a cold shower was zero steam. Making it easier to go right into combing back his dark hair that had become rather long in the last couple of months without a barber visit. He didn't mind it. And he didn't mind the stubble that had grown into more of a beard that week either. John Sparks would have called him a hippie for letting it all grow out, but Walker was tired of looking and acting how everyone else wanted him to.

He placed the comb by the sink and took a look at himself. He had actually leaned out a bit since making it to the lake. He always had a muscular, athletic frame, but lately he'd had more time to dedicate to real workouts, and the running was cutting his muscles even more. Looking in the mirror was hard for Walker. It always had been. It wasn't that he didn't like the way he looked; he just didn't like seeing the scars on his well-kept body.

Every time he took a trip down memory lane by tracing his scars, a darkness washed over him. He supposed any man felt the same who shared a childhood similar to his. But Walker's scars didn't stop forming after he left all the abusive homes. They'd only just begun. *Perks of the job*, he would always say to himself, to try to laugh the darkness away. But it never worked. He would always walk away from the mirror, remembering something terrible. He was getting better at shaking it off, though. Time away from the violence was helping with that.

Walker checked the clock on his phone, then sighed as he noticed the time. It seemed like he'd already lived a full day, yet it was only eight thirty in the morning.

All right, Carolyn, how 'bout an update on the Amy Turnberry situation. Maybe some good news?

Walker heard the news anchor on the television in the other room. He jogged around the corner to see what she had to say.

"Thank you, John. Unfortunately, there is no good news to report on the Soddy Daisy mayor's missing daughter, Amy Turnberry. Teams of men and women have been scouring the surrounding areas in what makes the fourth consecutive night. Law enforcement officials are trying to stay positive, but as you know, the longer these things drag out, the more worrisome they become. Hopefully, my report this afternoon will come with some more positive news. Back to you, John."

Walker felt his shoulders slump as he turned off the TV. In trying to understand why he suddenly cared so much about a case of a missing someone he had zero connections to, it was pretty obvious it was boredom. Like any out-of-work person, Walker had found something that meant nothing to him, and boredom had gone and morphed it into something important. So, like he had done four other times that week, he was going to go out and wash his car.

Even though his pride and joy was already spotless.

Maybe he would even crank some tunes and eat some bonbons. Wouldn't that be something.

3

Walker spent a couple of hours on his car. She had already been looking mighty fine, but last time he'd gone into town, he'd grabbed a container of wax. Now she was ready for the ball. Whatever that meant. It was just the first thing that came to Walker's mind. He needed a job. Something to occupy his time. More YouTube cooking videos, maybe?

The afternoon stretched on. He snacked on some deli meat and some Havarti cheese. He didn't have any idea what Havarti cheese was, but the woman at the deli counter had a beautiful smile, so obviously when she suggested Havarti, he bought it, as any self-respecting single man would. The cheese was good. Not a hell of a lot of flavor, but nice and creamy. Now he's a cheese critic?

Walker finished the novel, *The Fireman*, he was reading. Great book. He had another waiting in the wings, *Fairy Tale* by Stephen King, but he wasn't in the mood to start another five-hundred-page haul at the moment. So he did what any self-respecting lake goer would do on a Saturday afternoon:

he cleaned and sharpened his weapons. But only two of them. He wasn't crazy.

He'd taken apart and cleaned his Sig Sauer P365 XL hundreds of times, so he really did it on autopilot. All the while, his mind kept wandering to the woods, where he could envision herds of people out combing the land for Amy Turnberry. He wondered what the gain would be of taking the mayor's daughter if you weren't going to ask for a ransom. So it occurred to him, at least in theory, that maybe she just got lost. Or maybe a trafficker found her, but would they really be hanging around a lake trying to take twelve-year-olds? Wasn't that more of a city sort of grab?

He put the Sig back together, then grabbed the 500 grit whetstone (yet another Amazon package) and his Spyderco knife. He went to work sharpening the blade, but it didn't need much. Both tasks took up all of about fifteen minutes of his day. He was going to move on to his Daniel Defense AR15, but he'd just cleaned it two days ago. And he hadn't been to the shooting range that he'd been frequenting in nearby Hixson, Tennessee, in that time, so it hadn't had the chance to get dirty. Maybe he should go shoot. It would give him a chance to stay sharp—and an excuse to drive his car. Sounded like a win-win.

A couple of hours and a few hundred rounds later, Walker drove back through the neighborhood, turning heads everywhere he went. Literally the opposite of lying low. But to drive that car, a little attention was worth it. Plus, they didn't give a damn who was behind the wheel; the sound of her purring and her never-ending curves were the star of the show.

Walker pulled into the private driveway of the lake house, and Tim Lawson was just getting out of his pickup truck. Walker pulled to a stop and got out of the car as Tim took a lap around.

"Hey buddy," Tim said, offering a firm handshake. Then he nodded to the car. "I know I've said it before, but damn she's pretty."

Tim was wearing a royal-blue University of Kentucky polo shirt, with the white UK logo on his chest. He had a good, dark farmer tan going on. His buzz cut, short, salt-and-pepper hair said he was in his late fifties, early sixties. He wore small-framed reading glasses and seemed in good shape for a man who had no reason to be. Probably the work on his farm, which was pretty much just across the street. His matching salt and pepper goatee held a warm smile, and Walker could see in his brown eyes that he was genuinely happy to see him.

Walker pointed to the UK shirt. "You know I'm from Kentucky, right?"

"Hell no, but makes sense. I lived there for a few years for work. My son graduated from UK, so we root for the Cats together. You a fan?"

"Never got into sports," Walker said. "Never had anyone around me into them either, so I guess it rubbed off."

"Don't even watch football or NASCAR?"

"I'm more of a reader. Let's just say my lifestyle over the last decade or more has lent itself more to that."

"Did you tell me what you do for a living?"

"Nothing now," Walker said. "Maybe we can just leave it at that? I don't really want to lie to you."

"Yeah," Tim said, still smiling. "You put off that vibe. Military or something like it."

"I'm thirsty. You want a beer?"

"That secret, huh?" Tim laughed. A gut laugh with the wheeze of a smoker. Which Walker could smell on him.

Walker really liked that laugh. Probably because he hadn't been around many men in his life who ever even smiled, much less had a hearty ha-ha.

"Yeah, it's that secret."

The two of them went inside. Tim carried a bag full of stuff for burgers, and Walker cracked some beers. They ate big and "talked big," as Tim said. Tim told stories of his football days, some about his time running one of the largest chicken production facilities in the country, and even a few about chasing women. Walker realized he didn't relate well to *normal* people. He'd never had a regular job, played high school sports, or chased women. Though he wasn't bad at finding them.

So once Walker had a few drinks in him, and his trust in Tim had grown, he decided maybe it would be good therapy to tell a few of his own stories. Stories not even the highest office in the land knew about. They'd packed up the boat with some cold beer and a bottle of bourbon, and motored out to a quiet spot on the lake called Sail Creek. On the way there, Walker enjoyed looking at the sprawling homes that lined the lakeshore. Full of people living normal lives. Bankers, lawyers, entrepreneurs, people who had only heard stories and watched TV shows about guys like Tom Walker.

"Another beer?" Tim said.

"Won't say no." Walker took it from him; then they both stepped off the back onto the swim platform.

Walker watched Tim sit on the edge, dipping his legs in the water to about knee high, so he joined him. The water was cool, and the beer was cold. Which was good, because the sun above was sweltering. Walker had taken off his shirt, something he wasn't going to do, because with so many scars, questions inevitably cometh. But he was tired of hiding. He clanked his can of beer against Tim's. He could feel Tim look him over.

"Okay," Tim said, "two questions. Answering one of them is up to you, but the other I'm gonna have to know."

Walker smiled. "All right. Shoot."

"The way you're built, son, I bet you've had to beat the women off you with a stick. Am I right?"

"Honestly?" Walker said.

"Why not? Just me, you, and the water out here. But don't say anything you're uncomfortable with."

Walker nodded. "I've never talked about this with anyone outside the government program I was part of, but to answer your first question, I've been so busy hunting bad men my entire adult life that I've never really had time to hunt women."

"That's a damn shame," Tim said.

"Isn't it?" Walker agreed. "But . . ."

Tim smiled. "I knew there was going to be a *but*, probably a nice one or two." Tim laughed that hearty laugh. Walker couldn't help but join in.

"But . . ." Walker went on. "I've always had pretty good luck with the fairer sex when the opportunity came along."

Tim leaned over and patted Walker on his muscular arm. "Son, I doubt luck had much to do with it at all." They both drank. "You mind?"

Walker looked over. Tim had pulled out a pack of Marlboros.

"Not at all."

Tim lit one. Walker always did like the smell of a cigarette, as long as the smoke wasn't blown in his face.

"So, hunting bad men," Tim said as he took a puff. "You were military? Or CIA? You said the program you were a part of, so I assumed one or the other."

"Neither actually. They both have too many rules to follow. They put me in the program no one knows about, so we didn't have to ask permission to get things done. Or worry about how we went about doing them."

"Shi-it. Sounds dangerous. Judging by your scars, I'm assuming it was."

"You would assume right, but . . ."

Tim sensed Walker's hesitation. "Hey, listen. You don't want to talk about it, don't. I have more stories about chicken and football. Maybe some decent ones of some trouble I got into when I was young. Or we can just sit and stare at the water, for all I care. Don't feel obligated."

Walker took another drink, hurrying a bit so the beer didn't have time to get warm. "I was just going to say, you assumed right, but you can't really judge by my scars. I got a lot of these before they took me away."

Tim didn't say anything. Walker appreciated that he was letting him tell it in his own way.

Walker went on. "I've never had a family. I bounced around foster homes all my young life. I'm sure some people are good who take in orphans, but I didn't land in any of those homes. I always landed in the ones with people who took in boys like me because the government cut them a check. So they got to take their frustrations out on my body and make a little money in the process."

"I'm sorry to hear that, Tom. I—"

"It's okay. I made my peace with it a long time ago. But it did lead me straight into the life I've just left." Walker took a long pull of his beer. He was trying to decide whether or not he should go all the way there. Tim made him feel safe, and for some reason he just felt like he needed to get it off his chest. Tim waited patiently. "The last foster home I was in was the worst. He hit us kids because he was angry at how his life turned out. He hit my foster mom for sport."

"Son of a bitch," Tim said. "Man like that outta be put down."

Walker looked over at Tim. Tim finished his drink, looked over at Walker, and realized why he wasn't talking.

"Ah," Tim said, "that's how you got into the covert life. It may not be my place, but I'm glad you shot that asshole."

"I didn't shoot him," Walker said.

"Oh, I misunderstood. So, you got him put in jail?"

Walker cleared his throat. "I strangled the son of a bitch."

A hawk flew overhead and screeched as it went by. A nearby boat had sent over some waves, and their boat bobbed and weaved a bit in the moving water.

"Instead of putting me in jail, they took me into the program. Seemed I checked all the misfit boxes. Never even gave me a choice."

"Seems like you made it through all that shit and still managed to be a good man."

Walker appreciated Tim's attempt at positivity.

"Damn, am I a buzzkill or what," Walker said. "All this doom and gloom has made me hungry."

"Ready for another burger already?" Tim said. "You're like my son, you must have a hollow leg."

"I've been told that one before."

Tim hopped up and caught Walker by the arm before he made it off the swim platform. Walker looked into his eyes.

"Son, let me tell you something. I don't know what all you've been through, and I don't know how much of it you're still processing, but I just want to tell you one thing, and I want you to take it to heart from a man who has fought some battles of his own. The past isn't you. Good or bad, that's the man you used to be. Today, tomorrow . . . that's where a man becomes who he's meant to be."

Walker gave Tim a hard pat on his shoulder. Then he gave him a big smile. "One too many beers, maybe?"

Tim looked down at his Coors Light and laughed. "Shit, maybe so."

They both laughed, and Walker may have played it off, but he would never forget the words that Tim had just said to him. And all he could do was hope that his new friend was right.

4

Tom Walker and Tim Lawson brought the boat back to the house. Tim made a couple more burgers on the grill while Walker put another one of his YouTube video binges to good use and made fresh French fries in the air fryer. The video had said the key was to air fry them in batches so you could keep the fries all on one layer, making them extra crispy. The video was right—they were delicious. Dinner was fantastic, and the sun was getting lost on the other side of the house.

It had been a really good day. Walker's best since being at the lake. He got in a run, had some gun range time, spent some time with his girl—his '67 Mustang—cleaned his gun, made a friend, and ate a great meal . . . or two. Just as Walker was seeing Tim off at the door, his perfect day at the lake was ruined by the blue and red lights that were flashing as they came racing down the driveway.

"What the hell is this?" Tim said as he stepped out on the front porch.

Walker was thinking the same thing, except, unlike Tim, Walker always had a reason to believe a squad car could come for him at any moment. The police were better than some other people who could be coming after Walker, but still not a welcome sight. As he watched two police SUVs come to a stop, and a third car without lights on top coming in behind them, the scenarios began to spin in Walker's head.

His first mental reflex jumped him back to a month ago when he'd accidentally eradicated a drug infestation problem in his hometown of Ashland, Kentucky. But the woman he'd fought for ended up being the bad guy, and she was the one who ended up in jail. Walker had made a deal with the local sheriff, essentially killing his alternate identity, Evan Marshall, in a fire on the property. Walker knew this business was finished because his foster mother, Kim, had sent him a copy of *The Daily Independent*, Ashland's newspaper, and the cover story was the sheriff announcing that Evan Marshall, who'd been responsible for the murders in the mysterious car accident and for a large part of the drug operation, was dead. This enabled Ashland's law enforcement to stop searching for him, and more importantly to Walker, the government program he was a part of at Maxwell Solutions thought he was dead as well.

Tim turned back to Walker as the policemen exited their vehicles. "Whatever's going on, don't say a damn word. Understand?"

Walker was too much in his own head to worry about responding.

"Mr. Smith?" the officer closest to the house called out.

There were floodlights on the front of the house that were shining down on the driveway, making it easier to see the officers walking toward them. There were four of them in uniform and one in plain clothes just getting out of the unmarked car behind them.

"It's Mr. Lawson actually," Tim said. "Chuck and Tammy Smith are away on vacation for a while. What's the problem?"

Walker was just fine letting Tim do the talking, though he knew his time was coming.

"You staying here at the Smiths' house for the time being, Mr. Lawson?" the officer said.

"Well," Tim said as he walked down the porch steps to meet them in the driveway. "That's really none of your damn business."

The officer wasn't happy about Tim's tone. "Excuse me, sir?"

"Hold on, hold on," a woman's voice called from the shadows behind the police SUVs. "Officers, please take a few steps back. I told you to wait for me to do the talking."

The woman behind the voice stepped into the light. As she walked past the men in uniform, they dwarfed her. She was much shorter than they were, and because her open-collar, white button-down shirt was so tight, Walker could see that she was also very petite. Her dark hair was pulled into a ponytail, and the sharp lines in her face looked even more carved in the shadows.

"I'm very sorry, gentlemen. I tried to get down here to chat with you, without all of the show." She looked back at both police SUVs with their lights still flashing. "But as you can see, I don't run things." She looked at Tim. "Mr. Lawson, you said?"

Tim nodded.

The woman stepped forward and held out her hand. "I'm Detective Bailey."

Tim shook her hand. "Tim."

"Nice to meet you, Tim" she said. Then she looked up at

Walker who was still standing on the front porch. "Hello, I'm—"

"Detective Bailey," Walker said. Then he moved down the stairs. As he got closer, he towered over her. And now that her tight black slacks were in the light, he could see that she was even smaller than he thought. "David Walker." Walker held out his hand. When he'd had his new passport and driver's license made a few months back, he'd decided that keeping his real last name would avoid a lot of headaches in trying to remember to maintain his new identity.

The detective shook his hand; his swallowed hers. "David, nice to meet you."

"Call me Walker."

She took her hand back. "All right, Walker. Are you and Tim squatting here at the Smiths' residence? Or is there an arrangement we should know about?"

Tim started to speak, but Walker took over the conversation. "Was there a call to the police from Chuck or Tammy Smith?"

The detective looked back at the officers, then to Walker, shaking her head. "No. No calls made."

"All right then. It was nice meeting you, but it's been a long day. I'm going to bed."

Detective Bailey put her hands on her hips.

"I apologized for the flashing lights, Mr. Walker, and I'm being polite. Is it all right if I ask you a couple of questions?"

Walker ran his fingers through his hair. "Was I not polite, ma'am?"

She took a breath and let it out slow. "Let me start over." She looked between Tim and Walker. "I'm sorry to interrupt your evening, *gentlemen*." She let the word linger, as did her eyes on Walker. "But I'm not sure you are aware that there has been a kidnapping in the area."

Walker noted that it had been upgraded to a kidnapping. He knew exactly who Detective Bailey was talking about.

"Not much of a news guy," Walker said. "Hate to hear it, but what does that have to do with us?"

She nodded. "Maybe I should just come back in the morning." She took a step back. "After your early morning run. Sound good to you, Mr. Walker?"

Walker knew where the conversation was headed, and he didn't like it. "I get it," he said. "New guy in town who keeps to himself. Someone goes missing. Law enforcement has no leads and is getting pressured by the people in town who have the status to apply pressure. Detective gets antsy and starts following any silly leads, no matter where they lead, including an observation by someone else in the neighborhood that went sort of like this: '*Well, nothing out of the ordinary, Detective, except whoever the Smiths have watching their house, he is out in the mornings before daylight. Who runs in the dark? Might be something?*'" Walker gave a sheepish grin. "How'd I do, Detective?"

Walker could see Tim smile out of the corner of his eye.

Detective Bailey didn't say anything. Instead, she just produced two business cards from her back pocket. She handed one to Tim and one to Walker.

"If you gentlemen see or hear anything about the case that is on the news, please call me first. You two have a good night."

"You too, Detective," Tim said.

Walker didn't speak.

Detective Bailey turned and began walking back to her vehicle. "Let's go, boys," she said to the officers as she went by. She turned around to face Tim and Walker as she continued backpedaling toward her car. "I will be getting in touch with Mr. and Mrs. Smith. Not a threat, because I'm sure you've done nothing wrong. Just letting you know that I do in fact check *every* lead when I'm working a case. Especially one that involves a missing twelve-year-old girl."

Walker held his tongue.

"Have a nice night," Tim said.

The officers got back in their SUVs, turned off their flashing lights, then followed Detective Bailey's car up and out of the driveway. Tim turned back to Walker.

"She was a pistol," he said. "Not bad to look at either."

"They're getting desperate," Walker said.

"Yeah, well, it is the mayor's daughter. You seen it on the news?"

"I have."

"Probably just what you said," Tim said. "Mayor's probably up the ass of everyone with a badge. I know I would be if it was my daughter."

Walker nodded. "I suppose I would be too."

"Hard to understand till you have kids yourself."

Walker knew Tim was probably right about that. However, Walker had never had kids and probably never would. Yet something about this missing girl felt more personal than it should have. He knew a lot of it was because of the boredom of not currently working. But he also thought that maybe it was because of what happened last month in Kentucky. Even though he didn't end up fighting for the good guys, Walker's intentions were good. And it had been a really nice change of pace to use his skills for what *he* thought was good. His feelings of wanting to help Amy Turnberry must be some form of PTSD. Whatever it was, it didn't really matter. There was absolutely nothing he could do.

"Tim," Walker said, "hell of an evening, my friend. But I'm spent."

"Hell of an evening, buddy," Tim agreed and gave Walker a hard pat on the back. "Oh, and you don't have to drive out to that gun range. Just come over to the farm. I've got some targets set up. You can shoot as much as you want. I got a damn arsenal in my safes."

"Thanks, Tim. I might do that."

Tim smiled. "It'll give me a chance to teach you how to shoot."

"That right?" Walker laughed.

But he wasn't laughing at all on the inside. In fact, he was churning. Itching to get out and do something. Maybe he'd been lying to himself about just how much he'd been enjoying his downtime.

He waved good-bye to Tim; then he stood in the driveway next to Shelby and stared at Detective Ava Bailey's business card for a few minutes. Even taking the time to put the number in his phone. Then he got bit twice by mosquitoes, so he decided that was his cue to call it a night. It was early, but he'd eaten and drunk more that day than he had in the entire last week. He was definitely going to have to work it off in the morning.

That was before he knew how long his night was going to be.

5

Walker's eyes shot open, his hand whipped over to the nightstand for the butt of his pistol, and then he sat up, grabbed his phone, and tapped the notification that had just dinged him from his sleep. The first of his many Amazon purchases when he'd arrived at the lake house was a camera for every door of the house. The Smiths had their own security system, and Walker was using it, but he wanted direct notifications to his phone so he would be able to see from the bed if there was a problem, and see who the problem was.

The third night at the house, a wandering raccoon had sent a notification to his phone. But that didn't make Walker take this notification any less serious. And as the app opened, and he saw someone in a hooded sweatshirt go around the back, passing by the camera at the basement's sliding door, his quick action to his weapon had been justified.

Walker slid out of bed and threw on a pair of lounge shorts. He watched his phone, pulling up all three camera feeds on the same screen as he walked toward the hallway.

Walker had made sure when he installed the cameras to make them at least somewhat discreet. It was clear it was a decent job because the man had circled back to the basement sliding door and never looked in the direction of the camera. He was peering in the window now.

Walker moved down the first set of stairs to the main floor and slipped on his running shoes that were ready for his morning run at the front door. Then he watched the man try the door handle. When he pulled, of course it was locked. Walker started down the first part of the basement stairs. Once making the turn down the second set of stairs to the left, he would essentially be walking right toward the man who was trying to get in.

Walker pocketed his phone, raised his gun, and moved down into the basement. It only took a split second for the man at the sliding glass door to see Walker coming toward him. He bolted immediately. Walker flipped the lock, threw the sliding glass door open, and dashed down the deck stairs.

"I'll shoot you if you keep running!" Walker shouted.

But the man was all ass and elbows. And he was fast. He jumped down the hill that ran alongside the driveway and shot into the trees. Walker had planned on a run anyway, so he figured he might as well get in a hunt while he was at it. He dashed down the hill, sliding the last few feet. Not nearly as graceful as the man he was chasing. Walker wanted to fire a warning shot in hopes that it would stop him, but he couldn't. Not after having the police show up. If he didn't catch this man and there was a report of shots fired, even though he had video of the man, it would bring much unwanted scrutiny.

So he ran.

Walker bobbed and weaved through the trees, ducking

branches and jumping bushes. He couldn't really see what was directly in front of him, but the first major mistake the man made before he came to bother Walker was that while he did wear a black hoodie, the swooshes on his tennis shoes were reflective. There wasn't a lot of moonlight making it through the canopy, but there was enough that every so often Walker caught a glimpse and was able to stay on track.

The trees came to an abrupt stop because the neighbor on that side of the Smiths' house had horses. The land they grazed on began where the trees ended. There was what looked like a mini ranch that Walker had seen from the road. A barn in the back and a couple of paddocks where they would turn the horses out. As he watched the man go up and over the white three-rail horse fence of the farm, a shot of anxiety-ridden PTSD blasted Walker's system. After the time he'd spent a month ago on a farm, the last place he wanted to be was anywhere near a damn barn.

Of course, that was the exact direction the man was running in.

Walker was still holding his pistol in his right hand when he made it to the fence. He popped both hands on the top rail, and as he pushed himself up, he propelled that with a left foot on the bottom rail. He hit the ground running on the other side. Now he could gain on him, but there really was no need. He was clearly going for the barn. Smarts might not be at the top of the list for the man he was chasing. Especially on a clear night with a near full moon. The man's shoes were practically glowing.

The man ran into the barn, and Walker jogged up to the open entrance but pulled up short.

Walker took a couple of breaths. "Listen, I don't know who you are or what you were doing snooping around the house, but please don't make me kill you. It's been like thirty days since I've had to do something like that. My record is forty-five days without killing, and I was really hoping to break it."

Walker waited for a response. He could hear the man inside.

"I can hear you breathing. However you are thinking you can get out of this, you can't. And just to be sure, because it was dark back there in the basement. I do have a gun. And I am pretty damn good with it."

Walker took a couple of steps closer to the entrance. His gun was up, but he had his finger outside the trigger guard. If the man wasn't armed and Walker shot him, it wouldn't matter if the man was trying to break in or not—Walker would be in trouble. He wasn't even on the Smiths' property anymore.

"Last chance. Then I'm coming in."

Walker tuned his ears as he stepped forward. He could hear the man breathing. He was waiting on the left side of the barn's entrance for Walker to come in. Walker didn't see a gun in his hand back at the sliding door, and the way the man had been running suggested he didn't have one in his pocket either. So Walker stepped forward. He was just about inside. Leaning against the outside wall of the barn was a shovel. Walker picked it up, then tossed it through the entrance.

Before the shovel even hit the ground, a two-by-four came swinging down from the left. When it hit the ground, Walker kicked it out of the man's hands and stepped inside. Walker shot his empty hand up and grabbed a fistful of sweater. He yanked down hard and to the left, sending the man flying out of the barn into the moonlight. The baggy sweatshirt had given the appearance of a larger man, but it was clear with how easy it was for Walker to sling him to the ground that he didn't weigh much at all.

Walker brought up the gun as the man skidded to a stop in the dirt.

"Take off the hood," Walker said.

The man raised his left arm, palm out in a defensive pose. "Please, don't shoot. I was just . . . Please don't shoot me.

The person in the hooded sweatshirt was definitely more a boy than a man, judging by the pubescent squeak in his voice.

"I said, take off the hood. Now," Walker reiterated.

"Okay, okay. Just please. Don't shoot me."

The young man reached up and pulled the string on his hood. When he pulled it back off his head, some wavy blond hair sprang around a face that couldn't have been over sixteen.

Walker pulled the gun back and placed it in his waistband. "What the hell are you doing out here, kid? Trying to get yourself killed? For what? Money? Thinking you could score some drugs? Pills? What?"

The young man sat up on his butt and hung his head. "No, sir, nothing like that. I just . . ."

The crickets filled in the boy's silence.

"Sir?" Walker said. "What's a kid like you, with manners, doing trying to break into someone's house if it's not for money or pills?"

"I can't say, sir. But if you just let me go, please, I'll never come back. I swear."

"How old are you?" Walker said.

"Sixteen."

The kid didn't look sixteen, but Walker wasn't exactly an expert on the subject.

The kid went on. "I promise you I won't come back if you let me go."

"All right, I tell you what," Walker said as he walked over and extended his right hand.

The boy looked at his hand but didn't move.

"I'm not going to hit you."

The boy grabbed his hand, and Walker helped him up.

Walker continued. "Believe it or not, I was your age once. Got into my fair share of trouble too. So, if you answer a couple of questions for me, honestly, I'll let you go. But a word of warning. I used to do this sort of thing for a living, so I'll know if you're lying."

The boy came up to just above Walker's chest. Probably only about half his weight, however.

"O-okay. I'll tell the truth."

Walker nodded. "What's your name?"

The boy looked up at him like that wasn't an easy question for him to answer.

"Can we keep names out of it?"

"Why?" Walker said.

"Because if it gets out that I was out here, it will be on the news."

Walker's mind bounced around to the only news he'd heard while he had been in Soddy Daisy, and that involved a twelve-year-old girl who had hair about the same color as that of the boy who was standing in front of him.

"Turnberry," Walker said.

"Shit," the kid said. "I am going to be—"

"Don't worry about it. I'm someone who understands not wanting people to know his name."

The boy nodded.

"So," Walker said, "with all that's going on with your . . ." Walker didn't want to assume.

34

"Sister."

"Right. With all that's going on with that, what are you doing out here? And remember, only the truth."

The boy nodded again. "So you have heard what happened to my sister?"

Walker nodded.

"Well, the police have been looking for days now, with nothing. And I, well, I got sick of waiting on them to do something, you know?"

"I can understand that. But why at the house I'm in? That's awfully specific, and as far as I know, not a source of any suspicion."

Except the house call earlier from Detective Bailey, but that wasn't due to any actual suspicion.

"I was sitting on the stairs at my house when the detective lady was talking to my parents. She told them she'd been down here to this house but couldn't go in without any sort of warrant. But I heard my mom saying something about a strange man . . ." The boy pointed at Walker, "You, I guess. And how it was awfully suspicious that you were new here and then Amy up and went missing. The detective said she couldn't just go inside and look around, so . . ."

"So you thought you would," Walker said. "In hopes of what? Finding your sister?"

"I don't know, sir. I'm just getting desperate. She's little. And I'm worried about her. And I—"

"You don't have to explain anymore," Walker said.

"I-I don't?"

"No. If I was you, I would have done the same thing. Whatever it took."

The boy nodded, but stared at the ground.

"That doesn't mean it was smart. You could have gotten yourself hurt, or worse."

"Yes, sir."

"So, you want to look?" Walker said. "Ease your mind?"

The boy looked up, half shocked to hear Walker's suggestion. "I . . . shouldn't impose any more than I already have. It's late. But thank you."

"I'm already awake. Do me the favor of getting rid of your suspicions so this doesn't come up again?"

"Thank you. You don't have to do this."

"I kind of do now. It's fine. Let's just make it quick, deal?"

"Deal."

Walker extended his hand. "Walker."

"Daniel," the boy said as he gave a firm shake.

While Walker wasn't happy to have his sleep interrupted, the entire thing could have been much worse. And there might be a bright side to the disruption: maybe it would help keep anyone else from coming over and bothering him from here on out. Walker headed back the way they came. The boy followed. He checked his phone. It was already three-thirty in the morning. If Daniel was quick, Walker could still get his run in before daybreak.

That would prove to be wishful thinking.

6

W alker had been leading Daniel Turnberry through every corner of the Smiths' lakeside home. A couple of times he imagined that the Smiths probably wouldn't be too happy about a stranger going through every room in the house, but Walker felt the circumstances warranted it. The young man was clearly distraught about his sister being kidnapped, and Walker felt if it would ease Daniel's exhausted mind, if only a little, then it was worth it. Walker grabbed a T-shirt while Daniel poked around the bedroom. The two of them walked back up the stairs from the basement.

"That's it, Daniel. You've seen every room. Are you satisfied?"

"I am. And again, thank you. You didn't have to do that."

Walker checked his phone again. It was now four in the morning. "If you get going now, you might be able to get an hour or two of sleep before school."

Daniel looked over at the clock on the oven. "I haven't really been sleeping much, and tomorrow is Sunday."

"That's right," Walker said. "My days are running together out here."

"What are you doing here, if you don't mind me asking?"

Walker got the sense that the kid wasn't at all in a hurry to get home. Maybe his morning run wasn't going to happen after all.

"You want some coffee or something, Daniel?"

He actually perked up at the question. "You mean, you don't mind if I stay a while?"

"I'm not going back to bed, and you don't sleep, so you can stay a bit longer if you'd like. Seems like home doesn't feel so 'homey' to you right now."

"Yeah. Not since what happened with Amy. My mom's a wreck, and Dad just paces around for hours on end. Kind of maddening."

"So was that a no to coffee?" Walker said.

Daniel laughed. "I think I'm a little young for coffee, but I'll take a soda if you have one."

Walker's lack of child or teenager knowledge was apparent. But it was because his only experience with kids was his own childhood. He hadn't been around a single one in more than a decade. And when Walker was Daniel's age, he was already training knife techniques with John Sparks after his stint in prison for murdering his foster father.

Walker stepped to his right into the kitchen and flipped start on the coffee for himself. "I think the owners have some soda in the refrigerator." He opened it and saw a can of Coca-Cola. He held it up.

"That works, thank you."

"Have a seat."

At one end of the kitchen island, there was a round

granite countertop with three bar stools around it. Daniel took a seat.

"Play any sports, Daniel?" A riveting question, but quite literally the only one Walker had for the kid.

"Baseball."

"Any good?"

"Made varsity this year as a sophomore."

Walker had no idea what measurement of good that was, so he moved on. "You like it?"

"It's fine. My dad was really good in college."

"So you play because he wants you to?"

"No . . . I like it," Daniel said. "It's really my mom who likes me to play. She likes being able to tell her friends I'm good."

"Okay," Walker said, sensing a little frustration in Daniel. But what did Walker know—he'd never played sports or had a mother. "Well then, what do *you* like to do, when nobody's influencing your decisions?"

"I like baseball. Really. I do."

"Come on, kid. You don't have to put on for me. What do you really like?" Walker said as he got up to pour himself some coffee."

Daniel looked over at Walker's copy of *The Fireman* lying on the counter. "That yours?"

"Yeah, it's a good one. You read?"

"A lot. And that is a good one. I love Joe Hill. Have you read *Heart-Shaped Box*?"

"Of course," Walker said as he took his seat. "Another good one. So you like to read then."

"It's pretty much all I do," Daniel said. "I don't really watch TV. My friends make fun of me for it. Well, more so when I'm always scribbling in my notebook."

"Oh, you draw?"

"No, I meant scribbling as in writing. The only other thing I do when I'm not reading or playing baseball."

Walker and Daniel seemed to have a lot in common. His foster father always gave him shit for reading and writing too. Like it was a sissy thing to do. Walker wondered if Jim had thought Walker was a sissy when he was squeezing the life out of him.

"I have a stack of notebooks I write in all the time too."

"Really? That's awesome. I mean, I wouldn't have thought of you that way."

"Why's that?" Walker said.

"Well, you're just, I don't know . . . in really good shape and seem to really be able to handle yourself out there."

"That means I don't have a brain?" Walker said.

"What? Oh, no, I just—"

"I'm just messing with you, Daniel."

"Oh, okay. Cool." He laughed as he cracked open the soda and took a sip. "Don't spend a lot of time around teenagers, huh?"

"What makes you say that?" Walker sipped his coffee.

"Just a hunch. This might be too forward, and if it is, don't feel like you have to answer, but are you a cop or something? FBI maybe? You were just so quick to get your gun, and then the way you took me down so easy, and your build. I . . ."

"I am none of those things, actually."

"Really? I get it. You don't have to tell me. It's just kind of obvious."

"Yeah?" Walker said. "Because you have so much experience with such things?"

"No, I just read a lot. You fit the mold."

Walker smiled. The kid was smart. But dumb at the

same time. Probably a typical teenager trait, but it was endearing.

"You close with your sister?" Walker changed the subject. He never liked answering questions about himself. A life of secrecy will do that.

"Yeah, she's the best. The only one who really knows me and what I really like." Daniel laughed. "She read my notebook once. I was pissed at first, but then she told me I should see if I could get it published. She said it was really good."

"That's nice of her. And it's good that both of you can be yourselves around each other. Strict parents?"

"You could say that."

"That's tough."

"You too?" Daniel said.

"I never had parents. But the stand-ins I had were pretty rough."

"Sorry."

"I'm not a very good person to give life advice, Daniel, but I will tell you this." Walker looked him in the eyes. "The longer you live, the more hard times you are going to have. It's one of life's inevitabilities. The trick is that it is never about what happens to you, you can't control that. But you can control how you react to it. *That* is where you should always put your focus."

"Yeah, I guess that is what I was trying to do by coming here looking for my sister. I can't stand just waiting around while she might be hurting."

"That's why I didn't get upset about it," Walker said. "I understand wanting to try to make a difference in a bad situation."

Daniel took a sip of his Coke. "Walker?"

"Yeah?"

"Will you help me find my sister?"

Walker laughed it off. "What makes you think I would have any idea how to help you find her?"

"I don't know," Daniel said. "Call it intuition, maybe?"

"And your intuition about me is?"

Daniel was quiet for a moment.

"Don't be shy," Walker said.

"My intuition is that you're the type of guy who knows how to get things done."

"Why? Because I have a gun?"

"No . . ." Daniel was calculating his words carefully. "Because it's clear that you've dealt with a lot of things in your life, but you're still a positive person, giving positive advice. The only way that happens is that you believe you can still have an effect on everything around you. I read a lot, Mr. Walker. And all of the heroes in my stories have one thing in common. Perseverance. Whether it's a small obstacle in the story they have to get over or the main villain they must overcome at the end, they persevere. That's what I see when I look at you."

Walker sat back in his bar stool. The kid was impressive. Maybe too impressive. Walker was keenly aware that the kid was smart, but he was also buttering Walker up. He wasn't wrong necessarily, but he was selling as he was telling.

"Okay, Daniel. Let's say you're right. I know how to persevere. I'm still not a detective, nor do I have any experience in the matter. So I have nothing to offer you in that way."

"Maybe you're not a 'detective,' but you know you can help. I can see it in the way you carry yourself. It's my sister. I had to ask. I understand if you don't want to."

"It's not that, it's just that I don't have a badge. Therefore, there's nothing I can do."

"Can you just answer one thing, honestly? Then I promise I'll leave you alone."

"I can't make you any promises," Walker said, "but I'll try."

Daniel nodded. "You know you can help me find my sister, don't you?"

Walker was quiet. Now it was he who had to calculate his words. He had no reason to expose to this kid what he could and could not do, and what he was or was not capable of. Honestly, Daniel would never believe all of it anyway. No one would. But he also could see the pain in Daniel's eyes. And Walker could feel an aching of his own to help the innocent young girl be found. Could he help in that? Walker really didn't know. Because what he would be better at would be making the person pay for taking her once they found out who it was. And those were two completely different things.

Daniel got up from his seat and pulled his hood up over his head. "Never mind. I'm really sorry I ruined your night. And sorry for all the questions. I just want my sister to be okay."

Walker stood up with him. "Daniel, just because you ask a man a question and hope for a certain answer doesn't mean you'll get it. And can I be totally honest with you?"

"Yes, please. I'm not a kid. My parents keep trying to sugarcoat this thing and tell me it's going to be all right, but I know it's not. So just say what you have to say. It's not like you'll ever see me again anyway."

"All right," Walker said. "Like a man then?"

"Like a man."

"Okay. Daniel, I don't know if I can help you find your sister. Not because of what I can and can't do, but because she's probably already dead. You're a smart kid. I know you've read that much to know the statistics already, am I right?"

Daniel looked away, then mustered some gumption. "I have read that, but—"

"So the question you need to ask isn't *can* I help you find her. It's *will* I help you find out what happened to her."

"Isn't that the same thing?"

"No."

"Why not?" Daniel said.

"Because I'm not the kind of man who finds things that are broken, Daniel. I'm the man who breaks things once they're found. You need Detective Bailey or someone like her right now. I'm sure she's doing everything she can to find your sister."

Daniel didn't say anything. He just stared at his shoes. Walker knew as soon as he said all of it that it was probably too harsh for a sixteen-year-old. But hopes and wishes don't do you any damn good in life. Planning and hard work get things done. The sooner the kid learned that, the better off he would be.

"Sorry I bothered you, man," Daniel said as he started walking toward the door.

Walker wasn't *sir* anymore, now that he wasn't going to help. He was going to just let Daniel go, but his phone dinged. It was the camera up by the mailbox at the top of the driveway.

"Don't move," Walker said as he tapped the notification to pull up the incident that tripped the camera. As the software was loading on the app, they both saw headlights shine through the front windows. Walker grabbed Daniel by the back of the sweatshirt and pulled him around the corner into the kitchen. The software loaded. He knocked

Daniel's shoulder to look at his phone. A car went by, but Walker couldn't tell what kind it was.

"That's my dad's Tahoe," Daniel said. "What the hell are they doing here?"

Then a horn began honking in the driveway. Walker knew at that moment that taking Daniel back to the house had been a mistake. From the moment he'd seen Amy Turnberry's photo on the front page of the newspaper, he'd felt this story pulling him in. Now he'd been dragged right into the middle of it, whether he wanted to be there or not.

7

"I don't understand," Daniel said. "How could they know I'm here?"

As Walker watched Daniel's mother and father get out of their SUV in the driveway, via the camera's feed he'd installed at the front door, all he could do was shake his head. All he'd wanted to do was disappear, and now, twice in just a few hours, he was the attention of people he didn't know, about a local kidnapping case he had nothing to do with.

Walker stepped over to Daniel and held out his hand. "Give me your phone."

"What?"

"Just hand me your phone."

Daniel unlocked it and handed it to Walker. Walker scrolled through the many apps on Daniel's phone and finally saw the one he was looking for. The *Find My* app. He tapped on it, turned the screen toward Daniel, and showed him that his parents had simply followed his phone's GPS to where he was at the lake house.

Daniel hung his head. "Shit."

"Yeah," Walker said. "It's 2023, Daniel. You've got to do better than that if you want to sneak off."

There was pounding at the door. "Daniel!" a man's voice called. "Let my son go!"

"It's my dad," Daniel said. "Let me just go—"

Walker held up his hand to the boy's chest, stopping him from walking around the corner.

"Just hold on a second," Walker said.

He was trying to figure the best way out of the situation that Daniel had put him in. Walker knew there was footage of Daniel coming to the house. And Walker chasing off after him. And then it would show the two of them coming back to the house together. No one should be able to see that video, but if something else goes wrong somehow and the footage is subpoenaed . . . he had to think through his next move before he made it.

"What are we going to do?" Daniel said.

"I know my son is in there!" The man at the door was shouting as he pounded. "Daniel!"

Walker looked over at Daniel. Daniel was about to panic.

It was time to make a decision. Help Daniel find his sister, or stay the hell out of it. The easy answer was obvious. Leave it to the police. That was the smart and correct thing to do. And that is the decision that any normal human being would make.

Tom Walker was not a normal human being.

When Walker was leaving Ashland, Kentucky, a month ago, after an extremely long two days, Walker had felt good about fighting for what *he* thought was right. He'd spent nearly two decades at the whims of politicians and the world's elite. Killing in the name of their good, changing political structures in countries that he'd known nothing about before he was sent there, only to change the trajectory of that country with the swipe of his blade or the bullet from his gun.

Now, after convincing the government program, which he'd been married to by force since he was fifteen, that he was dead—the only way out of such a program—he had all the skills they'd taught him with nowhere to use them. Skills that some say make kings, but all Walker wanted to do with them was good. Good things maybe to erase some of the bad things they'd had him do. And saving a twelve-year-old girl, or at least trying to, from whatever evil had overtaken her, seemed to be just about as good as a man like Walker could do.

Daniel's father continued banging at the door. "The police are on the way! You won't get away with this!"

"Daniel!" Now his mother was shouting. "Let him go! Give us back our children, you monster!"

"What are we going to do?" Daniel said, with more panic this time. "I'm sorry I came here."

"You want my help finding your sister?"

Walker had made his decision.

"Yeah, but . . ." Daniel pointed at Walker's phone that was showing his parents going berserk at the front door. "It's too late."

Walker shook his head. "It's not too late, but you're going to have to trust me."

"You really think you can help?"

"I really don't know, Daniel. But I have a lot of skills that might, and a lot of free time on my hands. Might as well use it for something good."

Daniel jumped forward and threw his arms around Walker. It caught Walker so off guard that he nearly fell backward. Walker let the kid hug him, but he didn't reciprocate.

"Sorry." Daniel backed away. "I'm so sorry, I don't know —thank you. Amy is good, Mr. Walker. She doesn't deserve what's happening to her."

"All right. Let's start with one thing at a time. And right now, I have to get rid of your parents. But it might cost you."

"How do you mean?"

"I'm going to have to keep your phone and give it to them. It's the only way I can clear myself of doing anything wrong."

"But they'll know I've been here."

"They already know that," Walker said. "Just go down to the basement, slip out the sliding door, and get home. We never talked, and you never came in this house. Got it?"

"What do I say when they ask what happened?"

"That you came looking for your sister, and I ran you off. *Nothing* else. Got it?"

"Yeah, sure. But how will I get ahold of you, for you to help?"

"Can you make it back here tomorrow night? Without getting in trouble?"

"Yeah, I can. But what about my phone?" Daniel said. "They're obviously tracking it."

"If you can't figure that out, Daniel, then you won't be able to help me find your sister anyway. Understand?"

"I got it."

"All right, now go. I'll see you tomorrow night," Walker said as he led Daniel around the corner and started him down the basement stairs. His parents were still pounding at the door. "Oh, and do some homework for me."

Daniel turned around and looked up at Walker. "Like what?"

"I need to know everything you can get me on Amy's friends, teachers, coaches if she plays sports. Anyone who might be in her life at all. These things are almost always done by someone the victim knows. The more thorough you are, Daniel, the better chance we have of finding something that might help."

"Everything is on social media now," Daniel said. "I'll get all I can. I know her passwords. Maybe there are things in her social media accounts?"

"We'll look. Now, get going."

Daniel nodded, turned, took two steps down, then turned back to Lawson. "I know we're strangers, so I know how big of a deal this is. And I just . . . thank you. Thank you for helping me."

"I haven't done anything yet. Now, get the hell out of here, and don't let them see you."

Daniel took off. Walker pulled up the sliding door's camera and watched Daniel slink out into the night. Now it was time to deal with the parents. And just like dealing with a sixteen-year-old kid, it was going to be about a thousand percent out of Walker's comfort zone.

8

The incessant banging on the front door continued as Walker watched Daniel disappear into the night on his phone. He had a play in mind for Daniel's parents, but if they were irrational upon entering the house, there was definitely going to be a problem. He was going to have to suck it up and play overly nice, though he wasn't sure that trait was in his repertoire. He was just going to have to find out. Seemingly, a lot of what his life was going to be like this now that he wasn't a lone wolf hunting its prey. Life is a give-and-take, he supposed.

Walker unlocked the front door and braced himself as he opened it.

"What the hell do you think you're doing?" Daniel's mother shouted before the door was even fully opened. Her long, curly blond hair (Walker could see where the kids got their hair) was a mess, and her eyes were wide and wild. "Where are my children?"

At first Mr. Turnberry took a step forward, but when the door opened wide enough for him to get a good look at Walker, he took a couple of steps back.

"Can you please stop shouting?" Walker said.

"Stop shouting?" the woman shouted. Walker took that as a no. "My son is here, and I know that means you have my daughter too! Where are they? I want to see them right now!"

"Ma'am," Walker said, determined to remain calm, "if you would just—"

"Don't you *ma'am* me! Give me my kids!"

Walker shifted focus to Mr. Turnberry, who seemed—at least at the moment—to be the more rational of the two. "Sir, if you could just let me explain why your son's phone is here, I can—"

"You won't explain anything! You will bring them both to me! She's been missing for days! I'm coming in! Daniel!" She charged ahead as if Walker was just going to let her pass.

Walker didn't move from the doorway, and Mrs. Turnberry just about fell over backward down the front porch step, she bounced off him so hard. Walker made no move to catch her. Her husband leaned over to offer a hand, but she shooed him away and popped back up to her feet. Over her shocked face, Walker could see another vehicle coming down the driveway. What a night it had turned out to be. A regular party at the Smiths' lake house, but no one had been invited.

"You just pushed me to the ground!" Mrs. Turnberry shouted. Her brow was furrowed, making her look older, but Walker imagined she couldn't have been much over forty. Her husband, the mayor, looked at least five years older as he was beginning to gray at the sideburns.

"He didn't shove you, Emily," the mayor said. "You just ran into him. Let's not make a bad situation worse."

Emily turned on him like he was the devil. "*Worse?*

What the hell could possibly be worse, Clark? This man hanging their bodies from the roof for show?"

Over Emily's shoulder, Walker watched as Detective Bailey exited her vehicle. Walker imagined she'd been summoned to the lake house for the second time that evening. Or morning. Whatever the hell time of day it was then. Emily heard the car door shut and turned her rage toward Detective Bailey. Walker was trying to be understanding of her situation. She'd lost one child and was afraid another was gone. It was understandable that she was out of her mind at the moment.

"Detective! This man just tried to shove me down the stairs!"

"Emily!" The mayor followed her down the steps and onto the driveway. "That's not what happened. You have got to get a hold of yourself. This isn't helping matters at all."

Walker was happy to see at least one of the two was keeping their head. Yin and yang, he supposed.

"All right, all right," the detective said. She was still in the same outfit she'd shown up in earlier. Probably just threw it back on when Emily Turnberry called again. "Let's just calm down. We will get to the bottom of this, but we just need cooler heads."

"Cooler heads?" Emily shouted. She was about to blow her fuse.

"Emily!" the mayor shouted. Emily turned toward him like she wasn't used to hearing him raise his voice. "Take a walk up the driveway. Calm down. You're making this impossible."

Emily gave him a look that could melt steel, huffed, then walked away talking to herself. Detective Bailey stepped up the stairs and gave Walker a sheepish grin. Mayor Turnberry followed closely behind her.

"Mr. Walker." She nodded.

"Detective."

"Can you please clear this up for the mayor so we can go back home and we can leave you alone?"

Walker looked at Mayor Turnberry and nodded. "I'd be happy to."

The mayor nodded back. Walker could see *Sorry for her behavior* written all over his expression.

"Do you mind if we just step inside, Mr. Walker?" the detective said. "I think, if you're okay with it"— she nodded toward Daniel's mother in the driveway—"it might help defuse this unfortunate situation here that I'm sure you have a perfectly good explanation for."

Walker hadn't done anything wrong, and even though he did mind them coming inside, he agreed with Detective Bailey that it would help calm everyone down.

"Fine by me, detective," Walker said, then nodded to the mayor. "Mayor."

The mayor looked even more contrite after Walker actually okayed the entrance portion of the evening's show.

Detective Bailey walked inside, and after the mayor called for his wife, he held out his hand to Walker. "Clark Turnberry, real sorry about the ruckus, but you'd have to understand the full situation to get the chaos."

"I understand. Tough times make for difficult situations."

Emily walked up the stairs, then right past Walker and the mayor. Walker wasn't positive, but she might have even snarled at him as she went by. Walker shut the door and followed everyone into the living room.

"Where the hell is my son?" Emily said.

Walker had barely even had the chance to make it onto the rug.

Detective Bailey stepped forward to steer the conversation.

"Mr. Walker, the reason the Turnberrys are here, is because the *Find My* app on Mrs. Turnberry's phone shows this house as the location of her son Daniel's phone."

Emily stepped forward and shoved the cell phone's screen in Walker's face. "There, that dot is his phone. Right here where we are standing. So where is he?"

Detective Bailey put her hand on Emily's shoulder and got her to take a step back. Then she looked at Walker. "Are you familiar with the phone tracking app, Mr. Walker?"

"I am," he said.

"Any idea why her son's phone would be showing at this location?"

"Yes, ma'am," Walker said. Then he held up Daniel's cell phone.

Emily lunged at him and snatched the phone from Walker's hand. "I told you! Now where are my babies!"

"Damn it, Emily," Clark said as he took her by the shoulders and moved her back. "You have to be able to read the room. They aren't here. This man let us in. Will you let him explain why he has Daniel's phone, please?"

"Mr. Walker?" Detective Bailey said.

Walker nodded. "I was sleeping and thought I heard something. So I got up and checked the house. When I went down to the basement, I saw someone with blond hair poking out of a black hoodie, trying to open the sliding glass door."

"That's Daniel! Where is he?" Emily shouted.

"I don't know that. But the reason I have his phone is I chased him off the property. On my way back, I all but tripped over that phone. I was going to wait till morning to do anything about it, because it's, well, close to five in the morning now, I guess. So I went back to sleep. Albeit not for very long, because I heard a lot of banging at the front door."

"See, Emily?" Clark said. "Daniel is probably back home right now."

"Why the hell would he come here and try to break in?" Emily said. "Huh? That makes no sense." She was looking at Detective Bailey now. "If you knew my boy, you would know that there is no way he would do that!"

Detective Bailey was quick at putting something together. "Emily, Daniel probably heard our conversation at your house about Mr. Walker and what you had to say about him. He was probably just trying to be a good brother and find his sister."

"I'm really sorry to hear about your daughter," Walker said.

"Thank you," Clark said. "And we are sorry to have bothered you, but I hope you understand."

"I don't have kids, but I imagine if I did, I'd leave no stone unturned."

The detective turned to Emily. "Do you have a house phone?"

Emily seemed to snap out of a trance. "What? A house phone. Oh yes. Why?"

"Call it, Mrs. Turnberry," Detective Bailey said. "Maybe Daniel is already home?"

Emily walked away immediately, out the door, and onto the porch.

"Let us get out of your hair, Mr. Walker," Clark said.

"I hope you find your daughter," Walker said.

Clark nodded, then moved on.

"I'm going to walk them out," Detective Bailey said, "but

do you mind if you and I have a quick word before I go? I'll only take a minute of your time."

"Why not?" Walker said. "Not going to get any sleep now anyway."

"I'll be right back," she said.

Walker watched her walk the Turnberrys out of the house. She shut the door behind her. Walker imagined that Emily Turnberry had been making Detective Bailey's life a living hell for the past few days. But who could blame her? Her little girl was missing. And Walker had made a promise to her son that he was going to help find her.

The thing Walker needed to decide was just how much he was going to talk to Detective Bailey about the situation. At the moment, he had no idea.

9

Walker made more coffee. As Detective Bailey made her way back inside, he was pouring her a cup into a Carnival Cruise mug. One of many the Smiths had. He wondered for only a second what it must be like to love someone enough to travel the world with them. What a safe feeling that must be. One Walker doubted would ever befall a man such as himself.

"Oh my God, is that for me?" the detective said as she walked over to the kitchen.

"Figured you could use some," Walker said.

"I like you more already."

Walker just stared at her.

"I didn't mean . . . Sorry, I was just trying to be funny. I've been dragged out here twice in your name." She sighed. "Never mind. Not funny. But in my defense, it is early."

"What kind of conversation is this?" Walker said. "So I know whether I can laugh at your bad jokes or not."

She smiled. "It's casual, Mr. Walker. I obviously don't believe you've had anything to do with what's going on, but it is strange you've been involved twice."

"Trouble has a way of finding the troubled."

"That what you are?"

"Have a seat, Detective," Walker said as he pointed to the bar stool.

"Please, call me Ava. And thanks for the coffee." She took a sip as she took a seat. Walker noticed that her feet didn't hit the floor. In the yellow kitchen light, he could see that she was fairly young. No noticeable lines, but also not filled with BOTOX or other fillers . . . yet. Her dark brown eyes matched the coffee in her mug.

"Ava, you been doing this long?" Walker took a seat as well. Over Ava's shoulder, out the window and in the distance on the lake, he saw a light moving by. The fishermen were getting an early start.

"Been a cop since I graduated high school. So, about ten years. Been a detective for, well, almost a year now. Since about this time last year when half our force left for greener pastures. A lot of turnover every year, really. Not enough crazy stuff happens in this little town, I guess. Well, until lately."

"There's been more going on?"

"This is the third missing persons case in the last month. All unsolved, unfortunately," Ava said.

"Rough start."

Ava laughed. "Straight shooter, eh?"

"Probably to a fault," Walker said. "Any connection to the Turnberry case? The other two missing, I mean?"

"Nothing points to that, but there isn't really a lot to go on in any of them. They just up and disappeared. Like they walked out of town, avoiding all the cameras in the area, and never came back."

Walker sipped his coffee. "So, nothing like this has ever happened? This many missing?"

"No. Not this many. But there were two, about this time last year."

Walker raised an eyebrow. "You mean, around this time last year, two kids went missing and were never found?"

"Yeah, no, they never found them," Ava said.

"And then a bunch of people left the police force? Detectives or officers?"

Ava thought for a minute. "Both actually."

Walker shook his head. "That doesn't seem odd to you?"

"Well, maybe a little. But when they made me detective, they told me they hoped I could stick around a while because detectives seem to turnover a lot. Like it was nothing new." Ava eyed Walker for a minute as he stared at his coffee. "What?"

Walker shrugged. "Probably nothing. But since it happened around the same time last year, I might at least examine it a little. What about two years ago around this time?"

Ava shook her head. "I-I don't know. I was working more in Chattanooga. You think something is going on yearly? That makes no sense."

"I don't think anything. But if you have no leads, I would check everything that didn't sit just right. Know what I mean?"

Ava took a second, sipped some coffee, checked out the view through the windows behind her. "You know, I looked up David Walker."

"I figured you might. And?"

"And nothing. Like literally. It's like you don't exist except a Florida driver's license and a passport. But you don't sound like you're from Florida."

"I'm not. I'm from Kentucky."

"Okay. Well, you sound like you are pretty good at this sort of thing. You have a background in law enforcement?"

Now it was Walker's turn to take a second. His mind was churning on the information Ava had just shared about the others missing this year and last year. He wanted to help. Even if he didn't know whether he could actually be useful or not, he felt as though he'd been pulled into this one by forces beyond his control. But that meant divulging certain things about himself that could bring him trouble. And that's if she even believed anything he said anyway.

"Is all of this off the record, Detective?"

"I don't like the sound of that. And, I mean, I am a detective, so nothing is ever completely off the record. But if you have something you want to tell me, as long as you aren't confessing to kidnapping these kids, I won't hold it against you."

Walker eyed her for a moment. "You sure about that?"

"I am. Why?"

"I want to help. Maybe I can, maybe I can't, but you have to promise me that whatever I tell you about me, and about what happened tonight with the Turnberrys' son stays between you and me."

"Shit. Now I really don't like where this is going. So you did talk to Daniel Turnberry?"

Walker didn't speak.

"Let me rephrase," Ava said. "More happened here tonight with Daniel Turnberry. And before you answer, all I care about is doing the right thing and finding Amy Turnberry. I don't care about getting anyone else in trouble. But if you don't mind, start with you. You seem to have a law enforcement mentality at least, so any history?"

Walker didn't know why, but he believed Ava. She didn't

at all seem like the sort of detective who was chasing headlines.

"I definitely have never enforced any laws in my life," Walker said. "But I will say that I've had a very strong hand in influencing those who make the laws of the land, in many places around the globe."

Ava scrunched her nose. "What an odd and poetic answer, Walker. I saw the big thick book sitting over there. You a writer too?"

"It's a hobby."

"Interesting. So, CIA then? You some sort of superagent?"

"Let's just leave it as, something like that."

Ava nodded. "Okay. Do I want to know why your name shows no background, and why you're here in the middle of nowhere, with no connections to Chuck and Tammy Smith?"

"You don't. But I think I can help you with what's going on if you let me. If nothing else, I can be a fresh set of eyes."

"Off the books, of course," Ava said.

"I think it's best that I just stay the guy who is house-sitting for the Smiths."

"So what really happened with Daniel Turnberry? Then we'll get to why you want to help."

"They're the same answer, really," Walker said. "I told Daniel I would help him."

"Okay, we'll get to that, but why do you want to help him? You don't know him. Shouldn't you just leave it to us? The law?"

"That's what I told Daniel, but he doesn't have much faith in the law after four days of nothing. His words, not mine. Though, in all honesty, I can't say I disagree with him. It is his little sister, after all."

"Yeah?" Ava slid out of the bar stool to her feet. "And just what the hell would you know about any of it? What the television said? This was a bad idea, Mr. Walker. I'll just go and ask Daniel Turnberry what exactly happened here. Thank you for the coffee. I can see myself out."

Walker stood, but he didn't try to stop her. If she was someone who operated outside the realm of being able to be told the truth, she wouldn't be someone worth working with in the first place. Walker was good at a lot of things, but right or wrong, dancing around people's feelings was not one of them.

Ava stopped just before walking out the door. "And I'll have you know, I didn't ask for this job. It was thrown in my lap. And I'm sure the reason I'm storming out of here is because there is a ring of truth to what you just said. But I'm still leaving either way."

Walker just nodded to her. She walked out and shut the door behind her.

He would just have to wait and help Daniel on his own. But at least Ava had given him some contextual information that he could try to fill his day with.

A day whose light had yet to show its face. A day that no doubt was about to be a lot longer than the night he'd just had.

10

Walker didn't let the early morning intrusions by Daniel Turnberry, Mayor Clark and his wife Emily Turnberry, or Detective Ava Bailey deter him from getting in his morning run. It had not only been good for his body, but it was good to clear the mind as well. It also gave him time to sort through what he knew to that point and figure out what he wanted to do first. But before he got started helping total strangers with problems that had nothing to do with him, he did a long body-weight, muscle-building routine and then ate six scrambled eggs, a quarter pound of bacon, and a few sausage links. He'd been doing too much running, and he didn't want to lose muscle in the process. The weight training followed by copious amounts of protein would ensure he didn't lose any more weight.

He set his extra-large plate down on the counter beside his laptop and dug in as he pulled up an incognito window and went to the DuckDuckGo search website. The first thing he wanted to wrap his head around was why a major string of kidnappings had happened around the exact same time period two years in a row. If he could rule that out as a coincidence, instead of a pattern, it would be a good start. If somehow he could establish a pattern, then he would have a direction to run in. He would much rather talk to human beings about it than search the internet, but knowing no one and trying to stay unknown made for a rough go at in-person meetings.

As soon as he typed in the words *Soddy Daisy kidnappings 2022,* the camera notification app dinged on his phone.

"You've got to be kidding me."

Walker let his fork clank down hard on the plate. He picked up his phone and tapped on the notification. Then he watched a skinny, blond-haired teenage boy get out of his topless Jeep Wrangler and walk toward the front door. Walker's shoulders slumped. Not because he didn't want to talk to the kid, because he actually did, but because he just wanted to finish his breakfast in peace. Daniel knocked on the door.

When Walker opened the door, the Daniel in front of him looked even younger than he had last night. And he looked exhausted. He was holding a laptop computer in his hand.

"Long night?" Walker stated the obvious.

"Sorry to bother you again."

"I told you to come back here tonight."

Daniel looked up at him. "Another day might as well be a week for a missing little girl, Walker."

He had a point.

"Besides," Daniel went on, "my parents already know that I've been down here now. What's to hide?"

"Nothing for you," Walker said. "I, on the other hand, am trying not to grab any unnecessary attention."

"Shit, you're right. I'm sorry, man. I can come back later. Maybe then I can tell you that Amy is dead instead of just kidnapped."

Walker understood Daniel's frustration, but he didn't appreciate the sarcasm.

"Maybe you should take a nap. Then we can talk."

"Do you want to help or not, man? You don't have to, you just said you would. I have been up all night researching, and I have a few things I want to run by you. Please. I've got no one else."

Walker thought about Ava. If the kid found anything pertinent, she would need to hear it. Not Walker. But Daniel was right: Walker had told him he would help. He could always relay anything worth looking into to Ava after the fact.

Walker stepped aside and held the door open. Daniel walked in without saying thank you.

"Holy shit, it smells so good in here."

"You hungry?"

"Man, I don't even remember the last time I ate."

Walker followed him over to the kitchen. He pulled a plate from the cabinet as Daniel sat down. Then he went over and halved his portion, then slid the plate over to Daniel. He immediately dove in on the bacon while Walker fetched him a fork for the eggs.

"Dude, this is so good."

Walker filled a glass of water, then handed it over with the fork. "Stay hydrated."

"You sound like my mom."

"Yeah? Did she tear you a new one when they got home last night?"

Daniel's mouth was full, but that didn't stop him. "You

have no idea. But it's all good. She's just sad, I think, and doesn't know how to process it."

"You're probably right. So, tell me what you found."

Daniel shoved some more food into his mouth. "Okay, so you probably don't know this, 'cause the media is only really talking about my sister, but two other kids have gone missing over the past two weeks."

Walker swallowed some eggs. "Yeah, Ava—Detective Bailey mentioned that. A couple last year around the same time too."

"Yeah! And one the year before. Which could totally be a coincidence, but still . . . kinda weird, right?"

"Kinda weird," Walker agreed. "And all the detectives working the cases are now gone too, apparently."

"Right? I saw that too!"

Maybe the kid would actually be some help.

"Ava said they all left for other jobs," Walker said. "By *all*, I'm assuming she meant one or two. Not sure how many detectives this small town area has."

"Two. And I looked them up," Daniel said. He had a *"you're not going to believe this"* look on his face. The kid should stay away from poker.

"And?"

"One of them moved just across the state line to Ringgold, Georgia. Says he's the detective there on the police department website. Maybe he can help us with info on what happened with the two kidnapped last year."

"Maybe," Walker said as he finished the last of his bacon. The salty meat paired well with the sweet orange juice he'd decided to pour. "What about the second one?"

"Dead," Daniel said.

"Dead? That's it?"

"Yep. Hung himself in his house. It was in the Chattanooga newspaper archives online."

A person can find just about anything on the internet these days.

Walker swallowed some sausage. "You're wondering if it was really a suicide, aren't you?"

"You too?" Daniel said. "I definitely thought about it."

Walker was thinking about it too. "Well, it wouldn't really make sense that if someone wanted to cover something up, they would kill only one of the detectives. Unless of course the detective who's still alive had something to do with it."

"Damn, man, you think?"

"I don't know what to think," Walker said. "The problem with rabbit holes is a person's bias. Whatever you are chasing, the information is always skewed by what you already think or want to happen."

"Confirmation bias," Daniel said. "We just learned about that in history class. But I don't really have a bias here. I just want my sister back."

"Everyone always has a bias, Daniel. It's cooked into your DNA. Very few master the art of being able to deny it."

"Okay, Mister Miyagi, you want me to paint your fence next?" Daniel said with a laugh.

"I'm just impressed you know what *The Karate Kid* is. Quite a bit before your time."

"I like the older stuff. Everything now is just a remake of the oldies."

"Careful, kid. You might start to make me like you. And I don't want that."

Daniel laughed. "Why?"

"Bias. I start to like you, then I'll want to protect you.

And I need to find your sister. Can't let those two things interfere with each other."

"You're a strange dude, Walker. In a good way, I mean."

"I'd say thanks, but I'm not sure that was a compliment."

Daniel set down his fork on the empty plate and pushed the plate away. "Thanks for the food . . . so, what now?"

"What now is you get your ass back home and get some sleep. I'll run with this information you gave me, and we can meet back here tonight like we talked about."

"No way, man. I gotta be here with you. It's *my* sister, you know."

"I understand. But if you're dragging ass tonight because you haven't slept, what good are you to me or your sister anyway?"

Daniel was quiet for a minute. "Yeah, I am tired. But I can't go home and sleep now. I have to go to church. Mom said it's even more important now. I was dumb and said, 'More important than finding Amy?' Thought she was going to hit me."

"Maybe your mom is right. Get to church. Show her some support. Then go rest. I'll let you know what I find out tonight."

11

Walker had tried reaching Detective Foley––one of the two detectives who had worked the two unsolved kidnapping cases last year before leaving their jobs––by calling the Ringgold Police Department. The gentlemen who had answered the phone said Detective Foley never comes in on Sundays. Then he dodged Walker's couple of attempts at getting some more information. The man wasn't helpful at all, but Walker wasn't all that surprised. He was a stranger asking for personal information about a law enforcement officer, so of course he wasn't going to be told where Detective Foley lived or where he might be found on a sweltering summer afternoon in the South. So Walker decided the old-school, in-person approach was his only hope.

The drive over to Ringgold was a pleasant one. There wasn't much to see really, but with the windows down, the sun shining, and some Tom Petty pumping through the speakers, it didn't really matter. Though it seemed Walker may be growing bored living the same day over and over again at the lake, he felt like the reason he was loving it so much was because it was quite possibly the first time in his life he had ever actually felt free. His entire childhood, he was at the whims of adults, pushing and pulling him in every direction to find Tom the orphan a proper home. And while some of the people in his life at that time were trying to help him, none of them actually had. They did keep him from dying or starving to death, but there were plenty of moments when yet another leather belt was slapping against his skin, when he wasn't really all that sure that starving to death wouldn't be a better fate.

The only glimpses of freedom, or at least freedom of self, were when he would escape into his books. There he could be someone else. Someone living a fantastical life, which good or bad was at least of their own volition, even if it didn't turn out as planned. His dive into those imaginary worlds had kept him from going insane in his own reality. The writers of those novels, without knowing it, had saved his life. And he'd been a rather big fan of getting lost in the words of those authors ever since.

After he strangled his last foster father, because the man had nearly beaten his foster mother to death, freedom felt even more scarce. As he awaited trial, though, he still had books in his jail cell. And one might assume that when they "let" him out of jail and put him into the program at Maxwell Solutions, he was free, but that was when he might have been the least free of all. He was constantly in training, sometimes up to fifteen hours a day. Though there was no way Walker could have known it were true, the men bringing hell on his fifteen-year-old body told him his training outdid even a Navy Seal regimen. And that went on for three relentless years—the toughest three years of Walker's life—and he'd seen some doozies.

When his training period was over, and he was officially

an adult at eighteen, the real nightmare began. He had killed his foster father out of survival. Walker had believed with all his heart that Jim was going to kill either Kim or one of the three foster girls living with them. Killing Jim had been out of personal necessity. The first time he'd killed a man in Iran by sliding a knife across his throat didn't feel necessary at all. Mostly because he had no real idea who the man was. Just that the United States government needed him gone. And that Walker was doing his country a great service by ending him. Maybe that had been true. Maybe Walker had been able to make the United States safer. But in the moment, it sure didn't feel like anything but wrong.

Walker never forgot that day. He'd tried to block it out over the years, but it never worked. Hundreds of times he'd woken up, drenched in sweat, after another nightmare reliving the moment. Feeling the man's hot blood running out onto his hands. The copper and metallic smell that came along with it. The way the man's body slammed against the concrete when Walker let his lifeless body go. And even though he killed so many others for Maxwell over the years after that, it was the first one that never left him.

So, while Maxwell had allowed Walker to have his own place to live and some free time in between jobs, there had never been a feeling of being a free man. Not like Walker felt right then as he steered his Shelby Cobra around a long turn on a tree-lined two-lane road. And that's because he never was free. He was always at the behest of others, not like a free man in the United States who worked the job of his choosing. Walker knew that there was no leaving the "job" they'd placed him in. No 401K, no pension, only a casket. Or at least a fake one like he'd been able to manage back in Kentucky. Even then, in the back of Walker's mind, he knew his business wasn't finished with Karen Maxwell and the others who'd enslaved him. But he didn't let that truth sour the ride he was currently on. He enjoyed it all the way to the Ringgold Police Department parking lot.

Walker shut down the purring engine of his prized possession and stepped out into the sun. The square police building looked old, but the asphalt beneath him was brand-new. The smoky, oily, petroleum-like scent was still strong all around him. A stark contrast to the smell of cut grass and oak trees around the lake.

Walker headed inside, and he was happy to see a woman sitting behind the front desk. Not because he felt as though he could charm her, but because with the man he had spoken with earlier, there would have been no chance.

"What can I do for you today, sir?" The heavy-set, frizzy-haired woman was welcoming.

"How are you doing today, ma'am?" Walker said.

"I'm just fine, thank you for asking," she said with a wide smile. "What can I do for you?"

"Well, I just need a little help," Walker said.

"You came to the right place."

"Great. I'm looking for Detective Foley——Bill. I know he doesn't usually come in on Sundays, but I have something personal of his and I need to get it back to him. Is there any way you can help me out? Where can I find him? He isn't answering his phone, and we were supposed to meet up this morning."

"Oh yeah? Well, I wish you would have called and saved yourself the trip over here. He doesn't come in on Sundays unless there's a new case or something. And I'm sorry, but I can't tell you anything else."

"Yeah? No, I understand." Walker tried to play sheepish. He wasn't good at it and he knew it. "I was just thinking maybe you knew where he hangs out on a Sunday or something. I wasn't expecting you to give me his address or anything."

"Yeah, no. I certainly can't do that. I'm sorry, hon."

"All right. You sure? It's pretty important, but I'm sure it will be okay."

"Sorry."

"All right," Walker said, taking a step back. "Thank you anyway. I hope you have a great day."

"You too, sir," she said, then looked to her right, then to her left. Then back to Walker. "It is Sunday, you know. Lots of people are real churchgoers around here. There's a church just right down the road there if you feel like you need it. First Baptist. Preacher there is pretty darn good."

Walker smiled and gave her a nod. "Thank you. You know, I just might go see how good he is."

"All right, hon. Have you a good one."

"You too."

Walker backed his way out of the glass door and into the sunshine. It was good to know the old-fashioned, in-person approach still meant something in 2023, though he knew how lucky he was that she had been the one at the front desk. Either way, he was just happy the officer had clued him in and he had a next place to go to try to find Detective Foley. Walker had no idea if it would actually lead to anything in Amy Turnberry's case, but it was also the only lead he had. And he had absolutely nothing to do on a Sunday afternoon, so he might as well go get some religion.

And hopefully a clue as to whether the kidnappings a year ago at around the same time frame could possibly be related in any way.

Walker wasn't overly hopeful, but he was hoping it could lead somewhere.

12

The officer at the Ringgold PD front desk had eluded that the church was just up the road on the right. That wasn't exactly true, as Walker realized as he approached mile three from the department. And the road had gone from town to rural in about half that time. He was just about to open the navigation app on his phone when the trees on the right side cleared and there sitting inside the indention was a parking lot adjacent to a white A-frame building holding a cross above the open front door and just below a steeple.

Families holding hands as they walked across the parking lot filed in the front door. And just as Walker turned off the road, the church bells began ringing––the 11:00 a.m. service was just about to start. Walker pulled into one of the few remaining spaces, in between a years-worn blue pickup truck and a maroon minivan. Walker looked down at his blue jeans and his white T-shirt. He wasn't exactly dressed in his Sunday best, but most of the parishioners walking in before him seemed fairly casual. So he didn't feel too bad about it. He knew he was going to stand out either way. He was a stranger at a small-town church. He imagined most of the people inside had known everyone else in that building for many years.

Walker wanted to wait out in the car and watch to see if Detective Foley came out at the end. Then follow him. But that was an hour away at least, and if the preacher thought he was as good as the officer back at the station said he was, he might just be a bit long-winded for one short hour. Daniel had sent a picture of Foley over from the Ringgold PD's website. Walker knew what he looked like, and it wasn't a large church, so going on inside to see if he was sitting in one of the pews would be much quicker.

Walker made his way across the parking lot to the front door. There was a man greeting people as they came in. Probably one of the ushers. With the first foster home Walker could remember being in when he was six, his foster dad, Greg, was an usher at the church they attended. It was the last time Walker had been to church. It was perhaps the only foster home that had ever been a nice place to live for him. Greg had been a great guy. Everyone liked him. And from what little Walker could remember, he was always nice to Walker. That's why it was too bad––or sometimes what Walker felt was the TW (Tom Walker) bad luck––when Greg was killed in a car accident. The next home Walker went to wasn't nearly as nice, and it came with a hundred percent more bruises. That's where the TW luck started being a thing in his mind.

As Walker made his way to the door, the usher reached his hand forward and looked at Walker as if he was genuinely happy to see him. Walker took his hand. The man wrapped his other hand around Walker's as well, with one of those extra-good-to-see-you, two-hand shakes.

"Hello there, friend. It is awfully nice to see a new face

around here. I'm Steve Moore. An usher here at the church. What brings you to our house of worship today?"

Walker gave the man a grin with his firm handshake. "Rumor has it the preacher here can really call down the angels."

"Oh." Steve widened his already wide smile and took a big inhale. "Brother Stewart is the best. You're in for a real treat! He can make the demons give an amen."

"Looking forward to it."

"And your name, my friend?" Steve said, still smiling. His bushy white eyebrows fanned out above his gold-rimmed glasses. Walker imagined that Steve was probably the type of guy who, if you told him his dog just died, would have a silver-linings quote to share.

"David," Walker said.

"Well, it's real nice to meet you, David. And might I say, that is a mighty fine car I saw you get out of. Is it a '68?"

"Sixty-seven," Walker said. "And thank you."

"Yes, sir, well, you enjoy the sermon today, brother. I'll see you inside."

"I will, but before I go in, have you seen my friend Rob Foley?"

"Oh, you know Rob? He has been such a great addition to the church," Steve said as he paused to scratch his head. "Come to think of it, I don't think I've seen him today. But I did just go to the little boys room a couple of minutes ago. I easily could have missed him. The church isn't big. You should find him pretty fast if he's here."

"Thank you, Steve."

"Yes, sir. Enjoy the sermon."

Walker nodded as he moved inside the church. There was a small, rectangular holding area with restrooms on the right and left side behind him. The gray wall in front of him had a wooden double door right in the middle. It was closed.

Walker pushed open those double doors and took the aisle seat in the very back row. Then he immediately stood when the preacher took to the pulpit and the congregation all rose to their feet. Daniel had sent Walker a second picture of the detective from the man's Facebook page. It showed what Foley looked like in more casual attire. It was becoming increasingly difficult to stay private in a world where everyone was online. Walker checked the image of the detective on his phone, then scanned the crowd of about fifty people around him as the preacher said his hellos.

Steve was right: it was a fairly small church, at least it seemed so to Walker. He had very little experience with such matters. His entire adult life had been spent killing humans, so he was actually shocked that he didn't burst into flames when he walked through the door. The preacher was standing behind a pulpit, white with a wooden cross on the front. His stage was up a short set of stairs so everyone could have a view. Behind him stood a choir. Behind them, up another set of hidden stairs, there was a mural of a river running between mountains. Below it, a pool where people washed away their sins.

The choir began singing "*He Lives*" from the hymnal. A song Walker could faintly remember from being young in church. The couple beside him was holding hands and singing along. What a different life they led than Walker's. He knew people like the couple beside him had probably heard stories about men like Walker––killers––but they had no clue the extent to which violent acts were performed around the globe in the name of freedom. Walker probably looked normal enough in his blue jeans and white V-neck

T-shirt. But if they only knew the things he'd seen. The things he'd done.

Walker continued to search for the detective in the congregation, but there was no sign of him. Not really even anyone who resembled him. As the choir finished their song and everyone took their seats, Walker saw no reason to stick around. The detective wasn't there. As the preacher began speaking about the previous week the church had had, Walker stood and slinked out the door. But before he could make it all the way out, Steve caught him getting away.

"Leaving so soon, my friend?" Steve cut him off at the pass.

"Yeah, I really want to stick around, but I really need to find my friend. It's pretty important."

"It's actually really odd that Rob isn't here. Since moving over to Ringgold, I don't think he's missed a Sunday. But that doesn't mean you should miss out."

"I hate to, but I need to find him. Especially if he's missed being here today." Walker leaned in and used a whisper. "Between me and you, Steve, I'm pretty worried about him."

Steve's demeanor changed for the first time since Walker'd met him. Instead of over-the-top kindness, his face showed genuine concern.

"Oh no, are you with the police or something? Is he all right?"

Walker paused for dramatic effect. "Or something, Steve." He let that linger for a second. "And I'm not sure he is okay. I was hoping to find him here, because I only have his old address from where he used to work in Soddy Daisy. I'd go to the police department here, but I don't want to get him in trouble."

"Oh gosh," Steve said. Then he took Walker by the elbow and pulled him outside into the sunshine. "You're trying to help him, right? 'Cause I've heard that he's had a few problems. That's why he moved over here to Ringgold. You looking out for him?"

"I'm trying to. I know the problems you're talking about, and it's worse than you think." Walker didn't want to throw someone he didn't even know under the bus, but since he didn't actually know what the hell Steve, the town gossip apparently, was talking about, he thought maybe it could help him find Detective Foley. "But I can help him if I can find him."

"Well, I do know where he lives. It's actually just right up this road. But it would be wrong of me to say."

"I understand," Walker said. "I'd just hate for something ... *bad* to happen to him. You know?"

Steve looked around like someone might be watching him spill some top secret information. Then he leaned in close. "As long as you're trying to help ..."

Walker nodded.

"His house number is 3620. Not more than a mile or two, the way you were headed when you came to the church. It's a small white-siding ranch. He has an American flag hanging off the outside wall by his front porch. But you didn't hear any of that from me."

Walker pinched his fingers together and zipped his lips shut. Then he extended his hand. "Thank you, Steve. You've done a good thing here."

"Oh, I sure hope so. Please come back and enjoy a sermon sometime?"

"I just might do that."

Walker stepped away from Steve and moved down the steps.

"It was nice meeting you. I hope it goes okay," Steve said.

Walker waved to Steve, then got in his car. He'd been lucky with the help he'd received both from the woman at the police department and from Steve. Now all Walker could do was hope it paid off. He didn't like the fact that Steve said Detective Foley never missed a sermon and today he hadn't been there. He just hoped it was a coincidence and not a prelude to something Walker didn't want to step into.

13

Walker followed the road Steve told him to take to get to Detective Foley's house. As it wound up and around a thick layer of trees on both sides of the road, Walker reached over and pulled his Sig Sauer P365 from the glove box and set it in the passenger seat. The road took a turn back to the left and down the hill he'd just driven up. He could see toward the bottom of the hill in front of him that the trees began to clear. He let fourth gear slow him down as he coasted toward the bottom.

Once the trees backed away from the road, Walker could see a mailbox up ahead on his right. He glanced in his rearview as he continued to slow his Mustang. Finally, a house came into view. White siding, just like Steve had said, and the red and blue of Old Glory waving in the wind on the front porch popped against the white backdrop. Walker turned onto the driveway, and at a glance he saw a crooked number 3620 going down the wood base of the mailbox. This was Detective Foley's house. Now to see if anyone was home.

The driveway—what was left of it anyway—was broken-up old pavement with weeds sprouting up all over. The grass on both sides was overgrown. Walker bumped and shook all the way to the navy-blue Ford Crown Victoria that was sitting in front of the one-car garage. That was a cop car if Walker had ever seen one, so hopefully he would find Foley home.

Walker shut off his engine and stepped out of the car. He brought his pistol along with him, tucked in the concealed holster at the small of his back. The heat had risen at least another five degrees since the church parking lot. The humidity had to have been hovering around 90 percent, the air so thick he could feel the moisture. Walker ran his hand through his hair as he approached the front porch. Before he stepped on the first uneven step, he turned and had a look back out at the road.

There was nothing around. No sign of human life whatsoever. There was a slight breeze rustling the leaves around him, and other than the occasional call from some birds in the distance, there was absolutely nothing else.

Walker turned and stepped up the rickety wooden steps that led to the even more deteriorated wood-planked porch. The storm door was half off its hinge, and now that Walker was closer, he could see that the front door was ajar. He whipped his hand to his back and pulled his pistol.

"Hello?" Walker called out. Nothing came in response. He took a step closer to the door. He tried to peek inside, but it was dark. "Detective Foley? You here?"

Walker pulled the storm door back carefully. It groaned as he stepped forward and let it rest against his back. He used the muzzle of his pistol to nudge the door open a little farther.

"Detective Foley? You in there?" Nothing. "Everything all right?"

Walker hadn't used his instincts in over a month, but even then, they had been frazzled by his short-term memory loss. He could tell the years honing them hadn't let a little time off see them waver. He could feel it all through him that whatever he was about to find wasn't just going to be bad; it was going to create a ripple effect he'd be trying to wade through until he could somehow get out of the murky waters he'd stepped into down at the lake.

"I'm coming in, and I'm armed."

Walker pushed open the door and trained his gun on the dark room in front of him. He immediately knew his inclination was right. The living room he walked into was a mess. Not an "*I need a maid*" sort of mess, but an "at least two men came after me, and I put up a fight" sort of mess. Walker flipped on the light. The end table beside the tan couch on the back wall had been overturned. A lamp in pieces beside it. A mirror's faded rectangular outline clung to the white painted wall, the mirror itself shattered below. The drywall behind it had a man-sized indention cracked into it. Finally, the mahogany wood coffee table was broken, and the glass inlay was shattered, raindrop-sized glass shards pooled all around it.

Walker shut the door behind him and locked it. He didn't want any easy surprises sneaking up behind him. A couple of steps closer to the busted table and he could see a decent spray of blood on the khaki-colored carpet. His mind shot to Detective Bailey. He should call her. But he had to ensure his own safety first. Then he could worry about procedure. To get her attention quickly, he whipped out his phone and opened Ava's contact in the messages app. As he continued to scan the room around him, he dropped a pin showing his location, and the words "G*et here now.*" She would either come based on that or she wouldn't; it didn't really matter to him.

Walker pocketed his phone. As he stepped over to the couch, he could now see footprints in blood, the toe of the shoe moving to his right. There was a back door in that direction, and like the front door, it was still ajar. Walker moved over to it, again opening it with his gun to avoid fingerprints, and he could immediately see a body lying facedown in the grass just beyond the back deck. He stopped as his phone began vibrating in his pocket. He slipped it out of his front pocket, and Detective Bailey's name showed on the screen. He tapped the button to answer.

"Sorry for the brief message, but I can't talk. It's David Walker from the Smiths' lake house. Long story short, your former colleague Detective Foley's house has been broken into, and while I have yet to step over and check the dead body in the grass in front of me, I'm pretty sure he's the one lying there."

Silence.

Walker said, "I can't wait around for your mind to catch up with the surprise of this call. I might be in danger. I'll secure the perimeter and wait for you at the house."

"I-I-I'm on my way."

Walker ended the call and put the phone away. Before he took another step, he tuned his ears. Still nothing but the wind and a few of the birds that ride its invisible waves. He moved back inside the house, carefully stepping around the bloody footprints. He went to the front window to the right of the front door. Foley's car and Walker's Mustang sat alone in front of the quiet front yard. Beyond that, the road that brought him there.

If Walker hadn't lingered that split second longer as he looked out the window, he wouldn't have seen the front end of a vehicle come to a stop on the right side of the road. Walker could just make out a chrome grill; the trees covered the rest, hiding the make and model. His mind raced, first jumping to the obvious fact that whoever was in that vehicle was responsible for what happened to Foley. Otherwise, they would never have stopped in the middle of the road, and they wouldn't still be sitting there now. With that in mind, there were too many unknowns for Walker to give chase. There could be more than a couple of men. They could all be armed. And although Walker knew they wouldn't be trained like him, they could have some military background, and running roughshod at them would be a mistake.

However, waiting like a sitting duck for them to come and get him wasn't a great option either. It was clear to Walker that they had been driving by to see if anyone had found Foley yet, and when they saw Walker's car, the driver's instinct was to stop. This is where Walker's choice of vehicle immediately landed him in trouble. The '67 Mustang was unforgettable. So he was going to be easy to follow. So even if Walker made it away from Foley's house unscathed, his guard was going to be up. They would be watching.

After what seemed like an excruciatingly long few seconds, the vehicle backed away out of sight. Not what Walker wanted to see. He was inches away from having his first clue as to who might be responsible, and now it was leaving. And there was no way he could go out there right then to try to identify the vehicle. By the time he made it to the road, they would be long gone. The only clue left for Walker was that he could tell by the height of the vehicle that it was either a truck or an SUV. In a lake town in the South, that wouldn't exactly narrow it down. He realized the sarcasm in his own head wasn't helping, so he turned and went back out of the house.

Walker was at least going to positively identify the body as he waited, but the body's nose was straight down into the ground. And he wasn't about to touch it. Not until Ava made it to the scene. He'd more than likely already done enough for the police to find traces of him at the scene. He wasn't going to make it worse.

There were two deck chairs facing the backyard, facing a small, overgrown patch of grass, then more trees. Walker wiped the sweat from his brow, took a seat, rested his pistol in his lap—hand on the grip—and waited. For the first time in his life, there was a dead body in his presence and he wasn't the one responsible.

And he didn't like it one bit.

14

Walker's phone dinged in his hand. Detective Bailey. "Pulling in," she texted. Walker heard her vehicle approaching from the front. He texted her back: "In the back on the deck."

Walker was pretty much a pool of sweat by then. He watched out of the corner of his right eye as Ava walked around the corner, her pistol stretched out in front of her. He looked over at her. She lowered her weapon, and he watched her head volley between the dead body and Walker.

"I knew you were trouble the moment I met you," she said, her left hand now resting on her hip.

Walker stood and turned to face her. "Yeah, because this is how I wanted to spend my Sunday."

"Yet here you are." Ava walked over to the body and stood over the man dressed in jeans and a navy-blue sport coat. "What the hell are you doing here anyway, Mr. Walker?"

"Just Walker."

She looked up at him, using her hand to shield her eyes

from the sun. "Okay, Just Walker, how'd you come about being here at a detective's house, him facedown on the ground . . . dead? Let me guess, long story."

"Short one actually. Daniel did some digging—"

"Daniel Turnberry? As in the kidnap victim's brother, and the one who tried to break into your house last night? That Daniel?"

"You know which Daniel. Can I finish? It's hot. And I have some day drinking to do."

"Oh, so the heat makes Mr. Polite a little snippy?"

Walker wiped yet another collection of sweat from his forehead and took a breath. "Sorry. I haven't eaten either."

"Well, hot and hangry isn't a good combo," Ava said, giving Walker a pass. Then she bent down, pulled at the body's coat sleeve, and rolled it over. "Yep. That's Detective Foley all right." Then she looked up at Walker. "Let's step inside while I call this in."

Walker nodded. Sounded good to him. Ava called in the possible homicide, and he followed her inside the house. She put the phone away and eyed the smashed coffee table.

"I have to ask, Walker. Wasn't you that killed him, was it?"

"I have yet to kill anyone in Tennessee."

She smiled. "That's reassuring. So what happened?"

Walker stepped over to the front window, just to make certain the people watching earlier hadn't decided to come back. "After we talked this morning, my mind was stuck on whether or not there was a pattern with these year-over-year missing persons."

"It was just one year apart around the same time. Not sure that establishes a pattern."

Walker turned toward her after not finding the vehicle on the road. "Maybe not, but that coupled with the fact that none of the detectives stuck around, well, it stuck with me. But when Daniel showed up after you left, he'd been digging into the same thing. Found out that one of the detectives on last year's missing child was dead—"

"And found that Foley moved over here to Ringgold PD," Ava finished his thought.

"That's why I'm here."

"You didn't think to call me first?"

"I didn't expect to find the man dead. I just wanted to ask a couple of questions."

"Under what capacity exactly, Walker? Secret government agent? Concerned citizen? You had to know he wasn't going to open up to you."

Walker nodded. "I never said I was a detective."

"Then why are you trying to act like one? How'd you even find where he lives?"

"No comment."

Ava began shaking her head as she looked at the destroyed room around her. "You do realize what this looks like."

"I do. That's why I called you."

"And why am I not taking you to jail for murder? You are the only suspect I have."

"What have I stepped into here, Ava?" Walker changed the subject.

Ava hung her head. When she looked back up, she didn't exactly look confident. "I-I don't know. But I've got a big problem, don't I?"

"Just how many homicides or kidnappings have you investigated?"

Ava just stared blankly.

Walker stared back, but his glare was more of a knowing one.

"It's a small town," Ava said defensively. "And I've only been on the job a year. The worst trouble we ever usually have is somebody getting their wallet stolen out of their car, or Jimmy down the street caught with a bag of weed. I'm not ready for this, Walker. What the hell am I going to do?"

Walker felt bad for her. He could somewhat relate. The first mission he was sent on, he didn't think he was ready either. But he had been thoroughly and properly trained. It seemed to him that Ava hadn't been, and he knew that was where her lack of confidence was coming from.

"I wasn't trained for this," Ava went on. "This is *way* over my head."

"Don't you have a senior detective who can help you?" Walker was grasping at straws.

"Well, I did. Until a month ago. Bastard got drunk and got hit by a train."

"You've gotta be shitting me," Walker said.

"I wish I was. Though I'm not sure how much help he would have been anyway. He spent more time hitting on me than working cases. But at least he'd get the blame for this failure I'm currently riding on."

Walker watched for a minute as Ava stared at her shoes. This was not the confident woman he'd watched walking down the Smiths' driveway yesterday evening. If Walker was going to have a chance at helping Amy Turnberry, he was going to need that first-impression Ava back.

"You done?" Walker finally said.

Ava looked up, surprised. "Excuse me?"

"With this little pity party you're throwing here. You about finished with it?"

"I'm not . . ." Now both Ava's hands were on her hips. "Who the hell do you think you are?"

"I know who I am, Ava. What I'm trying to figure out is

just who in the hell you are. The detective I met yesterday had presence. Confidence. And whether that was just a front or not, I need you to find that woman and get rid of this one standing here now. 'Cause they are not the same person."

"Go to hell."

"That's better. Now, tell me what we're going to do next."

Ava looked around. Walker could see that her ego was bruised.

"*We,*" Ava said, pointing between herself and Walker, "aren't going to do anything. *I* am going to let you get the hell out of here before forensics gets here. Why? I'm not sure, really. But I will be watching you, Mr. Walker. If I were you, I would stop talking to Daniel Turnberry and go back to getting drunk on the lake like you should be doing. Do we understand each other? 'Cause I'm not asking you to do this. I'm telling you."

Walker smiled. "Okay, Detective Bailey. I hear you. Loud and clear. And you're probably right. I should just stay the hell out of this entire mess you've got here."

"Have a good afternoon," Ava said.

Walker nodded. He turned to the front door and nudged it open with his shoe. When he walked outside, he looked again where that vehicle had stopped earlier. Then he turned back to Ava.

"When I was in here earlier," Walker said, "just after I talked to you on the phone, I saw a vehicle stop out on the road there." He thumbed over his shoulder. "I couldn't see what kind it was, just the very front end, but it looked like a truck or an SUV. The rest was hidden by the trees. Anyway, they backed up and left, so I never fully saw it. I think they saw my car and got spooked. So, whoever it was, was probably responsible for this. And they'll probably be watching when you leave if they can stay hidden. Just wanted you to have all the information I had. Good luck, Detective."

Walker turned and walked down the front porch. Ava didn't move her hands from her hips. He got in his car, backed around Ava's, then drove slowly to the end of the driveway. He looked to his right, in the direction the vehicle he'd seen had been sitting. There was nothing but open road until it wound around to the right and disappeared into the trees. Walker considered turning that way for a moment. But only briefly. He didn't envy Ava's current position, but it wasn't his problem. And she'd made it clear that it wasn't his problem. So he made a left, hit the gas, and headed back toward the lake when his phone started ringing.

Tim Lawson.

"Damn, it sure is hot out today," Walker answered. "I could use some cold ones, but I'm afraid if I drink alone again, I'll start feeling like an alcoholic."

Tim laughed. "Say no more, buddy. I thought you had some things to do today?"

"It all just got filed under 'not my problem.'"

"I have a lot of those folders."

"See you in an hour?" Walker said.

"I'll come down on the boat. See you out on the dock."

"I'll be there."

Walker ended the call. Though he sounded jovial on the phone, he didn't really feel that way inside. Try though he might, he couldn't hide it from himself. Ava might have told him to get lost, but that didn't mean Amy Turnberry wasn't still missing. And it didn't mean her brother, Daniel, would all of a sudden stop wanting his help.

Walker had gotten really good at swallowing his own feelings about the jobs he'd been sent on over the years.

What he didn't think he could ever be good at now was suppressing those feelings when he was the one choosing the job. And though it felt more like Amy Turnberry had chosen him, he in some way had accepted. Turning his back on that now wasn't something he believed he could do. But as the wind blew in from his open window, with plans already made for another lazy afternoon on the water and Detective Bailey ordering him off the case, he didn't really see any other choice for the time being.

His hope was that the work he'd done to get Ava to Detective Foley's dead body would help her uncover something that might break Amy's case wide open. That would be enough for Walker. It wasn't like he was an actual detective. There was only so much an unemployed killer could do when official police business was involved. And force a detective to let him help was not one of those things.

Daniel Turnberry wasn't going to like it, but Walker didn't have a choice.

15

"There he is!"

Walker stepped down onto the lower dock where Tim Lawson had just pulled up in his Hurricane deck boat, sharing a wide smile. Walker didn't know much about boats, but the white-and-navy-blue, twenty-four-foot leisure boat with matching seats and gray canopy over the center console looked about as inviting right then as Walker figured anything could.

"We making a habit of this?" Walker said as he handed Tim a cooler. He'd mixed some sweet tea and bourbon and was keeping it on ice. One of his foster dads had made it his drink of choice. Walker had tried it one time as an adult out of a lack of any other mixer and fell in love with it himself. Few things went down better on a hot day.

"I have a lot of habits," Tim said. "This ain't one of the bad ones."

Walker took the seat beside the captain's chair. "'If this is wrong, I don't wanna be right' kind of deals, huh?"

"Exactly." Tim undid the rope from the cleat and

pushed off, then took a seat and fired up the engine. "Where to?"

Before Walker could answer, he felt a vibration in the pocket of his swimming trunks, and heard a loud and shrill beep that wasn't a common text or call. Tim reached for his pocket at the same time.

"One of those damn Amber Alerts," Tim said. "I always hate getting those."

They both checked their phones. The notification on the screen read: "EMERGENCY ALERT: Soddy Daisy Police activate Amber Alert. Victim is Riley Baker age 16. Suspected vehicle is a silver Dodge Caravan. Plate # ARBV 598. Last known location eastbound Mayflower Rd. If observed please call 911."

"Hang on now," Tim said. "I know Riley Baker. That's my grandson's little girlfriend, dammit. Let me check on my grandbabies before we take off. You mind?"

Walker shook his head. "No, of course." He got up and grabbed the cleat before the boat floated away from the dock, then tied off. His phone began vibrating again, but this time it was a regular phone call.

Daniel Turnberry.

Walker knew the call from Daniel was coming. He could either take it now and rip off the Band-Aid or risk getting a hundred more calls from him, and letting his anxiety build for no reason. Walker slid his thumb to answer.

"What the hell, man?" Daniel said before Walker could get out a hello. "You found the guy we were looking for dead, and you didn't call and tell me?"

Walker was about to respond, but Daniel butted back in.

"Wait, you didn't kill him, did you? What the hell happened out there?"

"First of all, calm down. Let me—"

"Calm down? My sister's missing, the detective you went to talk to is dead, and now Amy's friend Riley has been taken. This shit has gone nuclear, and you want me to calm down?"

Walker looked back at Tim on the boat and took a deep breath. Tim was still on the phone. Walker didn't want to be on the phone, but the poor kid who had slammed into Walker's life was currently having a meltdown over the phone.

"Daniel."

"I mean, it's nuts. This town is turning into one of those *Dateline NBC* specials or something."

"Daniel, take a breath."

"What am I going to do? Who's going to be next? We have to figure out what the hell is happening!"

"Daniel!" Walker was louder this time. "I'm off this. I'm sorry."

Finally, Daniel was silent.

"I'm sorry, Daniel. Detective Bailey told me to get lost. I'm not—" Walker had to back up in his mind for a moment. "Wait. How the hell did you know Detective Foley is dead?"

"I'm watching it right here on TV," Daniel said. "They just interviewed Detective Bailey. Said she got a tip something was wrong. That's all she knew. What really happened?"

Walker was very aware of the media hounds, but he felt like them being out to Detective Foley's house already was incredibly fast. Someone must have been monitoring the police scanners.

"Nothing happened, Daniel. I went to his house, found him lying in the back yard, and called Ava. Then she told me to get lost. So that's what I'm going to do."

"You can't! You promised you would help!"

"I'm not the police, Daniel. They aren't just going to let me help with anything. I'm a nobody here, and honestly, that's the way it needs to stay."

"But you know that Detective Foley being dead means that whatever happened last year is happening again. Or someone is covering up something. It has to be connected. Him dying is *way* too big of a coincidence. Whoever killed him has my sister. I know it!"

"And Detective Bailey is on it. I was with her earlier. She cares, Daniel. And she has the legal capacity to help. I don't."

"That's right. You don't. Don't care. But why would you? You're just a stranger here. Sorry I ever came to your house."

The call ended.

"Daniel?" Walker looked down at the phone to confirm. Daniel had hung up. "Shit."

As the sun was beating down on his shoulders, and his black T-shirt felt as though it was absorbing absolutely all of the sun's intense heat, Walker knew it was final decision time. If he got on the boat with Tim, tied one on, and came back to the house drunk or anywhere near it, the decision would be made for him. He'd be no use to anyone. The case would literally be closed for him. Whether he wanted to help or not.

"Everything okay, big guy?" Tim said.

Walker turned back toward the boat. Visions of bourbon and sweet tea no longer danced in his head. Without making the conscious decision, his mind turned to fight mode.

"Your grandkids okay?"

"Gauge is pretty shook up that his girlfriend is missing, but they're safe."

"You talk to Gauge yourself?"

"No, my daughter, Abby." Tim stepped off the boat onto the dock. He looked concerned. "Why? What is it?"

"You think it would be okay if I talked to him?"

Walker didn't have any idea what he would say, or if it would make any difference at all, but he felt compelled. And that's who he was now, it seemed—the man who follows his instincts instead of orders.

"What are you thinking?"

However, that didn't mean Walker wasn't torn. Stepping directly into the shit was never a good idea. Or a safe one. But that had never stopped him before.

"What are you thinking?"

"I'm thinking if I answer that question, we aren't going drinking out on your boat."

"I'm a sixty-five-year-old grandpa, Walker," Tim said with a cigarette dangling from his lips. "I'll have plenty of days to drink. But I may not get too many chances to help protect my grandbabies. If that's what you're implying that you're about to set your mind to, then to hell with that boat. You got a line on something? That where you were this morning?"

"Yeah. Amy Turnberry, the missing girl?"

"Yeah?"

"Her brother tried to break into the lake house last night."

Tim placed both hands on his hips as he listened.

"Said he thought maybe I had something to do with her going missing. Well, his mom did. You know, new guy in town house-sitting. Not a huge leap to be worried about me."

"I guess not," Tim said.

"Long story short, I ran him down, and somehow I

ended up telling him I would help him. He was losing his mind about the police not being very helpful so far. I should have stayed out of it, but I guess because of my past, I feel like I have quite a few things to atone for."

"Why does he think you can help find his sister but the police can't?"

"I don't really know. Probably like you, he thinks I'm an undercover agent or something. Which isn't really the case. But I do have quite a lot of experience in dealing with the sort of people who are capable of such things as kidnapping little kids and murdering detectives."

"Murdering detectives? Something happen to that spunky young woman who we talked to last night?"

"Detective Bailey? No. She's fine. But I did see her today. Twice actually, after you left. The second time was at Detective Foley's house. Where I found him dead."

"What?"

"Yeah, another long story short, Daniel and Detective Bailey—Ava—both told me about how there were kidnappings like this exactly one year ago. And that none of the detectives working those cases were still with the Soddy Daisy PD. Also, now neither one of them is alive. I went to talk to Detective Foley, over in Ringgold, just to see if there were any parallels between last year and this year. Guess someone didn't want him discussing that very same thing with me or anyone else. Or he just had a gambling debt he didn't pay and it's a coincidence. I have no damn idea right now."

"I've never been a fan of coincidences. My experience has always been where there's smoke."

"Yeah, me too. Anyway, Amy's brother just called, and I told him I couldn't help. That Ava had sent me home and told me to stay out of it."

"But you can't do that," Tim said.

They both looked out at the water as a couple of Jet Skis went zooming by. Tim threw them a mindless wave, then looked back at Walker.

"No, Tim. I don't think I can do that."

Tim nodded, then held up his lighter as a gesture to ask permission. Walker nodded, and Tim lit his cigarette. "And you think my grandson can help?"

"I think he knows his girlfriend, probably better than anyone else in the world knows her."

"Then let's get to it. He's home with my daughter. Seems to be girls being taken, but I sure as hell ain't gonna wait around for my grandson to be next. Let me get the boat back and change clothes. Come pick me up? I'll text you the address. It's literally just around the bend from this neighborhood."

"You don't have to come with me, Tim. People are being killed that are close to this . . . whatever this is. And you need to know that someone involved in that detective's murder might have seen my car at his house. I saw a vehicle watching, just couldn't see what kind of vehicle it was."

"Then I'd better grab a couple of my favorite trigger holders. I don't have a background like you do, but I do have a family. That means I'm willing to do whatever it takes to keep them safe. Don't underestimate the power of that."

"Okay. I won't. Just had to lay the cards out on the table."

"I'll see you in a half hour," Tim said as he turned back toward his boat.

"Sounds good."

Walker walked over and grabbed the cooler from the boat, untethered Tim's boat, and gave it a little push. As Tim pulled away, Walker could feel his phone vibrating in his pocket. He pulled it out as he walked back toward the house.

Ava Bailey was calling.

Walker didn't answer.

He figured it was better to ask forgiveness than permission. He decided that keeping her out of the loop was best for the time being. But he knew that if he actually found something, she was going to have to be the first person he called.

16

Walker let his right arm hang out the window of Tim's old Chevy pickup truck. The two of them decided it was better to take a much less conspicuous vehicle after discussing that someone may have seen Walker out at the recently deceased Detective Foley's house. Tim had run back by and picked him up. They were almost to the recently declared missing Riley Baker's house. Tim's grandson Gauge had informed them that the police had left, and Riley's mother wanted to talk to Walker. Apparently, Daniel Turnberry was a little more relentless than Walker had thought. He was friends with Gauge and had told him that Walker possessed certain skills that Walker had never mentioned to him.

Walker was pissed at first. The kid shouldn't be talking about Walker at all, much less assuming things about him, and even worse telling people he can help because Walker used to be a government super spy. The kid wasn't light years off, but Walker was not a spy. He was the man they called when spies went rogue. And though Walker didn't like it, he understood why Daniel was going the extra mile for help. He loved his sister and wanted her found. By any means necessary. If nothing else, Walker couldn't help but respect that.

Tim pulled the truck into a quaint little neighborhood. All the houses were custom, but they looked as though the builder had given everyone the same three choices of what plan they'd like to build. So, minus a few minor differences, the houses were all basically the same. Modern suburbia at its finest.

Tim turned down the radio. "I appreciate you coming along, even though you don't know these people, and they might be assuming things about you that may or may not be true."

Walker sighed. "I really do want to help, Tim. I'm just not a cop or anything else. So getting involved only means trouble for me and possibly falsely raising the hopes of people who are already hurting enough."

"I know. I get it. But if just one thing you hear, or see, gives them a different route that might lead to finding their daughter, you'd obviously change these people's lives forever."

Walker was quiet as they turned down a different street inside the neighborhood.

"But listen," Tim said, "I'll turn this damn truck around right now if you aren't comfortable. 'Cause you're right, none of this has anything to do with you, and I certainly don't want to cause you any more trouble than you've already had."

"I just don't think it matters, Tim."

"What's that, buddy?"

"I don't need someone to cause trouble for me. It just always has a way of finding me. Always has."

"Guess since you're still here, that means you've gotten pretty damn good at getting out of it."

Walker looked over at him. Tim gave him a wink. Walker didn't know what it was like to have a real father, but he imagined that Tim's kids and grandkids were awfully lucky to have him. Life is damn hard. Even for people who have a leg up in life with a good supportive family. So having someone who is so positive and encouraging all the time must be priceless.

"I like you, Tim," Walker said as he reached over and gave him a pat on the shoulder. "I'm glad fate threw us together."

"Me too, Walker. Me too."

Walker laughed.

"What?" Tim said.

"I just told you that trouble always has a way of finding me. So I wouldn't be too quick to be glad you met me."

"Yeah? Well," Tim said as he turned into the Baker's driveway, "I never did shy away from a little trouble." Tim returned the loving pat to Walker's shoulder, then put the truck in park.

A shaggy, blond-haired teenage boy walked over to Tim's side of the truck and gave Tim a hug. "Hey, pops."

"You doin' okay, buddy?" Tim asked him.

"Not really," the boy said as he hung his head.

"We'll find your girl, okay?" Tim nudged the boy in Walker's direction. "Gauge, meet my new friend, Walker."

Walker extended his hand. "Sorry about your girlfriend, Gauge. It's nice to meet you."

Gauge looked up at him and shook his hand. His brown eyes were bloodshot. "Nice to meet you too. My friend said you were like a spy or something. That true?"

"Not exactly, but I've been around quite a few of them."

"Oh. Have you killed people before?"

"Gauge," Tim said, "come on, buddy. That's not a question you ask someone. Especially someone you just met."

"Sorry." Gauge hung his head again.

"Not today," Walker said.

Gauge looked up. "What do you mean?"

Walker winked. "I mean, I haven't killed anyone today."

Gauge looked back at Tim and smiled. Walker thought it was best to leave him a carrot.

"My girlfriend's—Riley's—mom wants to talk to you, if that's okay?"

"Like I told your granddad, and your overly talkative friend, Daniel, I doubt I can be any help, but I'm willing to listen if it makes someone feel better about things."

"Well, I appreciate it," Gauge said. "She's a real sweet girl, Riley. She don't deserve being taken and who knows what else."

"I don't know her, Gauge, but I know I agree with you."

The front door opened, and a woman, late thirties, long brown hair pulled back into a ponytail, wearing a navy-blue T-shirt with SD TROJANS CHEERLEADING written in gold on the front, stepped out onto the front porch. Walker could see a tissue in her left hand. He could already feel himself getting uncomfortable. Never in his violent past had he every been trained to comfort anyone. But since quitting his killer day job, this was about to be the second woman inside of a month he was going to have to try to console. The last nearly ended up getting him killed. Somewhere in the back of his lizard brain something was telling him this just might end up the same way. Yet he stepped forward.

"This is Walker," Gauge said. "The guy Daniel was telling me about."

"Thank you so much for coming, Mr. Walker," she said.

"I'm Riley's mom"—she stopped for an emotional swallow —"Darla. Someone took my baby, and I'll try anything to get her back. You have kids, Mr. Walker?"

The lady was upset and nervous. Walker stepped toward the porch. "It's nice to meet you, Darla. I'm very sorry to hear about your daughter. I do not have children, but I hate to hear what you're going through."

Walker's dialogue felt forced. He had no idea what the hell to say. Darla didn't seem to mind as she stepped to the side. "Please, come in."

Walker nodded to Tim. He pushed Gauge along, and then Walker followed behind them inside the tan, vinyl-siding, two-story home. Gauge led them down a picture-lined hallway that dumped them out into the living room. A man stood and greeted Tim. He was in a light blue button-down shirt tucked into some khaki pants. His dark hair was balding on top, and he wore a pair of black-rimmed glasses. Walker was getting accountant vibes, for no other reason than stereotypes.

"Bob, this is my new friend, Walker."

Bob reached over and meekly shook Walker's hand. "Your reputation precedes you, sir. Thank you for coming."

Darla walked back into the room and stood beside her husband. All Walker wanted to do at that moment was get back in the truck, head out on the lake with Tim, and drink themselves silly. The room was heavy, and Walker felt like a fraud. He could see the hope in the eyes of two loving but lost parents in front of him, and the reality that Walker didn't know the first thing about investigating a kidnapping weighed on him like a forty-ton tractor trailer truck. His back began to sweat. He'd faced the worst of the human race countless times over during the last fifteen years, but this scared him more than all of them combined.

Walker looked over at Tim. Tim could see what Walker was feeling. Walker figured it was written all over his face.

"It is really nice to meet you both," Walker managed. "But I can't help you."

Gauge shot Walker an astonished look. Darla's and Bob's faces sank.

Walker stumbled over his words. "I, uh, I don't, um, I don't know what Daniel Turnberry told you or where he got his information, but I'm not the man he says I am. I'm really sorry."

"It's okay, buddy," Tim said. Then he turned to the Bakers. "I don't know what Daniel told you, but I get the feeling some wires have been crossed somewhere. We'll get out of your hair. I'm sure the police are going to find Riley really soon."

"Why did you come here?" Darla said. Her face read betrayal.

Walker wanted to shrink inside himself. He'd always thought of himself as an introvert; when you spend your entire life by yourself, that tends to happen. But it had never been more clear to him than in that moment just how backward and introverted he had truly become.

"I-I'm sorry," Walker said. "It was all just a misunderstanding. I wish you both luck."

Walker didn't wait for Tim. He just turned and walked out. He felt terrible, but he had to leave. There was just no other way. His skin was on fire, and there was a burning inside him that was completely frying his nerves.

He felt like he couldn't breathe until he pushed open the front door and walked out into the fresh air. It had been cool inside the house, but he was sweating profusely. His stomach was in knots, and while the first breath came easy, the second one didn't. Walker rushed over to the passenger side of Tim's truck and doubled over, hands on knees.

He heard the front door open and close.

"Walker?" It was Tim. "You okay?"

Walker was still bent over trying to get a good breath. He felt Tim's hand on his back.

"You're okay, bud," Tim said. "In through the nose, out through the mouth."

Walker tried, but the breath wasn't coming. And now he started to feel dizzy. He stumbled forward a bit, and he felt Tim's arms wrap around his shoulders, holding him up. Tim leaned him back against the door of the truck, then got down on one knee as he placed his hand against Walker's chest.

"With me now. You're okay. Look at me."

The ground swirled a bit, but Walker managed to find Tim's eyes.

"That's it. You're okay. With me now, ready?"

Walker needed a breath. He nodded.

"All right. In through your nose, out through your mouth. Start shallow, then we'll get more air."

Walker tried, but no air.

Tim smiled. Walker felt a little of his anxiety release.

"You're okay," Tim said. "The air will come. Just breathe with me."

Walker tried again. As Tim's face became blurry, he finally got a little air.

"That's it. It's coming. Just believe it and know that a good breath is coming next."

Walker believed Tim, and again he felt a little tension release. The burning sensation subsided a bit. The next breath came with a little more air. Then a little more. Until, finally, Tim wasn't blurry and the dizziness was gone.

"There you go. You got it now. You good?"

Walker found another full breath. Then he nodded. Tim opened the truck door for him. Walker got in. He glanced up at the front door. The Bakers were standing there with Gauge. All three of them looked disappointed. Walker melting down was not how they saw that situation going. They thought their hero had arrived. Walker understood in that moment that a killer and a hero were two completely different things.

Tim pulled out of the driveway and hit the gas.

"What the hell was that?" Walker said. "What happened to me?"

"You've never had a panic attack before?"

"That what that was?" Walker said, still trying to normalize his breathing.

"Yes, sir. Seen it happen a few times."

"Guess I'm not as tough as I thought I was," Walker said as he positioned the air vent to blow right on him.

"Bullshit now. That right there can happen to anyone. I promise you that."

They were quiet for bit. Tim weaved the truck out of the neighborhood, through the main roads, then back on the much more remote winding road that went up and down the hills before they got to the lake. Moving further away from people suddenly felt like a warm hug to Walker. Not something he'd ever thought he'd feel.

"Thank you, Tim."

"No need. I'm just glad you're all right."

"I want to help them. I really do. I just—"

"You don't have to explain a damn thing to me. I don't know what all your life has been about up until now, but I know you don't have to be a savior here. It's not your job."

Tim was about to say something else, but a vehicle

ramming into the back of his pickup truck stole his attention.

"What in the hell?" Tim said as he swerved to keep the truck on the road. The road was winding around a hill, and the incline on the opposite side dropped down through the trees all the way to the water.

"Just stop the truck before they can hit you again," Walker said as he turned in his seat to watch the white van speeding toward them from behind.

"What do you mean? You think they did it on purpose?"

The van was coming at them hard.

"They did. And they're about to do it again."

Tim hit the brakes like Walker had told him, but it was too late. The van smashed into the back of Tim's truck, but this time it clipped it at an angle. A bad angle. The back end of Tim's truck slid out to the left. He overcorrected in an attempt to dodge an oncoming car, and that sent them straight through the upcoming turn.

The pavement vanished beneath the pickup's tires. Tim pulled the steering wheel left, desperately trying to avoid the oncoming tree, but the front end on Walker's side slammed into the tree, sending the truck onto its side, then rolling. Walker went limp. His training taught him that when you try to fight your way through a car crash, that's when limbs get broken. The cab going end over end threw Walker and Tim around like they were stuck in a washing machine with no water.

After the split second of tumbling, which seemed more like minutes, came to a stop, Walker's shoulder slammed into his door. The truck had ended the fall on its side. Walker could feel Tim leaning against him. Then he realized the truck wasn't finished moving yet, and slowly, one final, slow rotation, and it finished upside down. Walker put his hands up to keep from hitting his head on the roof. Tim was suspended by his seat belt. The engine was hissing. Shattered glass had fallen like glitter. And quite a few parts on Walker's body were aching. But he was okay.

"Tim?" Walker grunted as he reached for his own seat belt release button. He worked his legs, feet, arms, and hands to make sure everything was still in working order. "Tim, you okay?"

Tim groaned.

Walker's seat belt wouldn't release. The button was jammed.

"That wasn't much fun," Tim said.

"You okay?" Walker said.

"Well, for now. But I'm not too sure that's gonna last." Tim managed to point out the glassless window beside him.

Walker didn't like the sound of that.

"What is it? They coming?"

"They're coming," Tim said.

Walker feverishly began to press the seat belt release. Still nothing. "How many?" He kept trying the button, forcing his thumb down on the button with his other hand.

"Five. One of them halfway down the hill. The other four just making it off the road."

Walker gave up on the button and reached in his jeans pocket for his Spyderco tactical knife. He thumbed open the blade, cut the lap belt, and eased his way onto his shoulder against the ceiling of the truck.

"Weapons?" Walker said.

"First guy has a ball bat. Can't see the rest."

Walker turned himself to where he was on his knees on the inside roof of the truck. He ducked down and looked past Tim through his window to see what was coming. He could only see the man with the bat.

"Cut me loose so I can help," Tim said.

Walker felt for his gun at the small of his back. His conceal holster was there, but the Sig must have slipped out in the tumble. He looked around but didn't spot it. He looked in the backseat for Tim's bag of weapons that he'd brought along, but he didn't see those either.

"The hell are you waiting for, son?" Tim said. "You're not having another panic attack, are you? Not sure we have time for that."

Walker couldn't help the smile that grew across his face. "Quite the opposite, Tim. Right now I couldn't feel more at home."

Tim was still upside down. He stared at Walker for a second. "Well, they're coming. So stop smiling and cut me loose before they get the jump on us."

"I'll cut you loose if you promise to stay in the truck," Walker said.

"You crazy? There's five of them. Even with me helping we'll be lucky to walk away from this."

Walker looked at him for a second, then shook his head. "No, Tim. I may not be much of a detective, and as I said, I wasn't any sort of CIA or FBI agent. But this?" Walker nodded up the hill in the direction of the men coming for them. "This is what I do."

Walker pulled the handle beside him and pushed his door open.

"You heard me say five of them, right?" Tim said.

Walker ducked and crawled out onto the leaf-covered ground outside the truck. Before he got up, he reached back in and cut Tim loose. He lowered him down to the inside roof of the truck.

"I heard you. Now, find a gun if you can, and stay behind the truck."

Walker helped Tim outside and got him upright. The first of the five men was almost to them.

"Don't be a hero," Tim said. "I'm older, but I can still throw a punch."

"I'm no hero, Tim," Walker said as he peeked up over the underside of the truck. The man was twenty yards up the hill, a wooden baseball bat in his right hand. Walker looked back at Tim. "I'm a trained killer. And these boys are about to find out exactly what that means."

17

Walker stepped away from Tim and walked around the front of the overturned truck. The man with the backward hat, scraggly beard, and baseball bat walked up and pulled his arms back to swing. As he brought the bat forward, Walker jumped back, and the bat whooshed by. The man was coming downhill and hadn't expected to miss, so his overswing pulled him off balance. Walker kicked his legs out from under him, and the man landed hard on his shoulder.

Walker bent over, snatched the wooden bat from the man's hands, and broke it over his knee. For a moment he considered shoving the sharp end the break had made through the man's neck. He showed mercy by soccer-kicking the man in the back of the head, leaving him unconscious but alive. Walker heard Tim say, "Holy shit," from behind the truck. But Walker knew the show had only just begun.

The second and third man coming down the hill toward Walker and the wreckage were moving at about the same pace. Walker tossed the broken bat to the ground and stalked uphill toward them.

"Tell me who sent you after us, and I'll go easy on you," Walker said.

The first man, in a black T-shirt with a white skull on the front, laughed as he walked toward Walker. "I don't think we're too worried about you, buddy." He looked over at his friend, whose tan muscles were bulging beneath a white tank top. "Are we?"

Tank Top shook his head and smiled. "I don't think we are."

Walker stepped forward and punched Skull Shirt in the groin before he could get his own shot off. The man dropped to his knees. As Tank Top planted his left leg to throw his overhand right, Walker kicked sideways and sent the man's knee cap in the wrong direction. Then Walker twisted his hips and fired a right hook down on Skull Shirt's left ear. He went limp like a freshly boiled noodle. As Tank Top tended to his leg, screaming, Walker stood over him.

"There are two more coming that I can get answers from, so if you hesitate, I'll break your jaw."

Tank Top was holding his leg, writhing in pain.

"Who's in charge?" Walker said.

In a labored voice, the man managed to say, "I don't have to tell you anything."

Walker took a knee beside him. "You realize you just ran me and my friend off the road, which could have killed us both."

"Yeah?" Tank Top looked down at his leg. "I think maybe we're even."

Walker pulled back his right arm, then jerked it down hard, smashing his elbow into Tank Top's jaw. It cracked horribly, and the man went unconscious.

Walker stood. "Now we're even."

The last two men stumbling down the foliage-covered hill paused for a moment. Walker started up the hill after them. The first three men were somewhere in their midtwenties. The last two looked younger. Barely out of high school. They looked at each other, then back to Walker, who was methodically making his way toward them.

"Don't be like them," Walker said. "Tell me who you work for and why you're after me. Don't make me hurt you."

They looked at each other again. Walker could see the fear on their faces. But instead of running from the fight, the fresh-faced young man with the shaggy hair revealed the knife he was holding in his hand.

"I'm not afraid of you," the kid said, his voice cracking. No way he was any older than nineteen. "I'll kill you if you come any closer."

Walker stopped. "Yeah? You're going to kill me?"

"I will. I'm not afraid."

"You said that already. You know, most people who aren't afraid usually don't have to announce it."

The kid stared at him for a second, then looked up at his friend, who seemed to want no part of the action. Then back to Walker. "I'm just saying. I'll do it if you make me."

"You ever killed a man, son?" Walker said.

"N-no."

"Think of the worst nightmare you've ever had. Then triple it. Then strap in, 'cause it will haunt you every night for the rest of your life."

Walker could hear Tim walking up the hill behind him.

Walker took a step forward.

"Don't move!" the kid shouted.

"Brent," the other kid said. "Let's just go."

"You should listen to your friend," Walker said. "Who's making you do this anyway?"

Instead of answering, the kid ran forward with his knife extended. When he jabbed it forward, Walker caught his hand at the wrist. He almost broke the kid's arm, but at the last second, he showed him mercy and knocked him out with an elbow to the temple. Walker let him down easy. Then he looked up at the kid's friend.

"Tell me who put you up to this, and I'll take care of it, I promise. They won't bother you anymore."

Walker was thirty feet from the boy, but he could see him shaking. Walker looked down at the kid he'd just knocked out and noticed a tattoo on the inside of his right wrist. He wouldn't have thought anything of it if he hadn't seen the same one on Tank Top's wrist a moment ago. Both of them had what looked like an upside-down cross, with a snake winding around the vertical piece. Walker looked back up at the kid.

"It's okay," Walker said. "I don't want to hurt you. But if you're in danger, I can help."

"You can't help me. No one can."

Walker started up the hill toward him.

"Don't come any closer!" he shouted.

The boy reached behind his back, and Walker knew right then he was pulling a gun. Walker held both hands above his head.

"Listen to me. I can help. Is this some sort of cult or something you've gotten caught up in?"

"What? No. Why would you ask that?"

"Do you have the same tattoo?"

On reflex, the kid looked down at his wrist, but quickly back to Walker. He had the tattoo.

"Tattoo? What are you talking about?"

Walker looked over at Tim who was now standing beside him. He could see that Tim had a pistol held down by his side. Walker shook his head.

"Doesn't matter," Walker said. "Listen. I'm not the police. I don't have to follow orders, and I'm not possibly in anybody's pocket, if that is something you're worried about. I can help you. You just have to let me. Do you know where Amy Turnberry is?"

"What? Why would I know where the missing girl is?"

"That what this is about?" Walker ignored the kid's question. "Were you sent after me because I was at that detective's house in Ringgold this morning?"

The kid didn't say anything; he just continued to hold the gun out in front of him.

"You don't want to do this, do you?" Walker said.

"He . . . ," the kid started, but trailed off as he looked around him.

"It's okay. Tell me and I can protect you. He what?"

The kid looked around again, then lowered the gun. "You can really help me? You some sort of FBI agent or something?"

Walker could hear hopefulness in the kid's question.

"Something like that," Walker said as he took a step forward. The kid didn't raise the gun.

"He told us this is the only way."

"Who told you? And what is the only way?"

The boy paused. This was hard for him. He was visibly scared.

"He told us that if we want to live for—"

"Shut your mouth, Cameron!" a man shouted from behind Walker and Tim. Walker whipped his head around and saw Skull Shirt sitting up. "Stop talking right now! You'll get us all killed!"

That set the hairs on the back of Walker's neck to attention. He could feel the fear that was driving this group of young men.

"It's all right. I can help you too," Walker said. "All of you. Right, Tim?"

"We can, boys. You just have to trust us."

"Bullshit," Skull Shirt said. "You have no idea what you've walked into here. They're going to kill you. It's just a matter of time." Skull Shirt looked up at Cameron. "And you're not going to drag us down with you. So shut your mouth, Cam. And let's get the hell out of here."

Walker turned his attention to Cameron up the hill. "Don't listen to him, Cameron. This is one of those crossroad moments in your life. Whatever you're caught up in here, I can help you out of it. I promise you that. I just need you to help me help you."

Cameron looked at Walker, then past him to Skull Shirt.

Skull Shirt spoke again. "Don't listen to him, Cam. He has no idea."

"No idea of what?" Walker said.

Cameron looked back over at Walker. Then to Skull Shirt. Then back to Walker. Then he raised the gun, put it to his head, and pulled the trigger.

"No!" Walker shouted as he watched Cameron fold over and fall to the ground.

"Damn it!" Tim shouted as he pulled the pistol from his back and turned to face Skull Shirt, who was about thirty yards down the hill. "Start talking right now, or I shoot you dead. Who was that boy afraid of? Why would he kill himself like that?"

Walker let Tim talk to Skull Shirt as he scanned the area. Things had gone as sideways as he'd ever seen. And though he hadn't been at all prepared for it, he had to start thinking of a way out.

"Don't shoot!" Skull Shirt said.

"Then start talking!" Tim shouted.

"Okay!" Skull Shirt held up his hands, then looked at Walker. "You sure you can keep me safe?"

Before Walker could answer, a loud crack sounded from the top of the hill. Walker knew without looking that it was a hunting rifle. But the hole made by the round in Skull Shirt's neck confirmed it. And Walker knew Tim would be next. He reached over, grabbed Tim by the collar of his white polo shirt, and yanked him down the hill. He snatched the pistol from his hand as he pulled him down, turned it around, and began firing up the hill.

"Get behind the truck!" Walker shouted.

Walker continued firing as he backed his way down the hill with Tim.

"See if you can find my Sig," Walker shouted. He fired a couple more times before diving behind the truck just before another round from the rifle was fired.

As he got back to his feet, Walker was wondering how he hadn't been hit. Whoever was firing the rifle clearly knew how to shoot. Skull Shirt had been an easy target. Walker moved past Tim who was scouring the inside of the truck for weapons, and just when he made it to where he could see around the front, another shot fired. It was immediately clear why Walker hadn't been shot. Whoever was firing the rifle was picking off the men who'd come after Walker and Tim.

The shooter was making sure none of them could talk.

18

Tim reached up from inside the truck; he was holding Walker's Sig Sauer in his hand. Walker took it from him, but it was too late. The person with the rifle had only shown up to make sure none of their own would be able to be questioned by Walker or the police. They heard tires squeal as the shooter left the scene, a handful of grizzly murders left in their wake.

"What the hell have we stumbled into?" Walker said, mostly to himself.

Tim was busy digging in the truck for his bag of weapons. But they weren't going to need them. Not right then anyway. Walker holstered the gun and pulled out his phone. There was only one person he knew to call, and it was going to be the second time that day he called her with a dead body at his feet.

"Walker," Detective Bailey answered, "I told you that you needed to stay out of this. I can't—"

"Ava I need you to listen. Okay?"

Ava was quiet. She must have sensed his tone.

"Wherever you are, you aren't safe. Someone is watching you."

"Walker? What are you talking about. What is going on?"

"I'm going to drop a pin at my current location. You need to get ambulances and police here ASAP. People are dead. Hopefully some injured here can be saved."

"Walker, what the hell is happening? What do you mean people are dead?"

Walker sent a pin to Ava's phone, showing exactly where he was on a map.

"Walker? Talk to me."

With the dead bodies lying on the ground just over his shoulder, the twisting metal of the truck tumbling down the hill still reverberating in his system, and sinister people he didn't know trying to do him harm, Walker felt a wave of darkness moving over him. And in stark contrast to the panic attack he'd had a while ago, this feeling was familiar. Like an old friend stopping by to say hello. His old self, the violent man the government program had turned him into, was making his way back to the surface.

The thing that sent a shiver down Walker's spine in that moment was that not only was he not upset about feeling like his old self again; he liked it.

Walker ended the call and pulled Tim up from his position on the ground.

"What is it?" Tim said. "You all right?"

"After the police run you through all their questions, go back to the farm, have your family meet you there, and hole up until I've put an end to this thing and it's safe to come back out."

Tim's face scrunched behind his glasses. "You can't fight

this thing on your own. You don't even know what you're up against."

"I don't know what I'm up against *yet.* But I will. Before the night is over. But this isn't business for you, Tim. Do what I say, and go home. And stay ready in case someone follows you."

"Whoever did *this*," Tim said, gesturing with his hand toward his ruined truck, "made it my business. I'm not just going to sit around and wait for someone to come after me or my family. And I'm not going to let you fight this alone. Talk about not someone's business, Walker. You don't know any of these people. This isn't your concern. Get out now before it's too late."

"This is what I do, Tim."

"What, Walker? What the hell is it that you do? I don't even know."

Walker took a step toward Tim and looked him dead in the eyes. "I'm a killer, Tim. Maybe the best one there is. It's the only thing I've trained to do since I was fifteen years old."

Tim caught Walker off guard when he placed his hand on his shoulder and spoke with a soft voice. "You don't have to be the man they made you anymore, Walker. And you don't have to let these people you don't even know, who are into God knows what, turn you back into that man either."

Walker's jaw set, and he spoke through clinched teeth. "There is no turning back into anything. It's who I am. And whoever's behind what's going on here is about to find that out."

"You don't have to—"

Walker swiped at Tim's arm, knocking his hand from his shoulder. Tim took a step back.

"Go home after this, Tim. I'll let you know when it's safe."

Walker turned and walked around the front of the overturned truck. His phone started to vibrate from Ava trying to call him back. Instead of answering, he swiped over to the camera app as he approached Tank Top who was lying in a pool of his own blood. Walker crouched down beside him and turned over his left arm, palm up. He wiped away the blood pooled at his wrist, then snapped a picture of the snake-covered upside-down-cross tattoo.

"Son, I know you don't want to hear this," Tim said from the truck. "But this isn't your fight. Let it go."

Walker stood and looked at Tim.

Tim continued. "You can, you know. You can let this go. Let the police handle it."

Walker just turned and started up the hill. He could hear sirens in the distance, and he could hear his own heartbeat hammering in his chest. He could appreciate what Tim was trying to do, but Tim was wrong. Walker couldn't just let it go. It wasn't in his DNA. He decided right then, as he stepped over the young man who'd killed himself because he was too afraid to face what Walker was about to, that not only was he going to find Amy Turnberry, but whatever else was going on that led to what just happened, he was going to find the source of that too. Even if the two had nothing to do with each other.

It didn't matter what he had to do.

It didn't matter how nasty things got.

Walker didn't mind if things got dark. That's where he thrived. And he just couldn't help but get the feeling that he'd wound up in Soddy Daisy, Tennessee, for this very reason.

19

Walker jogged the two and a half miles back to the house with relative ease. The length he'd been running in the mornings had more than prepared him for the easy run to the lake house. However, it was much hotter in the waning evening sun than it ever had been before sunrise. He'd managed to send Daniel Turnberry a picture of the snake-and-cross tattoo he'd snapped; it seemed to be the theme of the men who'd run Walker and Tim off the road. Daniel sent back a snarky "I thought you weren't going to help" text, but then followed it up with a message saying he thought he'd seen the image somewhere before and that he would see what he could find out.

Once inside, Walker moved quickly. He changed clothes and gathered his weapons, including all the spare magazines he'd already filled. He realized as he packed his backpack that it seemed as if he were preparing for war. He hoped that wasn't the case, but judging by the ruthlessness of whoever had silenced the young men on the hill, it just might turn out that way.

He didn't really have a plan, just that he knew he

couldn't stay at the lake house. He didn't know who was after him, but Walker was well aware that they knew him. He wondered if going off on his own that morning to find Detective Foley had been a bad decision. He certainly wouldn't be in the position he was in right then. But he also wouldn't be any closer to finding Amy Turnberry either. Like everything else in life, nothing good is easy. And usually, that something good is right around the corner from bad—you just have to keep driving.

He also thought that Amy Turnberry, more than likely, was just the tip of the iceberg to something much larger that was going on in that small town. If this was just one person going around kidnapping innocent victims, there would be no way those men would have been sent after Walker. And no way they would have been gunned down just to keep them quiet. There was always the possibility that Amy Turnberry's case and Detective Foley's murder were two separate things. But every fiber of his being told him they were connected. And his early deduction, with everything that was going on, was that maybe he had stumbled into a human trafficking ring.

The kidnappings year over year would certainly point to that. The team of bad guys coming to stop Walker because of what he saw at Detective Foley's house would point to that, and maybe even the tattooed symbol spoke to some sort of gang that was facilitating the kidnappings.

The only thing that Walker couldn't quite understand was why it would happen only once a year, at around the same time of year. That part was strange. But for the time being, it had no bearing on what Walker had to do next, which was to find the silver Dodge Caravan reported in the Amber Alert. The one that had taken Riley Baker. The girl who Walker had just told her parents he couldn't help because he was in the middle of a full-blown panic attack. He still couldn't wrap his head around how it happened.

Walker had read that change can bring on a lot of different feelings and realities for people. It seemed to him that walking away from a violent life would be helpful to his psyche. But no matter how flawed that life was, it was the one he knew, and it had structure. It made sense. He was comfortable. Standing in front of strangers whose daughter had just been taken, seeing expectations of him in their eyes —that had been foreign. And he still couldn't believe the way his body had shut down on him.

So, like most people who feel uncomfortable, Walker was just going to throw himself into what seemed right to him. Violent, insane, and terrible things. That's where his comfort level seemed highest. And lucky for him, there was plenty of that going on in the small, sleepy town of Soddy Daisy, Tennessee.

Walker's phone began ringing. He pulled it from his pocket. Ava was calling.

"Detective Bailey," Walker answered.

"What in God's name did you leave behind, Walker? What have you done?"

"Did you talk to Tim?"

"Yes, I talked to Tim. He's lucky he knows the sheriff, or he'd be explaining himself down at the police station. He'll have to later, and so will you. You can't just walk away from a crime scene, Walker. I have to come and take you in."

"If you come and take me to jail, more people are going to die," Walker said.

"There's no way you can know that. And there's no way I can do police business that way. I have orders. I have laws. And I have channels I have to follow. And that first channel is to come and get you, and bring you in for questioning."

"Where are you right now?" Walker said, ignoring Ava's words.

"The question is, where are you?"

Walker ignored her again. "Wherever you are, you're in danger. Now, have you ever seen a tattoo or a symbol of an inverted cross with a snake winding around it?"

"Walker, I'm on my way to the lake house. Don't leave. If you do, there will be a manhunt for you."

"That's good." Walker sounded sarcastic. "Pull resources from the massacre that just happened on that hill. Pull much-needed officers away from trying to find Riley Baker and Amy Turnberry. All to go and get a guy that you know is only trying to help."

"How do I know that, Walker? I don't know you. How do I know you didn't kill Detective Foley and that you didn't instigate what happened out on that hill?"

"That's right, Detective, you don't know me. But you've looked into my eyes and you know you didn't see a bad man. Just a man who's willing to do bad things for the right reasons. What you don't know about me is that I might be the most qualified person in Soddy Daisy to go and shut down whatever in the hell is going on here."

"Why is that, Walker? Why are *you* so qualified to do it?"

"Because whatever is going on, searching for clues and dusting for fingerprints isn't going to stop the violence and get those girls back if they are alive."

"Oh yeah? Since you're so qualified, just what will get them back?"

"Violence. And if you don't believe another word I say, believe me when I tell you that I am overqualified for that."

Ava went quiet. Walker could hear car noise in the background. She was driving toward him. Then his phone dinged a notification from the camera at the top of the driveway. He quickly switched from the phone app to the camera's app. It was a car he didn't recognize.

"Someone's here, I have to go. But understand I'm going to help Daniel get his sister back. And I'm going to help Tim make sure his family is safe now that these people think he is involved with me. You'll just have to decide if you want to make it harder on me to do those things or not. But either way, that's what I'm going to do."

Walker ended the call and swapped his phone for his Sig Sauer. He sidled up to the large uncovered window in the front room, poked his head out around the wood trim, and watched the Toyota move down the driveway. He moved over to the front door and watched through the small windows at the top. The car stopped. The door opened. And Tim Lawson got out of the car—a shotgun in his left hand and a cigarette hanging from his lips.

Walker let out a sigh and opened the door. "What the hell are you doing here, Tim? I told you to go home."

Tim walked up the stairs and got right in Walker's face. "And I stopped taking orders from other men when I moved out of my daddy's house more than forty years ago."

Neither of them backed down.

Tim looked Walker up and down. "Now, I believe you when you tell me this business is suited for you. What I'm telling you is believe me when I tell you I know how to keep my family safe. Sitting around on my ass waiting for things to happen has never been my way. I make them happen. Now, I'm a good shot. And I might not be the toughest son of a bitch out here, but you push me, I can sure as hell be the meanest. Those people came after you *and* me back there. That was my damn truck that's getting towed to the dump. And it's my grandson's girlfriend who's been kidnapped. I'm not one for keeping score, but we both know that puts me with a whole hell of a lot more skin in this game than it does you. Now, just because you're trained to do this doesn't mean you're better suited than I am right now. Just means you're better suited to lead us. And I don't wanna hear shit about how I could get hurt or worse. I was right back down on that hill with you. I saw what they're capable of, whoever's behind this. And yet here I am standing here in front of you. I know what's at stake. Now, let's get down to business."

Walker took a step back and holstered his pistol. "Well . . ."—his face was stern, and he didn't look away from Tim—"that's about as good of a damn speech as I've ever heard. You're a grown-ass man. You'll get no other argument from me."

"Good. Now where do we start?"

Walker's phone beeped again. Someone else was coming down the driveway. He knew without looking that it was Ava Bailey.

Walker nodded toward the driveway.

Tim turned to have a look. "That the detective who was here last night?"

"It is. And we're about to find out how this thing is going to go. Hopefully she won't make it any harder on us than it's already going to be."

20

Detective Bailey got out of her car and began walking toward the front porch where Walker and Tim were standing. She was shaking her head before she even got around the front of her car.

"Feels like a little déjà vu seeing the two of you here again. How'd you beat me here, Mr. Lawson?"

"Patrol car dropped me at the farm, and I came right over," Tim said.

"You two planning another boat outing then? 'Cause I know you're not thinking about getting involved in what's going on."

"*Getting* involved?" Tim said. "Sounds like you didn't see what happened down the road back there. Whoever is doing this involved us."

Ava stopped at the bottom of the steps. "Maybe, but now you just need to take yourself out of it."

"Cut the shit, Detective," Walker said. "I'm done talking about whether or not we all are involved. The only thing I want to talk about now is how we find who's doing all this. If you have anything else in mind by coming here, feel free to leave. Or arrest us. But I'd prefer we work together. Because I want to find these missing girls, and I want to stay alive. Both of which you can make easier or harder, but both are going to happen."

Ava put her hands up. "All right . . . all right. I don't like it. But I suppose I have to play the hand I've been dealt. And I decided the best way to do that is together, because I'm getting pushback from everyone up the ranks, and frankly, I'm tired of it. I'm like you, I want to live. Something that seems to get harder to do the more we're involved."

"You could have just led with that, you know?" Walker said.

"I just wanted to make sure that you two were sure. If this goes sideways, it's at best jail time. At worst . . . well, it seems the two of you get it. Just know, I can't keep you out of jail. But I can do my best to keep you alive."

"Let me worry keeping us alive," Walker said.

Tim cleared his throat. "You all mind if we move this inside? My sweat is sweating, it's so damn hot out here."

Walker didn't move. He stood staring at Ava. She shifted her weight and crossed her arms over her chest.

"Is there something you want to say, Walker?" Ava said.

"My job right now is to make the decisions that will optimize the chances of finding these missing girls and eradicating the people responsible for their kidnapping, and for coming after me and Tim earlier. If they are, in fact, the same people."

"So what does staring at me have to do with that?"

Walker stepped down from the porch to get on Ava's level. He looked down into her eyes. "Because I am trying to determine if you're what's best for me in accomplishing those two goals."

Ava laughed. "Me? I'm the only one here who is even allowed to be doing this. How could—"

"That's exactly my point, Ava," Walker said, cutting her off. "If you walk inside with us, I need you to understand that you're crossing a line you can't go back on. You can't do what you did at Detective Foley's house earlier. You can't tell us to back off if you get uncomfortable."

Ava let her arms drop. "I don't understand. What do you mean 'uncomfortable'?"

"I mean, the things I'm going to have to do to have a chance at making this right are going to be things that your badge doesn't allow you to do. And if you're not okay with that, you need to go."

"What do you mean by 'things my badge won't let me do,' Walker?"

"I think you know what I mean. And there is no turning back."

"I'm not sure she does understand what you mean, son," Tim said. "Now is probably not a good time to leave things unsaid."

Tim was right. Walker could assume things all day long, but what they were about to have to do needed 100 percent clarity. Maybe Tim needed to hear it too.

Walker stepped back so he could have both Tim and Ava in view. "The only way to deal with the type of people who are responsible for the mess here in Soddy Daisy is to fight the way they fight. Only dirtier." Walker focused on Ava. "Tim and I watched a man shoot his own people, just to keep them from talking. Can you even comprehend what people like this are capable of, Ava?"

Ava was quiet. Walker could see her calculating. He wanted to see confidence from Ava, but he also wanted to see her be honest with herself. There was nothing in her life that could prepare her for what was coming. Walker knew this from experience. But he needed her to understand that she didn't know. And that she needed a man who had stared the devil in the face and still managed to come out alive.

"I can imagine what they are capable of," Ava said. "But only because I've seen innocent young girls go missing and people murdered. The problem that I think you've already figured out, Walker, is that I also know what I'm capable of, and I realize I can't fight this on my own. The question is, how do I know you can?"

It was a fair question. Tim had caught a very small glimpse of what Walker could do back at the scene of the accident, but Ava had not. He was happy to hear that her mind was in the right place. Because it was the only way she was going to survive.

Tim spoke up. "I can tell you he's better qualified than both of us, just from what I saw earlier."

Walker looked over at Tim. "Tim, you need to understand this too. People like this, if we fail, your family will suffer. They'll come after everyone you love to keep whatever operation they have here running."

"I get it. But they'll have to come through me first."

"They will," Walker said. Then he turned to Ava. "You too. They'll destroy everything. I've seen it happen. I don't have a family. So the only thing on the line here is me."

"Then we better not lose," Ava said.

"I haven't yet," Walker said. "And I don't plan on starting now."

Walker's phone buzzed. It was a message from Daniel: "*We need to talk. Now.*"

"It's Daniel Turnberry," Walker said. "He says we need to talk now."

Walker messaged Daniel back: "*Busy right now. You find something?*"

"Walker, I can't involve a minor in this," Ava said.

"You think this is what I want?" Walker said. "Unfortunately, it's his sister. And I can tell you, you aren't going to keep him out of it. So I might as well keep him close so I can protect him."

"And if you can't?" Ava said.

"I gave him the speech, Ava. I told him to stay out of it. That he could get hurt. But I would do the same thing if I was in his shoes."

Ava gave a begrudging shrug that seemed to match the scowl on her face. "You think he knows something?"

Walker's phone buzzed again. Daniel messaged back: "*I found what the snake-and-cross tattoo stands for. We have to talk* NOW!"

Walker read Daniel's text aloud.

"Is he talking about the matching tattoos on the wrists of the men who came after you? The snake and cross? 'Cause I have someone at the precinct looking into that too."

"Yeah?" Walker said. "Daniel is way ahead of them. Still don't think we can involve him?"

"Yes, Walker, I still don't think we should involve him. But now we have to. Especially if he can give us any sort of clue as to who is involved or what is going on."

Walker texted Daniel back: "*Come to the lake house. Make sure* no *one sees you or follows you.*"

Daniel: "*Already on my way.*"

"Looks like we're about to find out, because he's headed over now."

21

Daniel walked in, and as soon as he walked through the front door, he stopped dead in his tracks.

"D-detective Bailey?" Daniel said. Then he looked at Walker. "You didn't tell me she was here. I—"

"It's fine, Daniel. She knows everything."

"Yeah, but if she tells my parents I'm here, I'm screwed. Royally."

Ava turned in her chair to face Daniel. "To be honest, I should be telling your parents where you are. Right now. But somehow I've let Walker convince me to let you help. But this is it, you hear me? You share with us what you know, and then we'll handle it from there. Got it?"

Daniel looked at Walker.

"Uh uh," Ava said. "Don't look at him. I'm speaking for all of us. Okay?"

Daniel glanced quickly at Walker, but directly back to Ava and nodded his head.

Ava looked up at Walker. "Got it?"

Walker nodded.

Ava turned to Tim, but he beat her to it.

"I got it."

Walker watched as Daniel looked eager to get going. "Come on then, before you explode."

Daniel rushed over and put his laptop on the bar between Ava and Tim. Walker pulled the chair out of the way and stood looking over Daniel's shoulder. He opened the laptop, typed in a password, then scrolled over to the internet tab.

"You know the picture of the tattoo you sent me, Walker?" Daniel looked back over his shoulder.

Walker nodded.

"Bring everyone up to speed so we can all be on the same page, please," Ava said.

A picture of someone's wrist adorned with an upside-down cross with a snake wrapping around it filled the computer screen.

"Back on the hill, amidst the chaos," Walker said, "I managed to notice that two of the guys had that tattooed on their wrist."

"Only one of the men on that hill didn't have that tattoo, actually," Ava said.

"So I asked Daniel to look it up. Daniel, it seems like you've found something?"

"You guys aren't going to believe this," Daniel said. "You ready?"

Daniel punched another button on his computer.

"I don't like the sound of this," Tim said.

Daniel looked over at Tim. "It's worse than you think."

The hair on the back of Walker's neck stood on end. The way Daniel said that, coupled with the image of a bunch of people in robes standing around a fire on the screen, gave Walker a chill.

"When I first started searching for the tattoo, there was obviously a lot of stuff about religion that came up," Daniel said. "But none of the images or stories on Google brought back anything significant. Which, to be honest, is pretty much what I expected."

Daniel paused and looked over at Ava for a second.

"I can't get in trouble for any of this, right?"

"I'm not sure what you mean," Ava said. She then glanced up at Walker. Her face wore concern.

"Well, technically I'm working with the police right now, right? So I can't get in trouble for telling you stuff or anything?"

"Technically, no, Daniel, you are not working with the police. Technically, you're not here, and I am not involving civilians in an ongoing police investigation."

"Oh, so even better, right? None of this"—Daniel made air quotes with his fingers—"is technically happening."

"I'm not going to tell on you or take you to jail, if that is what you are worried about."

"Bussin," Daniel said.

Tim looked over at Walker and raised an eyebrow. Walker shrugged. He didn't have a clue what Daniel said, or what it meant. Walker just figured it must be New Age slang meaning something good.

"What are we looking at here, Daniel?" Walker said.

"Okay, so, last year my friend and I watched a movie called *Into the Black*. A super underground horror movie about the dark web. And well, it creeped us out so much that we kinda became obsessed with what the dark web actually is and what you can do on it."

"Hence why you asked if you could get in trouble for what you say here," Ava said.

"Right," Daniel said, without looking up from his

computer. "Probably needless to say, we found some really messed-up stuff going on. Not only around the country, but right here around Chattanooga. People selling guns illegally, drugs, sex—"

"Can we keep this focused to what's going on with the tattoo?" Walker said. "We're losing daylight."

"Right," Daniel said. "Anyway, when Walker texted me a picture of the tattoo, I knew I would end up using my experience on the dark web to find something. And I did. And it's pretty terrifying. And I hope the guys you found this tattoo on don't have anything to do with my sister being taken." Daniel paused for a second. When no one spoke, he went on. "I found a match for the tattoo image buried way down deep in some local thread. Here it is."

Daniel pulled up a page that looked similar to a Reddit thread. Basically a bunch of people talking about a certain topic. Inside one of the messages were the images Walker saw a moment ago: the tattoo and the group of robed people standing around a fire.

"Can you summarize for us?" Ava said.

"Sure. Somebody started a thread with a question about cults in Southern Tennessee. A lot of people were chiming in. One person would say they knew of one, and someone else would call them a liar and talk about how it was all myths and BS. 'Prove it then' came up several times, and this went on for a while. But then I noticed one account in particular. The screen name was *BaphometsSon*."

Daniel looked around at everyone as if they were supposed to have a reaction to the name. When they didn't, he helped them out.

"You know, Baphomet? The satanic deity?"

Tim chuckled. "Only deity I know about is the devil. Outside of that, I only pay attention to God."

"You sound like my mom," Daniel said. "There isn't much to know. Baphomet is just a goat-headed man with long horns that Satan followers worship. The reason I know about it is because Baphomet is supposedly a genderless deity, and in Hollywood, the Satan worshippers are said to be steering their children toward being transgenders in a sacrifice to Baphomet."

"You serious?" Tim said. "That's sick right there."

Walker just listened. He wasn't concerned with what Hollywood was up to. Never had been and never would be.

"I've seen some videos on Instagram about this stuff," Ava said. "It is messed up."

"Anyway," Walker said.

"Yeah, anyway," Daniel said. "This *BaphometsSon* kept insisting in this thread that not only was there a cult in the Chattanooga area, but he was a part of it. The 'prove it' thread went on for a long time until finally they challenged *BaphometsSon* to post a picture from the next cult gathering that they went to. Long story short, they did, along with a picture of the tattoo that Walker had sent me."

Ava leaned in, eyes squinting, trying to get a better look at the picture of the people in robes. "Any context given on the picture of the people?"

Daniel looked over at Ava. "This is where it gets scary."

Daniel turned and looked at Walker. He could see the concern in Daniel's eyes.

"There was a little back and forth trying to get BaphometsSon to give more information. Finally, they got them to say that it was a preparation ritual they were performing."

"Preparation for what?" Walker said.

"The Buck Moon sacrifice."

The words didn't mean anything to Walker, but the fear in Daniel's eyes when he said it told the story.

"I'm assuming the Buck Moon is a bad thing to Satan worshippers?" Tim said.

"Well," Daniel said. "It's a good thing for them I guess, but bad for the . . . sacrifice."

"Is there information on the Buck Moon's significance to these people?" Walker said.

"Not, um, not these people in particular with this cult, I don't guess. But the information on the internet about the Buck Moon and satanic worship is there. The moon in July is called the Buck Moon because it's said to be when a buck deer grows his antlers. To Baphomet worshippers, I guess they interpret it to mean the growing of Baphomet's horns. There isn't much on it after that, but I assume in this local cult's case, they are going to sacrifice something in honor of Baphomet's horns."

Daniel swallowed hard and stared down at his feet. Walker knew exactly what was troubling Daniel, because it was now troubling Walker as well. Daniel was worried that the sacrifice just might be his sister.

"Listen, Daniel. Great job looking into all of this. But this doesn't mean it has anything to do with your sister's kidnapping. The men with the tattoo don't have any connection to anything going on with kidnappings that we can see."

"Don't do that," Daniel said.

"Do what?"

"Don't patronize me. You know you are thinking it too. Because the men who had the snake-cross tattoo came after you, Walker. And the only reason they would do that is because you went to see that detective in Ringgold, right?"

Ava chimed in. "There is no way we can know that, Daniel."

"Bullshit," he said to Ava, then looked at Walker. "That's BS and you know it, don't you?"

Walker didn't want to worry the kid more, but even more than that, he didn't want to lie to him. "I don't know anything for sure, Daniel. But it's the only reason these men would come after me."

"You don't know that, Walker," Ava said. "So there is no sense making it harder on Daniel with speculation."

"Daniel's a big boy. And besides, it's not really speculation, is it? Have you read this all the way through in your mind, Ava?"

"I have, Walker. But without concrete evidence there is no way—"

"Just spell it out for me, Walker," Daniel said. "I already know Amy's in trouble if she's still alive, so just lay it out."

Walker glanced at Ava. She was shaking her head. Daniel was in a fragile state, but Walker decided to talk to Daniel like he would have wanted to be talked to if this had happened to him at fifteen.

"Detective Foley was involved in investigating the kidnappings this time last year," Walker started, but was interrupted when Ava scoffed and walked away.

"I want no part of this," Ava said. "He's too young."

"He already knows what I'm about to tell him," Walker said. "He just wants it clarified. The kid is smart. Don't underestimate him."

Ava whipped around. "You said it, Walker. The 'kid' is smart. But he's still just a kid."

"Yep. And some bad people took his kid sister. And he wants answers. I'm going to do my best to do what no one else seems to want to do."

"Want to do?"

Walker could see Ava's face turning red. She was about to blow.

Ava continued. "Want to do? You don't think I want to help Daniel by solving this case for him? You don't think that's what I've been doing since the very first second the information that Amy was missing came across my desk? How dare you question what I'm trying to do to solve this?"

"Detective Bailey, this isn't about you." Walker didn't measure his words.

"This was a mistake. I should never have involved any of you."

"You didn't," Walker said. "Daniel did. That's why your feelings matter less to me than explaining exactly what I think is going on with his sister."

Ava stomped toward Walker. "And you think speculating about something you don't actually know anything about is the way to do it?"

Walker kept calm in the face of Ava's fury. "No. I think linking what I now know to what has happened in the last twenty-four hours—to me, Detective Foley, Tim, and the men who died on that hill trying to kill us a couple of hours ago—is the way to do it. Then speculating with your help after that on what we should do next is what I was hoping for."

That cooled Ava a bit.

"The boy knows what's going on here," Tim said. "He just wants the cards on the table so he can help play the hand, am I right?" Tim looked at Daniel.

Daniel nodded, then looked at Ava. "I know it's bad. I just want to know what is going to happen next."

Walker took control of the conversation. "Daniel, I think the men with the tattoo who came after me and Tim killed

Detective Foley so that he couldn't talk about what he knew. About what got him to take a job at another police force other than Soddy Daisy last year. I think someone from the tattoo group saw me at Detective Foley's house, and that's why they came after me, because they thought I was sticking my nose into this thing to try to find your sister. Are you sure you want to know what I think that means now, especially since you've found this information about a cult preparing for this Buck Moon thing?"

Daniel nodded without hesitation. "Yes. I mean, I know what it means. I just need to hear you say it, and then I need to hear you tell me you can stop it."

Walker looked at Ava. She just hung her head.

"Daniel, I think these people took your sister, and maybe the others as well, to sacrifice her in this cult. And I can stop it." Walker looked at Ava again. "But I'm going to need some help."

Ava looked up, found Walker looking at her, then gave a nod of her own.

"How . . . how are we going to stop them?" Daniel said. He was fighting back his emotions from the tough words Walker had just told him.

"Find this BaphometsSon. Then make them talk. Have you looked up when exactly this Buck Moon is, so we at least know how much time we have?"

Walker wasn't sure, but he thought maybe he could see the color drain from Daniel's face.

"It . . . it's a three-night full moon."

"Okay," Walker said. "When is the first night?"

Daniel hung his head and his shoulders slumped just before he looked up at Walker. "Tonight."

22

The sun was setting outside. The orange glow had settled over the four of them from the surrounding windows. While the setting was pretty, the mood of the room was anything but. However, even though the information they had uncovered was horrible, they at least had some leads, and Walker had to put them to work immediately if they were going to have a chance to find Amy Turnberry before it was too late.

"Okay, Daniel, do what you can—including calling your dark web friend—to find out who this BaphometsSon is and where they might be. But before you do that, send Ava the picture of the robed people around the fire." Walker looked at Ava. "See if anyone on your team can decipher the location of that picture. Maybe we can get lucky and someone recognizes something." Walker addressed everyone now. "Just understand that both of these things are a long shot. Especially in the short time window we are dealing with now. But at least we have something to go on."

Daniel had already turned and was typing on his computer.

"Let me know you understood everything, Daniel," Walker said.

Daniel turned around. "Oh, yeah, sorry. I had already been talking to Ricky about this. He just messaged me back."

"Ricky?" Ava said.

"The one who went into the dark web with me."

There was a beep from Daniel's phone. Daniel picked it up and read a message, then looked up at Walker. Walker read his expression as hopeful.

"He already found him."

"BaphometsSon?" Walker said.

"Yeah!"

"Already? How?"

Daniel read another message, tapped on his phone, then looked back up at Walker. "The moron's Facebook profile, Bapho666." Daniel turned the screen of his phone toward Walker. "And his profile picture is Baphomet smoking a joint."

Walker looked at the Facebook profile. He saw the picture Daniel was talking about, and behind that small one was a bigger rectangular picture of a winged demon with red eyes.

"How did he find him so fast?" Tim asked. "I don't understand any of this technology shit. Except that it's the damn devil itself."

"Ricky is a computer genius," Daniel said. "But it sounds like this BaphometsSon is exactly the opposite and left an easy trail for Ricky to follow. He's combing through the Facebook page now to see if BaphometsSon has ever been dumb enough to geotag himself."

"Geo *what*?" Tim said.

"Tag a location on a post or a photo," Daniel said, "showing where you are or where the pic was taken."

"Why the hell would anyone ever want to do that?" Tim said. "There's too many crazies out there that will follow you or come and steal your stuff."

"You'd be surprised," Ava said. "It's how we catch people a lot of the time."

"You've actually caught people?" Walker said.

"Ha-ha. Very funny, Mr. Mysterious. You're probably just some accountant from a little town in Kentucky who thought it would be fun to go try to play hero."

"Impossible," Walker said.

"But is it?" Ava said.

"Yeah. 'Cause I hate math."

The four of them stole a rare laugh from the overwhelmingly somber situation. Then Ava walked away to make a phone call. Daniel went back to his computer, and Tim got up and walked over to the window overlooking the lake. The pinks, yellows, and oranges were reflecting off the top of the water. Walker went over to join him.

"Life is a strange existence, isn't it?" Tim said.

Walker thought he understood what Tim meant, but he wanted to hear Tim's thoughts. "How so?"

"Just look at all that beauty. It's all around us, all the time. It's in the trees, the water, and the sky. It's everywhere."

Walker followed Tim's gaze and took in what he was seeing.

"But . . . ," Tim said. "So is the ugly. And the evil. Even though it hides itself a lot better than the beautiful things all around us, it's there all the same." Tim looked over at Walker. "I realize I'm talking to someone who's seen more evil than I'll ever know, but when you have kids, it's almost as if your senses sharpen to see that evil even better. And if you let it, it can drive you crazy trying to worry about keeping your kids away from it. But that's all I am now, Walker. My kids are grown. And both of them are great parents to my grandbabies. They don't need me in their everyday lives anymore. But a great parent, one who did things right as they raised their kids, is with them every day, even when they aren't. And all I can do is hope I left enough of me with them to make good decisions and protect their own kids. Just like everything else in life, though, you always wonder if you did enough."

Walker could see that Tim was having a moment. He would have given anything to have a father like Tim when he was growing up.

"I don't have a good reference point, Tim, because I never had a dad. But I can tell you beyond a shadow of a doubt that you have done more than enough. And I don't need to know your kids to know that. You're there for them when they need you. Most kids don't understand like I do that, that is the most important gift a child could ever receive."

Tim placed his hand on Walker's shoulder. "I'm sorry you never had that, son. But I sure am glad I met you. Even though you dragged me into all this shit."

Walker looked over and found Tim smiling. "Glad I met you too, old man."

"We gonna get the people who did this? 'Cause I want to find who took Daniel's sister and my grandson's girlfriend, and I want to keep them from being able to do it to somebody else's kids or grandkids."

Walker looked over at Daniel. Then back to Tim. Then he lowered his voice. "We're going to find them. I just hope it's not too late."

"He says he found him!" Daniel shouted.

Everyone walked over to the kitchen.

"Ricky says he thinks he knows where BaphometsSon lives! They tagged their location about a week ago as the 'Pit of Hell.' It's a neighborhood not far from here! Let's go get them!"

Daniel had turned around and was looking at Walker wide-eyed.

"That's great news, Daniel, but you are staying right here."

Daniel stood from the stool. "The hell I am. This person knows where my sister is. I'm going!"

"Daniel," Walker said, "you are nothing but a liability out there. But you can do us a lot of good from here. Especially with your friend Ricky's help if we should need to find something else."

"I'm going, Walker. You can't stop me."

"I can stop you. And you're not going. We have no idea what we are going to find when we get to this location. It could be nothing. I need you right here working on plan B while we check it out. I need to know the real name of this BaphometsSon if you can find it. This is a good lead, but it may lead to nothing."

Daniel hung his head. "But it's good, right? I'm helping to find Amy, right?"

"We wouldn't even have had a chance without you, Daniel. But now we do. And I need you to keep doing what you do best, while I go and do what I do best."

"Yeah?" Daniel said. "And what's that?"

"Make bad people disappear."

23

"Make bad people disappear?" Ava said with a laugh. "Did you really say that?"

Tim pulled out of the driveway at the lake house. He couldn't hold back a chuckle of his own.

"Ah, I see," Walker said. "I try to give the kid some hope, some confidence in us, and I get shit from Tweedledee and Tweedledum here."

"No, no, it was a good line," Tim said, still laughing. "I was just surprised that before you walked out the door, you didn't turn back to him to tell him, 'I'll be back!'"

The two of them busted out laughing.

Ava wiped a laughing tear and said in her best Arnold Schwarzenegger voice, "Get to da choppa! Get down!"

Tim changed his voice to sound like Rocky Balboa. "Adrian!" He pounded the steering wheel as he laughed. Ava was bent over holding her stomach laughing in the passenger seat. Walker just sat back and had a laugh himself. He could see where what he'd said sounded a little cliché action movie hero.

"I hate to break up a fun moment," Tim said, "but just

what in the hell are we going to do right now? Just roll up to this address and knock on the door? And say what to whoever answers the door, '*Hello, are you a cult member who writes in chat forums on the dark web about Satan worshipping?*'"

Tim had a good point.

"I don't really have a good answer for that," Walker said.

"Uh," Ava said, "first of all, it's going to be me who goes to the door and asks the questions. You know, the only person with a badge? Depending on what we get if someone actually does come to the door, we can take it from there."

"Sounds good," Walker said. "Any word from your people about the photo of the robed cult members?"

"We have a good tech guy on the team—Jimmy—he's looking into it. Hopefully he can pull some sort of clue from it."

"Hopefully," Walker agreed. "I have a feeling we're going to need a plan B to fall back on after this little house visit. The odds this turns out to be something worthwhile are slim to none."

"Agreed," Ava said.

Tim drove Ava's unmarked car through a yellow light, then turned off the main road.

Ava held up the GPS on her phone. "Should be just about a mile up here on the right. I think I know this subdivision."

"A satanic cult member living in a regular old subdivision," Tim said. "You just never know what the hell is going on around you, do you?"

"You have no idea," Walker said.

Tim flipped on the car's headlights as the last of the day's light disappeared. Walker noticed Tim looking at him in the rearview mirror.

"What? You want a story?" Walker said.

"We have a couple of minutes. But only if you feel like sharing."

Ava turned around in her seat. "I wouldn't mind knowing at least one thing about you as we walk into this sinister thing together."

"Oh, you want a confidence boost, do you?"

"Yeah." Ava smiled. "Just leave out the cheesy hero lines."

Walker nodded, then watched some trees pass by his window in the glow of the yellow headlights.

"The third job I ever went on, when I was at the ripe old age of nineteen, they sent me to Lake Como in Northern Italy."

"They?" Ava said.

Walker looked over from the window to her shadowed face in front of him. "Yeah, they."

"Don't ruin story time now, Detective," Tim said.

Ave held up her hands and let Walker continue.

"Don't know if you've ever been to Lake Como, but it is about as quaint of a small town as you'll find. Surrounded by beautiful homes all around the massive lake. Lots of families who run the restaurants and local businesses all live in a very neighborly area. To Tim's point, you just have no idea what is going on around you.

"When I arrived, I had an espresso out by the water. I hated it, but it seemed like the thing to do. Families were buzzing about. Locals were doing their work, enjoying their days, and travelers were doing the same with the help of those locals. All of them, completely oblivious. Two days later, just about a block away from that very spot where I sat, I slid the blade of my knife across a man's neck who had been living among these people for half a year.

Constructing the final blueprints for a nuclear weapon that had been in its final phase of construction after a decade of building.

"My handler told me that if the man I killed had had another week to finish the blueprint, there was a good chance half the Eastern seaboard in the US would have looked completely different. And not in a good way."

"Wow," Tim said. "That is nuts."

Ava turned around as Tim turned right, into a neighborhood. "Any idea what the nuclear weapon was?"

"My handler said something about an undetectable, fully automated sea weapon. The only thing I saw when I collected the blueprints, and all of the files on his computer, revealed something in the shape of a dolphin. Point is, that beautiful town full of lively families and blissful travelers had no idea that man existed for evil. And when I was sitting among them, ordering my food, choking down espressos, they had no idea I was a killer either."

The car was quiet. Ava's GPS announced that their destination was just ahead on the left. Even though Walker felt his pistol in his concealed holster pushing into his side, out of habit he ran his hand over it. He supposed it was subconsciously soothing.

"We just going to roll up and knock on the door?" Tim said.

"We have nothing to hide," Ava said. "And whether or not the person who lives at this address does or not, we're going to find that out." Ava turned to Walker. "How is your BS meter these days?"

"Might be rusty, but between the two of us, we can probably sniff it out."

"Tim," Ava said, "you stay in the car. If something goes

sideways, don't be afraid to get the hell out of here and call the police."

Tim gave the pistol at his hip a pat with his hand. "I'll call the police, but I ain't leaving."

"Suit yourself," Ava said. "Walker, just let me do the talking. Get my back if it gets itchy."

Tim pulled the car into the driveway of the suspected BaphometsSon's house. There was a sliver of daylight left, and with the help of the car's headlights Walker could see that it was a two-story, brown brick home. The roof was a darker shade of something. Ava reached for the door, but Walker stopped her before she got out.

"I think I should go around back while you hit the front door. Just in case someone makes a run for it."

Ava shook her head. "No. I don't like the idea of going up to this house alone. We need to stick together."

"I'll go around back while you two go to the front," Tim said.

"Absolutely not. I can't let civilians make life-or-death decisions without me being with you."

"I'm not going to shoot the person. I'll leave that to you all. Just want to be able to give a heads-up."

"No, Tim. Just stay in the car like I—"

"I think it's a good idea," Walker interrupted.

Ava swung her head around to face him.

Walker held up his hands. "He said he will just shout if someone runs out the back. That's just smart."

"But I said no."

"Then Tim might as well turn the car around and head back to the lake house, Detective. What good is having us come along if you aren't going to use us wisely?"

"I *am* using you wisely. You have experience, Walker. More than all of us, so you say. Tim does not."

"I have experience shouting. Now, damn it, Walker's right. Why the hell did you tell us to come along for if someone we need to talk to can just run out the back door into the damn woods?"

Ava turned back and sat forward in her seat. Then she let out a heavy sigh. "Fine," she said, turning her full attention to Tim. "But if you touch your weapon, I swear to God I'll have you arrested myself."

"Unless he has to defend himself," Walker said.

"Jesus H, you two. Both of you just get the hell out of the car and do whatever the hell you want then. You kill somebody, I'll just say I had no idea where you came from and that I feared for my own damn life. Now, can we go? Or do you all want to argue a bit more about who's doing what?"

Tim turned around to face Walker. He was wearing a shit-eatin' grin. "I think we're good now, right?" he said with a nod.

Walker laughed and got out of the car. The evening cooldown had yet to kick in. The air was thick with moisture. Tim got out and walked over to the far-right side of the house.

"Ava's right, Tim. Don't be a hero. That's my job, remember?"

Tim laughed. "I'll just yell 'Adrian' if I see something."

Ava walked around the front of the car. "Apparently cheesy lines are your job."

"Yeah, maybe," Walker said. "But at least I meant that one as a joke."

Ava scrunched her nose. "But did you?"

They laughed it off as they approached the front door. There was a light on in one of the upstairs bedrooms, but there were no cars in the driveway. Walker calculated a 50/50 shot that someone was home. And if BaphometsSon actually lived here, he gave it more of a 10 percent chance that they would get someone at the door.

"Here goes nothing," Ava said as she reached forward and touched the doorbell. The ding-dong was louder than Walker had expected.

A muffled female voice called out, "Just a minute!"

Ava looked back at Walker, stuck out her chin, and shrugged her shoulders. Two bright yellow lights on each side of the door lit up. Then the door opened. A very homely, fairly overweight, middle-aged woman stood staring at Ava and Walker.

"Pretty late to be ringin' people's doors. Everything all right?"

"Everything's fine, ma'am. Sorry about the late hour. My partner and I were wondering if we could ask you a couple of questions?"

"Partner? Ya'll police or somethin'? My boy didn't do nothin' dumb again, now did he?"

Walker couldn't help but think they just might be in the right place. And judging by the woman's lighthearted demeanor, if her son was a troublemaker, Walker imagined she had no idea exactly what he was into. Especially since she was wearing a gold chain with a cross dangling from it.

"Well, we don't think he has, ma'am, but he might just have some information about the Amy Turnberry kidnapping that could help us."

"My boy? Know something about that poor girl missin' on the TV?"

From somewhere behind the house, a large crash sounded. Followed by a scream of agony.

The woman at the door turned and looked behind her. "What in *thee* hell is that boy doin' now?"

"We got a runner!" Tim shouted. "Well, sort of. More of a limper."

"Who the hell was that?" the woman said.

Walker took off jogging in Tim's direction. As he rounded the house, he could just make out Tim standing with his hand on his hip, watching something intently.

Walker ran up. "What's going on?"

Tim laughed his smoker laugh. The one that always turned into a cough. "Chubby fella broke through the back porch awning trying to climb out the back window. I didn't think he was going to get up, but there he goes limping away."

"Arnold! Get your ass back here!" the lady from the front door yelled out the back toward the limping figure. "Right now! Or you're *really* gonna be in trouble!"

The limping figure stopped. Walker didn't have to run anybody down. Now all he could do was hope this little visit was worth it. The kid running was a good sign, but Walker's confidence level that any of this was connected couldn't have been lower.

"Let's go see what this shithead has to say," Tim said, slapping Walker on the stomach as he walked away.

Walker fell in behind him. "After you."

24

Ava, Tim, and Walker were standing in the strangers' living room. It was pretty run-down. The white paint was full of scuff marks and little holes. The brown couch—maybe suede, maybe leather—looked like it had been handed down more than one generation. And the light brown carpet was full of stains and what looked like cigarette burns. That explained the lingering smoky smell that seemed to cling to every single inch of the home.

In front of them, a young man, at least a hundred pounds overweight, maybe twenty-five years old, sat trying to catch his breath. His rosy cheeks were covered in a scruff that looked like he'd been trying to grow a beard since birth, to no avail. The rest of him was pale, like he didn't much care for leaving the house, and his dark shaggy hair said about the same for caring about his appearance. The *Slipknot* T-shirt didn't mean he was in fact the Satan worshipper the dark web said he was, but like it or not, it did seem a step in that direction. The final and most glaring piece of Arnold's appearance that Walker noticed being missing was the snake and cross tattoo.

"I'm Detective Bailey, and these are my associates. Arnold, your mother has given me permission to ask you a few questions, is that okay?"

Arnold looked up at his mom.

"Just answer the damn questions," Arnold's momma said.

Arnold looked back up at Ava and gave a nod.

"Have you ever heard the name BaphometsSon?"

Walker liked the way Ava had gone right after Arnold to catch him off guard. And it clearly worked. The rosiness in his cheeks turned ghost white as he swallowed hard and looked up at his mother. Then back at Ava.

"I-I, how did you . . ." Arnold's words were hard to find.

"I just want you to know that you aren't in trouble. Yet. But I need to know everything you know about the cult here in Chattanooga."

"BaphometsSon?" his mother said. "Cult? I told you to quit listenin' to that devil music, Arnie. Now what the hell have you gone and done?"

Walker could see that Arnold was churning on exactly how to handle the situation. Walker gave him a little nudge over the edge. "Arnold, the next thing you say is very important. We already know the things you've claimed on the dark web. If you lie to us now, you're not going to see this house again for a very long time."

"Dark web?" Arnold's mom said. "What in the—"

"I was lying about all of it. I swear!" Arnold blurted out. "I was just trying to be cool." He turned both of his chubby arms over, wrists facing up. "See, no tattoo. I promise I'm not in the cult." He looked over at his mother. "I swear,

Momma. I was just havin' some fun with some people on the internet!"

Everyone was quiet for a moment. Ava was letting Arnold work it out.

"I'm tellin' you, I don't have nothin' to do with no cult."

Ava took a step forward. "I believe you, Arnold. But that's not good enough. I need to know where you got the information you did post on the dark web forum."

"What in the hell is a dark web?" Arnold's mom said. "How many times have I told you that you've been spendin' way too much damn time in front of that screen. You'd better tell these people what they want to know, then I'm tossin' that thing in the garbage!"

"Arnold," Walker said, "this is your chance to take the mistake you made and turn it into a positive. If you tell us everything you know, you just might be able to help a missing girl be found before something bad happens to you. Don't you think that would make your mother proud?"

"You think he can really help like that?" Arnold's mother said.

"I do, ma'am."

"Tell 'em every damn thing you know, baby. You hear me?"

"Yes, Mom. Where do you want me to start?"

"Same place you started the thread about the cult," Ava said. "And where you got the information."

"All right. But do I have to tell you everything I've been lookin' at?" Arnold said. Then he looked with a face full of guilt at his mother.

"No, Arnold. Stick to the cult. Whatever else you do on there you probably shouldn't do, but it's not our concern today."

Arnold nodded. That seemed to bring him some relief.

"Okay. I read a long blog post once about the dark web, so I started studyin' on it. Once I figured out how to move around on the dark web, I started talking to people who liked some of the bands I like. My mom thinks because they like Satan that I do. But that ain't true. It just interests me."

His mom shook her head in an "I don't know what I'm going to do with you" way.

"After a couple of months, I saw where somebody in one of the local forums was talking about a cult. I couldn't believe there was one around here, so I pretended like I might want to join and started asking questions. To be honest, I was afraid it was people from that cult here to get me or somethin'. I've been paranoid ever since I posted those two pictures."

"We know the pictures," Ava said. "Let's get to those in a second. You said you started asking questions. Where did that lead?"

"The guy said he was a member of a cult here in Soddy Daisy. I guess because of my stupid name—BaphometsSon—he thought he was speakin' to someone who worshipped Satan too."

"You could probably see where someone might think that?" Tim said.

Arnold hung his head. "Yeah, I do. I guess that was kinda the point, if I'm being honest. But it was just me being curious, I swear!"

"What the hell is a Bafomet—or whatever the hell you named yourself?" Arnold's mother asked.

"Do you mind if he explains everything to you later, ma'am?" Walker said. "We're pretty short on time."

"Oh, he's gonna explain all right. As I burn his damn computer."

"Please go on, Arnold," Ava said. "No judgment here. We just want the truth."

Arnold nodded. "Right, so, he told me about the cult. Said the name of it was SIK—Satan Is King."

Tim looked over at Walker. He must have been thinking the same as Walker, that he couldn't believe what they had gotten themselves mixed up in.

Arnold continued, "I told him that was cool and all, but I didn't believe him. But that if it was true, I would definitely be down to join. I just wanted more info, you know?"

"It's okay, Arnold," Ava said. "We all get curious once in a while."

Arnold gave a thankful smile. "I basically told him to prove it. Same as the people were saying to me on the thread you read of mine. So he first sent over the picture of the tattoo. Told me it symbolized the serpent gaining control of the cross and all that the cross symbolized. I told him I thought the name and the tattoo were cool, but that he could have easily made that stuff up. Then he sent me the video."

"Video?" Ava said. "I thought the robed people was just a photo?"

"It was, in the forum. I read somewhere that videos get flagged a whole lot quicker by cops or agents or whoever watches the dark web sometimes. So I just took a screenshot of the video he sent and posted it. I didn't think anyone would believe it, but they kinda did, I guess."

"Pretty convincing photo of some kind of cult going on," Tim said.

Arnold nodded.

"How'd you end it with the person who sent you the video?"

"That's when things got a little weird, and I quit talking

about any of it altogether. He was relentless. Said they needed new recruits to help the cause."

"The cause?" Ava said.

"I didn't ask. I was creeped out after the video. It wasn't fun anymore knowing it was real."

"So he just left you alone?" Walker said.

"Sort of. This was only a couple of days ago."

"Sort of?" Ava said.

"Yeah. I gave him one of my emails that I never use just so he would back off."

Ava hung her head. Walker knew why. It would be easy to trace him from his email.

"You know you can't share real-world info on the dark web," Ava said. "They can find you."

"I know, I know. But he threatened me. And I didn't know what to do. Before you guys showed up, I thought it would be okay. But if you found me . . ."

"Boy," Arnold's mother said, "if you invited some devil-worshippin' people to my house, you're going to meet the damn devil yourself when I'm through with you."

"I'm sure it's fine, ma'am," Ava said. "But I need that video, Arnold. Send it to me now, please. Here's my phone."

Ava walked over and handed Arnold her phone. He began pushing buttons, and as Walker watched, he couldn't help but let what happened back on the winding road where he and Tim were ambushed creep into his subconscious. He took a step back, then walked over to the window to the right of the front door. It was covered by a paisley curtain. He pulled it back and gave the outside front of the house a once-over. At first he didn't see anything. On his second pass, a shadow moved in the light of the front door.

"Everybody down!" Walker shouted as he pulled his gun from his holster.

Before he could bring up his gun, two men stepped out from behind Ava's vehicle, and both of them were holding semiautomatic rifles. Walker turned and found Ava walking toward him. He lowered his shoulder and tackled her onto the floor, just as the glass shattered from the front door and the living room window. Walker turned and kicked Tim's legs out from under him. As Tim dropped, the wall he would have been standing in front of was littered with bullet holes. Tim looked behind him at the holes in the wall and nodded a thank-you to Walker as the gunfire continued.

Arnold and his mother had dived as best as two heavyset people could toward the kitchen. Walker saw another shadow pass by the back window.

"Everyone stay down!" he shouted. "If you have a basement, get to it. Now!"

Arnold's eyes shot toward the door in front of him, and he rolled that way until he made it there. As Walker was making sure they were getting to safety, Ava managed to get up, and Walker just about lost it.

"I said stay down!" he shouted as he reached for Ava's wrist. He got a solid grip and nearly yanked her shoulder out of socket to get her to the floor.

"We have to fire back!" Ava said. "We're all dead if we wait for them to come in!"

Walker shook his head. Calm. The chaos of the continuous gunshots around them held no bearing over his demeanor. "Just get to the basement, and stay there until I come and get you."

"You're crazy! There's at least four of them!"

Walker pulled himself up to a crouch, and pulled her again by her arm with his right hand as he shoved Tim with his left, getting both of them in front of the basement door.

He ushered them in until they were on the stairs looking back at him.

"Stay down here until I come back for you. You understand me?"

Tim nodded.

"Did you understand *me*, Walker?" Ava said in a panic. "I said there are at least four of them!"

Walker took the doorknob in his right hand as he held his pistol down by his side with the other.

"They should have brought ten."

Then he slammed the basement door shut. Now that they were safe, he could really go to work.

25

Walker slammed the basement door shut and opened his tactical mind. He knew he could run circles around the men sent to kill him, but that didn't mean he didn't have to use his tools. When stray bullets are flying, any decision can accidentally be a bad one. He didn't see the shadow at the back any longer, so his first move would be to take out the men in front before one of them made their way in.

Outside the house, they didn't pose much of a threat to Walker. But inside, bullets can penetrate walls much more easily, and the angles are a lot harder to navigate. Walker stayed low and moved to the edge of the wall. The front window was gone, but a lot of the curtains covering it still remained, albeit decorating the space quite a bit differently than they were a couple of minutes ago.

One of the men had stopped firing, most likely exchanging his empty magazine for a hot one. Their lack of experience was evident in a lot of ways, but how long it was taking for the man to swap mags was a glaring sign. As the other gunman sprayed more rounds toward the outside wall, Walker took his shot and moved down the wall toward the front door, immediately sprinting up the stairs out of harm's way.

He could hear gunfire now erupting from the back. They were coming from more than one rifle, so he switched gears to focus on the back, rushing through what must have been Arnold's room. If the heavy metal posters on the wall weren't a giveaway, the crumpled roof of the back porch where Arnold trying to escape collapsed it, solidified the theory.

Arnold had left the window open, and seeing as how there were no rounds being fired toward the upper half of the house, Walker poked his Sig Sauer out the window and with two shots took down the only man he could see. Before the second gunman—who Walker could now tell was firing from the other side of the crumpled roof—had a chance to change course, Walker squeezed through the window, jumped down onto the dodgy roof, took two steps over so he could see the gunman, and two more bullets left the back of the house quiet.

Then the entire outside of the house was quiet. Either the shooters out front had heard Walker take down their gunmen in the back, or they were satisfied with the amount of holes they'd put in the front of the house. They were either going to leave, or they were going to go in and make sure the job was finished. Walker wasn't going to wait around to find out.

He jumped down off the mostly fallen porch roof and jogged over to the outside corner of the house. It was clear, so he advanced forward along the side of the house. He was shrouded in darkness. The only two men he could see when he peeked around the corner, however, were shining like lightbulbs from the front porch light. Walker took a step left, raised his weapon, and shot the man in front twice, then the man behind him twice.

Before he saw them fall, he moved again to the back of the house. As he rounded the corner, he kept his gun held high. Just as he reached where he could see around the porch, one more gunman was coming around the corner. This time instead of firing kill-shots, he wounded the man with a round to his trigger hand, then shot him once in the leg so he would go down. He fell backward at the side of the house. Alive.

Walker wanted some answers.

Before he could advance to get them, he heard a crack in the distance, and a piece of the head of the gunman he'd spared went missing. Someone had once again silenced the enemy before Walker could question him. This time Walker wasn't going to let him get away with it.

Walker pulled himself up the destroyed porch roof and sprinted for the open window. He dove through, did a front roll, then rushed through the hallway to a different bedroom that faced the front yard. He threw back the curtains, located a man jumping into a pickup truck, and fired his last four shots directly through the glass as the truck pulled away.

Walker knew this was their best chance at gaining information about Amy Turnberry. Maybe their last if the video Arnold handed over didn't produce any information. So he wasn't going to give up on running this man down. He swapped his magazine for a fresh one as he ran into the hallway, then dashed down the stairs. He heard Ava call for him as he threw open the front door, but he just kept running. Down the porch steps, through the grass, and into Ava's vehicle.

As Walker threw it into reverse and stomped on the gas,

his headlights showed Tim and Ava rushing out the front door. He turned the wheel right to maneuver onto the main road, put it in drive, then sped away. His adrenaline was pumping, so he cranked the AC. The cool air relaxed him, and he focused forward. He made a hard left out of the neighborhood, sending the car forward like a slingshot, almost losing the pavement on the right side.

The car straightened up, and he squeezed the steering wheel with both hands. His headlights only showed pavement in front of him, along with trees waving hello on both sides. He knew if he didn't make it to where the turn onto the main road was visible, he would never find the man in the pickup truck.

A few seconds and about a hundred miles per hour later, Walker saw red taillights a couple hundred yards in front of him, turning right onto Highway 27. He had him. Walker's left side was clear of trees and buildings, so it was easy to see that no cars were coming. As he approached the turn, he grabbed the emergency brake, pulled it as he kept his foot on the gas, and drifted out onto the highway. He closed the brake, turned back into the slide, and when the front end straightened, he was on the gas again.

He was gaining on the truck fairly quickly, but that's when he spotted red and blue lights flashing in the distance. Arnold's neighbors must have reported shots fired. Now they were going to see Walker and the pickup truck he was chasing, racing away from the direction of the neighborhood they were called to. He couldn't let that deter him.

As Walker closed in on the pickup truck that was swerving in and out of traffic, the police cars went flying by. Walker steered around a minivan, then glanced up at the rearview mirror to find one of the police cars had peeled away and was circling to come after him. His window of getting answers just got a little closer to fully shut. It was go time. He would have to worry about the consequences once everything was over.

The patrol car was now fully giving chase. Walker swerved around a motorcycle, then gave the car all it had as the pickup truck was now directly in front of him. There was a siren, people blasting their horns, and a red light not far in front of them. The truck slowed a bit as Walker tried to decide if he could make it through the light cleanly. Walker needed to take advantage. He checked every mirror, then glanced ahead. No cars. He had to act immediately.

Walker touched the floor with the gas pedal and steered the front end of the car right, meeting the truck's back right bumper. When he connected, at first he thought it wasn't going to be enough. The truck swerved a little left, then right, then the driver overcorrected, sending the truck flopping over on its side. Metal and fiberglass sparked against the pavement as the truck slid across two lanes, then flipped gloriously into the air when the front end connected with the pole of the red light on the left side of the road.

Walker pulled up behind the truck and was out of the car before the truck was at a complete stop. The truck landed on its roof, with the driver's side door facing Walker. As he ran for the driver, he glanced over his shoulder and saw the police car swerving around the last few cars that had slowed to stay out of harm's way. He would only have a couple of seconds with the driver.

Walker made it to the door. The window was blown out, and the driver was slumped forward. He grabbed the driver by the shirt and yanked him out of the truck. His head wobbled around like a bobblehead doll, and his eyes were closed. There was a gash in his forehead, and blood from the man's nose had pooled in the mustache portion of his dark beard.

"Wake up, you son of a bitch!" Walker yelled, then smacked the man on the face. "Wake up and tell me who you work for!"

No response. He clamped his right hand on the man's jaw and shook his head. "Wake up!"

"Hands above your head, right now!" a man shouted from behind Walker.

Walker stayed focused because for the first time the gunman's eyes began trying to open.

"Wake up!" Walker shouted again.

"I'm not going to tell you again. Put your hands above your head and back away from him!"

The officer's tone told Walker he was going to shoot if he had to. He could hear the wail of an ambulance siren growing closer. The gunman was in and out of consciousness. Walker wasn't going to get the information he needed. All he could do was hope the man came around in the hospital so Ava could get in to ask him some questions. But Walker knew the man wouldn't talk. Right there, half dead on the pavement was the only time Walker would have been able to get any sort of truth out of the man. That ship had sailed.

Walker put his hands up as the gunman's head slumped back over to the right.

"Don't move! On your knees. Hands behind your head!"

Walker did as told. He waited for the officer to come to him. Walker had never been arrested before, but he knew enough to know that the first way to get yourself hurt when an officer is risking his life to do his job is to not do exactly what he or she says. The officer came up behind him, took him one wrist at a time, until both hands were cuffed behind his back. He stood Walker up, and Walker towered over the man.

"What the hell is going on here?" the officer said.

"No Miranda, Officer?" Walker said. He meant for the comment to have some snap, but he was defeated. He couldn't believe the opportunity to get a key piece of information was lying just feet from him, and there was nothing he could do to get out of it. Well, almost nothing . . .

The officer tugged at Walker's cuffs, then pushed him toward the squad car. But Walker stiffened up and didn't budge. "I know what you just saw looked bad, Officer. But I need one favor before you put me in your cruiser."

"This isn't the time for favors, and if you don't move where I move you again, you can add resisting arrest to whatever else you did tonight."

"Just one thing and I'll go wherever you want me to go."

"You're going to go where I want you to anyway, bud," the officer said with a forceful push.

Walker let him push him, but he needed to see one thing, just for himself, before he left the scene. "You know Detective Bailey, right?" he said as he let the officer steer him.

"What of it?"

"She's a friend. I helped her out tonight with the Amy Turnberry case. I just need two seconds and then you can take me in."

Walker felt the officer stop. "You know I can just ask Bailey if you know her or not, right?"

"I do. That's why I mentioned her."

"If she says she doesn't know you, I'm going to add withholding evidence to the charges."

Walker knew that wasn't what was happening here, but he bit his tongue. "I know. Two seconds."

The officer sighed as the ambulance pulled up to the right side of the overturned pickup truck. "What is it?"

Out of nowhere, Walker heard an engine at high rev, and out of the corner of his eye, over the policeman's shoulder, a white van was coming straight for them. There was only time for one move. But even if he could actually pull it off, it would be a miracle if he survived.

26

Time, as Walker knew it, ceased to exist. As soon as he noticed the white van going full speed right at them, everything slowed down. He could feel that the police officer had a hold of the link between Walker's cuffs, so Walker twisted his wrists to wrap around the officer's hand, and he dove forward with every ounce of power his legs could muster.

He felt the hot air the van was carrying with it as it flew by, not more than inches away from Walker's body. As Walker hit the pavement, a lot of things happened at once. He had turned his head to see what the van was going to hit. Doing so let him witness the first EMT out of the ambulance nearly explode in a burst of bloodied smashed bones and skinned flesh. This happened while Walker's skin on the right side of his face peeled back from sliding on the pavement. With his hands linked behind his back, there was nothing he could do.

As the officer shouted and landed on top of Walker's back, Walker saw the van's left tire pop the dying gunman's head like an exploding pumpkin. Then the van slammed into the pickup truck on the other side of the gunman and just kept on going. The officer was still screaming behind him. Walker craned his neck to see what the problem was. He had been able to save the officer's life, but what was left of his leg didn't look like it was going to make it.

Walker was pinned on his stomach. He didn't want to move too fast and put the officer in an even more painful position, so he just tried to take a couple of deep breaths to steady himself. Then he heard tires screeching against pavement like someone had just harshly applied the brakes.

Walker looked past the EMT, who was crouched over her dead friend, sobbing, and saw the white reverse lights of the white van light up.

They were coming back to finish the job.

The officer shrieked in pain when Walker tossed him off his back. The van reversed and swerved its tail-end right. They were turning around so they could see what they hit.

Walker rolled back over and shouted ferociously at the officer. "Uncuff me or we're all going to die! Now!"

Walker didn't feel the officer's hands on the cuffs. The van had whipped around, and Walker heard the driver put the transmission in drive.

"Now or you're dead!" Walker shouted again. Just as the tires squealed from the van's forward thrust, Walker felt the officer's hands on the cuffs. As soon as he heard the right cuff click open, he yanked away from the officer, pushed himself to his feet as he turned, grabbed the officer's shirt with both hands, and threw him as hard as he could to the right. Then he spun as he ripped his pistol from its holster and started running headfirst toward the oncoming van that was only about forty yards away.

"Watch out!" Walker shouted to the EMT who was so wrapped up in her shock as she stood over her dead colleague that she had no idea the van was coming back. Walker raised his gun as he ran, shouting, "Get out of the way or you're dead! Run!"

Like a deer in headlights, the woman looked at Walker instead of the direction of the now speeding van. He fired three rounds, all three much closer to the EMT's head than he would have ever felt comfortable with, but he had no choice. The van was coming right at her. All three bullets hit the van, but not where they needed to in order to stop the driver.

"Move!" he shouted one last time, but she was frozen. She had pulled into herself even further when she saw Walker firing his gun in her direction.

The van was a mere few feet away now. Too late to shoot. Walker dove one more time and pulled the woman by her arm as he rolled left. The van whizzed by and immediately hit the brakes this time. Whoever was driving was not going to give Walker a second to recover this time.

As Walker rolled with the woman, he tossed her as far to the other side of the ambulance as he could. He heard her hit with a thud and finally let out a scream. While Walker finished his final roll, he twisted his hips and flipped over on his stomach. Just when he managed to get his pistol pointed at the van, the back door slid open, and Walker shot the man getting out three times. That only left three rounds in his magazine, with no spare to follow.

The driver-side door opened. As Walker trained his pistol on the inside of the door, he watched two pairs of legs hit the pavement on the other side at the bottom of the van. Walker was a great shot, but he was not going to be able to kill all three of these men with the only three rounds he had left. He looked left, inside the ambulance's window. He knew the keys were in the ignition, but his lizard brain needed to know for certain that the keys were in the ignition before committing to his next move. And there they were, dangling, along with a florescent-green-haired troll doll key chain.

Walker fired once at the van's back tire, popping it, then opened the passenger door of the ambulance, hopped in, and jumped into the driver's seat. It was time to give these monsters a little taste of their own medicine. He threw the ambulance in drive and stomped on the gas. His window was open, so when the driver of the van showed himself and his gun, Walker fired twice with his offhand. He wasn't trying to hit the driver; he just wanted to keep him in the van so he couldn't shoot the police officer on the ground to Walker's left before he could get the ambulance up the van's ass.

The shots worked, the driver retreated, and just as the two gunmen were rounding the back end of the van from the passenger side, Walker steered right at them, first smashing the back of the van, then running directly into both of them. Then he slammed on the brakes, hit reverse, and rolled back over them. The van had done an entire spin, all the way back to the same position it was in when Walker hit it, only a few feet from the same spot. With one bullet left, Walker stuck his pistol out the window, ready to fire when he got back on the driver's side of the van. But Ava had already beat him to it.

Walker stopped the ambulance as the van's driver dropped to the pavement. Ava was standing behind the driver's side door of a car he didn't recognize, still holding her shooter's pose, just in case the gunman wasn't dead. But he was.

Walker stepped out of the ambulance. He looked back to his left where the EMT he'd saved was already beginning to tend to the police officer's leg. Then he looked back at Ava. She had lowered her weapon. Tim got out of the passenger side of the same car and started walking over to him. Walker just bent over, hands on his knees, exhausted.

The scene around them could only be described as carnage. Walker couldn't believe how far the cult, or whatever they were, was willing to go to keep themselves from being discovered. Sirens were blaring all around. Every potential lead they had was dead.

"You okay, buddy?" Tim said, giving Walker a pat on the back.

"Fine." Walker stood up straight. "Just disappointed."

"Disappointed? You just saved all of us back at that house and likely a couple of these people here. How the hell could you be disappointed?"

Walker looked at Tim. He understood what Tim was saying, but it still felt like a loss. "Because all of this brought us zero percent closer to finding Amy Turnberry."

"Hell, son. Don't beat yourself up. You did a hell of a thing here tonight."

Walker gave Tim what little smile he could muster and a hard pat on the arm. Then he walked over to the gunman that Ava had shot dead. More ambulance and police would be there in seconds. Before they arrived, Walker just wanted to know for sure it was all connected. He crouched down over the body. Again, it was a young man. He couldn't have been older than twenty-five.

"Please don't touch anything," Ava said as she walked over to him.

Walker looked up at her. "Really?"

"It's a crime scene. It's my job at least to say it out loud before you move something."

Walker looked back down at the man, then grabbed his

right arm by the wrist and turned it over so his palm was facing up. Just as he'd expected, the snake-and-cross tattoo was there.

"I can't believe this is happening," Ava said. "Right here in the quaintest little lake town on earth."

Walker stood. "Believe it."

She let out a sigh as she took in the scene. "Thank you, Walker. You saved my life back there. I wouldn't have made it out of there alive."

"Stop selling yourself short. It's keeping you from reaching your potential. You're better than you think you are."

Ava cocked her head. "Um, thank . . . you . . . I think?"

"Have you looked at the video Arnold sent you?"

"Yeah . . . no. Been a little busy since ten minutes ago in the living room."

"Tim," Walker said, "let's get out of here."

Tim stepped around a body in the road.

"You guys can't just leave," the police officer said through labored breath. "Detective Bailey, you have to help me go through all of this mess." He grunted again in pain as the EMT began wrapping his leg.

"You can handle it, Officer," Ava said. "I have to go make sure this doesn't happen somewhere else."

"But I've never written up anything like this."

Ava turned to face him. "I'm not sure anyone has, Officer Whitlock. But we know what happened here. What we don't know is who is behind it all. That's where I have to use my time."

They turned to walk away but the officer spoke up again. "Hey, sir!"

Walker turned to face him.

"Thank you."

The EMT looked up. There was just enough light to see sadness on her face, but she had the same thing to say to Walker. "Thank you. You saved my life."

Walker nodded. "Sorry about your friend."

The EMT just looked down, then back toward the body.

"See, son," Tim said, "all that stuff you went through, whether they used you for good or not, there's still plenty of good you can do with those skills."

Walker appreciated Tim's support, but when shit was hitting the fan, he had a one-track mind. They could talk feelings after everything was over.

27

"Pull up the video," Walker said as soon as he, Tim, and Ava got in the car. "Whose car is this anyway?"

"Arnold's mom's," Ava said. "We have to take it back. I already radioed for someone to come pick us up. But we have nowhere to go."

Tim had already turned Arnold's mom's car around and was driving back in Arnold's direction. They remembered to get the rest of the weapons from Ava's car that Walker had trashed before they headed back to Arnold's house.

"Maybe the video can give one of you a clue since you grew up around here," Walker said. "It's our only shot. By the time leads are followed on these guys and their addresses are known, Amy and the others could be dead."

"We sure you got everything out of that Arnold kid?" Tim said.

"I think so, don't you, Walker?" Ava said.

"I do. He was caught up in something he never meant to be. His reasons really don't matter, but I think he gave us all he had."

"Video's not very long," Ava said from the front seat.

"Go ahead and watch it. It won't mean anything to me. Tim, you can give it a look when we park the car. Maybe we'll get lucky and one of you recognizes something."

"If it's anything at all, right?" Tim said. "Just because some no-name person on the black web, or whatever you call it, sent Arnold a video, that doesn't mean it's legit either."

Tim was right. Walker had thought the same thing, but he was trying to keep that prospect out of his head. They were dead in the water if the video wasn't really from this cult.

"I'm trying to stay positive," Walker said.

"Here goes nothing," Ava said.

Walker said it would mean nothing to him. And it wouldn't. He didn't know the area. There would be no clues to gain from watching it. But that didn't mean he wasn't curious. Of all the sinister people he'd encountered in his life, it was always about political or financial gain. Power. Never about religion, and certainly not about the devil himself. Walker edged forward and watched over Ava's shoulder.

The video started out shaky and was almost pitch black. Ava turned up the volume, and they heard the rustling of tree branches, accompanied by labored breathing from whoever was controlling the camera. After a few seconds of that, the camera lens reached beyond the leaves, and the video showed the same scene of the screen-shot of the robed people that Daniel had found posted by Arnold.

The video was shooting downward, as if shot from a hilltop. There were a number of people in robes lined up in two straight lines, then a circle of fire in the middle. One robed individual stood on their own in front of the fire.

"Is there something over the fire?" Ava said as she looked over her shoulder at Walker.

Walker strained his eyes, but the imagery was too dark. "Can't really make anything out. Is your brightness all the way up?"

Ava paused the video, adjusted the brightness of her screen, and when she went back to the video, it was clear that something was in fact suspended over the fire.

"There is!" Ava said. She moved the phone right in front of her eyes, her nose almost touching it. "Still can't see what it is, though. You don't think it's a body, do you?"

Tim laughed.

"What?" Ava said.

"Oh, you were serious? You think they could have a body cooking over that fire?"

Ava looked over at Tim. "How many dead bodies have you seen in the last day? I'm pretty sure that wouldn't be too far-fetched."

In the glow of the dashboard Walker watched Tim shake his head. "No, you're right. I guess it's just that, if you told me all of this a week ago, I would have thought you were out of your damn mind."

Tim turned into Arnold's neighborhood. Ava pressed play on the video. The person standing by the fire began to speak, but their words were inaudible. The voice sounded either like a low woman's voice or a high-pitched man's voice, but it was too close to tell. After almost every sentence, the group of people surrounding the fire would collectively make some sort of grunting noise. Like they were part of the ritual.

"What did Daniel say this thing was called?" Ava said.

"Preparation ceremony," Walker said.

"That's right. For the Buck Moon sacrifice or something?"

"Yeah," Walker said as he slid over to the window on his right. It didn't take him long to locate the full moon. And though he'd seen hundreds of them in his lifetime, this was the first one that gave him a chill that ran the length of his spine. "A three-night full moon, according to Daniel."

"This is night one?" Tim said.

"That's what the kid said he found." Walker slid back over to the video. They were still doing some sort of chant, but none of the words were discernible to him. "Anything?"

"Nothing to see," Ava said. "Clearly this was shot by someone who wasn't supposed to be there. All I see is a hill, some trees, and a bunch of nuts."

Tim wheezed as he laughed. "That was a pretty good one there, Detective. Maybe you aren't so bad after all."

Ava glanced back with a smile on her face. Walker didn't greet her with the same amused look. He'd heard the joke, and he appreciated it. But after the last hour of chaos, he wasn't really in a joking mood.

"All right. I get it," Ava said. "I just thought I'd lighten the mood."

Walker watched as the video came to an end. Tim put the car in park out on the street. The police cars and an ambulance were blocking Arnold's driveway.

"There," Walker said as the video finished. "Back it up. I saw something right before the camera shut off. Just after the person recording moved. Tim, watch this. See if anything comes of it."

Tim leaned over as Ava backed it up, then pushed play.

"Right when the camera moves left," Walker said. "There was something lit up on the left side of the screen."

There was a lot going on around the outside of the car.

Policemen looking at evidence, EMTs checking on people, and the coroner picking up the dead bodies that Walker had left behind. But inside the car, the three of them didn't notice any of it. There was complete focus on the six-inch phone in Ava's hands.

"Stop!" Walker said.

Ava hit pause, and the illuminated object that Walker had seen was still on the screen.

"Can you zoom in?" Walker said.

"Not on the video. Let me take a screenshot."

Ava pressed two buttons on the phone, and the screen flashed. Walker could feel his phone vibrating in his pocket. He knew it was Daniel asking for an update. Or Kim was day drunk in Hawaii again. Either way, he didn't have time for it. Ava pulled up the photo of the lighted object and pinched out with her fingers to zoom in.

"Is that a . . . flagpole?" Ava said.

"Could be," Walker said.

Tim leaned over even further. "May I?"

Ava handed him the phone.

"My eyes are for shit," Tim said as he took the phone. He looked closely, then zoomed out. "I'll be damned."

"What?" Walker leaned forward.

"I think I know where the hell this is."

"You're shitting me?" Ava said. "How?"

"Well, just down the road from my farm there's a little grassy knoll. I pass it every night. Noticed the light when it first got put in a long time ago. It stuck with me 'cause I was happy to see that someone else other than me actually loved our country with all the damn trying to tear it down going on these days. Anyway, it is a big-ass American flag. Only one I know of sitting out by itself like that. Right next to a hill. Obviously, could be many more of them, but it's at least worth checking out."

A spark of hope flickered inside Walker. It felt good, but he didn't like it. The life he'd led had taught him over and over again that hope usually only leads to letdown. Every time when he was a kid and he hoped the new home they were sending him to would be different, he was let down. When Maxwell Solutions "saved" him from a lengthy prison sentence when he was fifteen, he hoped it was the end of his bad luck. He was murdering people for a living only three years later. And he'd never even felt hopeful about love. Never been romantically close enough to anyone to be let down. But he knew it would probably be the same. He was conditioned at that point. Hope meant letdown. So he stomped out the spark and kept expectations where they belonged: low.

"Well, that's great news!" Ava said.

Both Tim and Ava turned to see Walker's reaction. He fizzled their spark with his less than excited expression.

"Long shot, but it's better than anything we had a minute ago," Walker said. It was his best effort not to stomp on their dreams entirely.

Another vehicle pulled up alongside them.

"Here's our ride," Ava said. "We're going straight to the flagpole, right?"

"You're in charge," Walker said as he got out of the car. "Remember?"

"I do remember, Walker. But after what I've seen, you're going to call the shots from now on. You made a believer out of me."

"Me too, buddy," Tim said.

Walker had never worked with a team before. Not once

in his career. He wouldn't say that he liked the attention, but the positive feedback didn't feel . . . bad.

"Let's just hope this lead actually pays off."

The three of them got into the car.

"I really like you, Walker," Tim said. "I really do. But you've gotta figure out how to see the good sometimes. The lead we just got here with Arnold paid off. The video gave us our next clue. And even though getting run off the road and nearly getting shot wasn't good, it paid off too. You noticing the tattoo led us to Arnold. Sometimes a positive mind can lead to positive outcomes."

"Yeah? That might be how it is in your line of work, Tim. Or in your personal life. I've never had a positive outcome in what I did for a living. Even a successful mission was deemed successful because somebody died."

"Yeah, a bad somebody," Tim said. "Just because your endings seemed negative doesn't mean they were. The bad endings you created probably saved thousands of lives or more. And correct me if I'm wrong, but that's good."

"Maybe," Walker said. "And maybe not. I don't even know the answer to that, so I'm pretty sure you don't either."

The car went quiet as Tim pulled away from Arnold's house. Walker didn't want to talk about the past. It was over. Good, bad, or ugly. All he cared about was getting a missing girl out of trouble. Tim and Ava could talk about happy endings when that happened. Everything else, to Walker, was just noise.

28

Tim turned off the winding road, and sure enough, ahead of them, lighting up the darkness, was Old Glory herself. Right in the middle of a field, which looked like it dropped off a cliff on the other side.

"If that's not a beautiful sight, I don't know what is," Tim said.

Walker stepped out of the car. The flag was flapping in the breeze, the Buck Moon glowing behind it. Walker had refreshed his Sig Sauer's magazine on the ride over. He now also had his AR-15 slung over his shoulder and a spare thirty-round magazine attached to the side of the rifle. He was through getting caught with his pants down.

His phone began buzzing again. He pulled it out this time, and it was in fact Daniel who was calling.

"Busy here, Daniel," Walker answered.

"There you are!" Daniel was excited. "You've got to start answering your phone!"

"Like I said, it's been rather busy."

"Where are you? How'd it go with BaphometsSon?"

Walker stepped around the vehicle and stood beside

Tim and Ava as they looked up at the flag, waiting for Walker to finish his call.

"Uh, well, I killed at least six or seven people, Daniel. But we did get a video lead from Arnold before it all went down."

"Come on! If you're not going to be serious, just let me talk to the detective or something. This isn't a game, Walker. This is my sister's life!"

Walker looked down at the AR slung around his neck, and then down at the pistol holstered at his hip. "Yeah, Daniel, I'm pretty aware it isn't a game. Do you have something new? Because we are checking out a lead on where the cult might be having their little get-togethers."

"You're effin serious? You had to kill people at BaphometsSon's?"

"I'm effin serious, Daniel. And now I have to effin go."

Walker ended the call.

"Gotta be hard for him to just sit there and know nothing," Ava said.

"Hard shooting people too," Walker said. Then he looked around. "No cars. No noise. This doesn't look promising."

"We were just saying the same thing," Ava said.

"Let's at least go check it out," Tim said. Then he pointed to their right. "Those must be the trees they took the video from. Looks like if you walked down in there a ways, it would be the same angle they took it from."

Walker agreed. But he knew it didn't matter. No one was there now.

"Let's go walk the perimeter," Ava said. "Maybe we can find something that will tell a story."

"Lead the way, Detective," Walker said.

Ava started by walking up the hill to the lit flag pole. Off in the distance Walker saw a city whose lights were shining brightly. Down the hill on the other side it was nearly pitch black.

"Anyone think to bring a flashlight?" Ava said.

"If my truck hadn't gotten totaled, I'd have one," Tim said "But, well, you know. I do have a lighter." Tim pulled out a cigarette and went ahead and lit one up.

Walker clicked on the Scout Light Pro tactical flashlight attached to his AR-15. "Guess I'll lead the way."

"Nice," Ava said. "I do have my phone flashlight. Better than nothing, I guess."

Walker took the lead. He moved down the hill toward where the people were standing in the video. A coyote called out in the distance, letting the three of them know they weren't alone. The hill was a gradual decline, so it wasn't hard to keep their footing.

"Anything in particular we're looking for?" Tim said.

"Just signs that we are in the right place. Maybe remnants of the big fire they built? Directions to where they are now?"

"That'd be nice," Tim said.

Walker focused forward. The grass had grown up enough to prevent seeing any sort of footprints or even where they perhaps had worn down the grass a month ago. They were at the bottom of the hill. The land flattened out. Just ahead was where the fire would have been. Walker went forward, following the beam of his flashlight. All he saw was grass until finally a stone appeared.

Walker stopped and pointed his flashlight upward. The beam revealed stones stacked on top of each other, and when he moved his light around, it revealed a makeshift fire pit.

"Well, there you go," Ava said. "This is the right spot."

"Key word *was.*"

"Negative damn Nancy," Tim said.

Walker brought his gun around to where the flashlight spotlighted Tim. "If you see something positive here, please say it. 'Cause all I see is a pile of stones and no Amy Turnberry."

"Come on, Walker," Ava said. "We're trying to remain positive here. Every step we're taking is at least leading to something. It's more than we had before."

"Is it?" Walker put the flashlight on Ava. "Please, do tell what's next then."

"Asshole," Ava said.

Walker moved to his right and walked around the fire pit, leaving Ava's name calling alone. Somewhat because it wasn't the first time he'd been called that name, but mostly because he didn't really care what she thought. What he was saying was true. Although the video led to where the people had once been, it was where they were last month. Not now. So now they had nothing.

"You said this is night one of the Buck Moon, right?" Tim said.

"Yeah," Ava answered.

"And you said the video was a preparation ceremony, right?"

"Yes."

"So maybe they do their thing for the Buck Moon on the second night? Maybe we found the place where they will be tomorrow?"

Walker stopped for a second, then shined the light back on Ava and Tim. "You're right, Tim. That could be the case, actually. Sorry about being so negative. Old habits and such."

"It's all right. This is some intense shit," Tim said.

"You've been through things like this before, probably why you're more pessimistic."

"Either way, it isn't helpful."

"Yeah, well, you weren't wrong either, though," Ava said. "Because now what? We can't just sit around until tomorrow, hoping they show up here. They could be somewhere doing some sick Satanic stuff to these poor girls right now. We need to find a next move. Fast."

"Now we're talking," Walker said. "We don't have a day. We don't have hours. We—"

A branch snapped off to their right.

"Shit, get down!" Tim shouted.

Walker dropped to a knee, brought his Sightmark Wraith night-vision scope to his eye, and scanned the area that was now lit in the classic night-vision green light. He could see a bright green light behind a tree. Something was there. He held the rifle steady as he rested it on his knee.

"Stay down," Walker said.

"You see something?" Ava whispered.

Walker was quiet, focused on the bright green light. If it moved, he was going to shoot it. They'd been blindsided too many times for him to let it happen again.

"Walker?" Ava whispered again.

"Let him alone," Tim said quietly.

Walker assumed whoever it was must be hiding behind the tree and waiting after they knew they had been heard. Walker didn't mind waiting. He wasn't a hunter of animals, but he'd once spent more than four hours looking through a scope into a man's window. Patience had paid off in Munich, and he knew it would pay off now.

Then the bright green light moved, and he let out a sigh of relief. In front of him was the outline of a deer. It must have been bent over eating behind the tree. Walker let his gun—and his guard—down.

"What? What's going on?" Ava said.

"Deer."

"Good God. I thought we were goners."

Tim helped Ava to her feet. Walker looked around. "Anything we can take away from this? Other than the pat on our backs that we found where the cult had been before?"

Ava wiped some loose grass from the knees of her pants. "Afraid not. I'll put an officer on this place to watch it. 'Bout the best I can—"

"Don't do that," Walker said.

"Why not? You don't want to know if they come here and set up for tomorrow?"

"Of course, but if they do, I don't want them to be scared off by an officer on watch. Then we'll never find them."

"Well, that does make sense."

"Anyone you know a hunter?"

"My nephew," Tim said. "Why?"

"You think he'll come out here in the trees and watch? I'm happy to pay him. Just need him to stay hidden like he would from a deer."

"Nah, he owes me a favor. Won't have to pay him. He's a good guy. He'll do it."

"Great. Give him a call, if you don't mind," Walker said.

"Let's get out of here," Ava said. "This place is giving me heebie-jeebies."

Tim laughed. "You mean you don't like being somewhere used for the calling of the Dark Lord?"

"I really don't."

"Where we going? I've got security at the lake house, but

there's a good chance these people know I'm there. Which I think is a good thing, but you might not."

"How could that be good?" Ava said.

"If they come to us, it's a lot easier than us trying to find them. All we have to do is just keep one of them alive."

Ava laughed. "Forgive me, Walker, but keeping people alive doesn't seem to be your strong suit."

Walker started back up the hill toward the car. "I've kept you alive so far, haven't I?"

He turned around and aimed the flashlight toward her face. She shrugged her shoulders and laughed again.

"Touché, Walker. Touché."

29

"Good God, I'm glad you guys are back," Daniel said as he stood in the living room.

Walker, Ava, and Tim had barely even made it through the door.

"Why?" Walker said. "Something wrong here? I didn't see any notifications on my phone from the perimeter cameras."

"No . . . but this stuff we're looking into is creepy as hell."

"Sure is, kid," Tim said.

"Do you really think these are the people who have my sister?"

Walker opened the refrigerator and grabbed three bottles of Kona Big Wave beer. "I don't see how it couldn't be."

The answer disappointed Daniel. "Yeah. You don't think they've done any weird culty stuff to her, do you?"

Walker handed Ava and Tim each a beer. Then he popped the tops off them and his own. He took a swig. "I know it's hard, but you just can't think that way. I could give you a million scenarios of what could be going on with your sister, and all million of them could be wrong. So, when you don't know something, it's best not to dwell on it."

"Easier said than done," Ava said.

"Yeah, that's why I prefaced with 'I know this will be hard.'"

"Prefaced?" Ava raised an eyebrow. "Did they teach you that when they were teaching you how to break people?"

"He's a big reader," Daniel answered for him. "He would have learned it there."

Ava looked at Walker and smiled. He knew what she was thinking. That Daniel was beginning to look up to him. Walker knew that would be misplaced idolatry.

Walker sat with them and drank his beer as he caught Daniel up on everything that had happened. With Tim and Ava ad-libbing about how amazing Walker was when things went down, Walker could see Daniel's admiration grow. Which was bad. Because Walker feared he would only let him down. Walker finished with them finding nothing at the site of the preparation ritual, and that's when Daniel opened his laptop.

"Right before you all got back, Ricky messaged me back. He sent me a link to a forum. The only thing he said was that the Satan Is King cult is mentioned in a two-paragraph spot in this long thread. I found it just before you walked in."

Daniel turned the laptop's screen toward Walker. Walker reached for it and took it in his hands. There were no graphics on the screen like you might find on regular internet forums. This was just a black background with white words, broken up when someone with a new name posted something to it.

"What am I looking at?" Walker said.

Daniel reached around the screen and pointed to the name ConduitOfSouls. "Start here."

Walker started to read when Ava interrupted.

"Out loud, if you don't mind?"

Walker gave her a nod. "Okay, ConduitOfSouls says—"

"ConduitOfSouls?" Ava said. "Charming."

"Indeed," Walker said, then continued. "'I don't have to prove anything to you about the Buck Moon or SIK.' Then a name called SquatZilla says, 'Sounds like something a poser would say.' ConduitOfSouls says, 'Okay, smart-ass, a Buck Moon to most of the blind and lost souls of the world means the time around when a male deer grows his antlers. But to the more knowledgeable in what really matters, a Buck Moon is the time we present a sacrifice to Baphomet. Two sacrifices, to be exact.'" Walker looked up at Daniel. "You sure you want me to read this?"

"I've already read it," Daniel said. "I know it's bad. But just wait till the end. I think it will help us find Amy."

Walker nodded. "'Two sacrifices to be exact. A God loving virgin and a God loving whore, to show the hypocrisy of Christianity.' Then Squatzilla said, 'Whatever, bro, you read that on some lame wannabe satanic website. I know how they have to be sacrificed. Bet you don't.' ConduitOfSouls replied, 'Please. Under the second full moon—.'" Walker looked up at Daniel who was smiling. He knew it meant they hadn't hurt his sister yet because tomorrow night would be the second full moon. "'Under the second full moon, both the virgin and the whore will be sacrificed by baptism. The way they washed away their sins for Christ is the way Baphomet wants to greet them in hell.'"

"Wow. Good to know all of this is going on right under our noses," Ava said.

Tim finished his beer and set down the bottle. "What the hell do they mean 'hypocrisy of Christianity'? From a virgin and a whore?"

"I guess they mean you can do anything you want as a Christian as long as you ask forgiveness?" Ava said.

Tim scoffed. "Well, all that does is prove Christianity isn't hypocrisy, right? If you're allowed to make mistakes and be human and still get into heaven, that shows anyone can as long as you believe."

Tim was looking at Walker when he finished.

"Don't look at me," Walker said. "I was never taught anything about religion. So I wouldn't know. I was only taught if you talk when foster dad is drunk, you get the shit beat out of you. That in the Bible anywhere?"

"Well, yeah," Tim said. "But I'll spare you the sermon. I don't know everything either."

"All I know is that this thread is good news," Walker said. "We just have to catch a break and find out where this is going to happen."

"Well, they said it was baptism, so it's going to be somewhere around water," Daniel said, excited. "That has to help, right?"

All three of the adults hesitated. They didn't want to break the news to him that Lake Chickamauga alone had 810 miles of shoreline.

"I know, it's a huge damn lake," Daniel said. "But it's better to know that it's in water than having to include all of the land around it in our search too."

"The kid has a point," Tim said.

"Good attitude, Daniel," Ava said. "Maybe you can teach Walker here a thing or two about positivity."

Walker gave her a fake smile. She returned it with a swig of beer.

"All right. So what's next then?" Daniel said.

Just as he finished the sentence, Walker's phone dinged. It was the chime made by the camera at the top of the driveway. Then two more chimes came in at the same time.

"Somebody's blowing you up," Tim said.

Walker reached over and picked up his phone. The notifications were from movement at the top of the driveway, the basement sliding glass door, and the front door.

"Must be some sort of glitch with my cameras," Walker said as he pulled up the app.

"Why?" Ava said.

"Because all three cameras detected motion at the same time. And that's impossible."

Walker turned so that the three of them could see the app along with him when it opened. What they saw shocked them all. Standing in front of each camera was someone with a goat mask on and antlers.

Walker dropped the phone and nearly ran right over Daniel as he raced out of the kitchen. He pulled his pistol from its holster as he sprinted for the front door, and nearly threw the door off its hinges when he flung it open. To his surprise, no one was there.

He turned in a few half circles, his gun extended in front of him, but he only saw trees and driveway. He ran up the driveway with all he had, but when he reached the top, there was nothing. Only the sound of crickets in the woods, wind through the trees, and his breath as he did his best to control his heart rate.

As he walked back down the driveway, his head on a swivel, he saw Ava step out onto the front porch, her gun extended as well. "Anything?" she called to him.

He walked until he was in the light of the front porch and shook his head.

"Tim went to check the basement," she said. "What the hell was that, Walker? How'd they get away so fast?"

Walker turned and gave the driveway one more look. "I have no idea."

"I mean, you shot out of that kitchen. There's no way they could run away that fast. What happened?"

"I said I don't know, Ava." His tone was harsher than he meant. But he was frustrated.

Ava walked back inside. Walker followed. Tim was walking up from the basement and met them in the living room.

"Anything for you?" Tim said. "'Cause I didn't see a thing."

"Same," Walker said. Then he looked at Ava. "Sorry I was harsh."

She waved him off. "We're all on edge. Don't worry about it."

Daniel walked into the living room. He was holding Walker's phone. "There wasn't anybody here."

"What the hell are you talking about?" Tim said. "We all saw them."

"You saw what they wanted you to see."

"Elaborate," Walker said. "And dumb it down for the electronically challenged."

"Okay, when the three people showed up on all the cameras, you all saw the mask. Me too, but I noticed they were all wearing the same pants too. When you ran out, I picked up your phone and checked it. No one ran away, they just disappeared."

"I am definitely one of the electronically challenged," Tim said. "What are you saying?"

"Sorry." Daniel grabbed his laptop and pulled up a settings tab. "I've been monitoring your servers and your

Wi-Fi today, Walker. Ricky said it would be a good idea. So, when I saw the three guys just disappear from your cameras, I checked who had accessed your Wi-Fi here, and there was a new access just a minute ago."

"Catch us up," Ava said.

"They hacked your Wi-Fi and made it look like they were in front of your cameras, but they really weren't. They were just trying to scare you."

"It worked," Ava said.

"Sounds like an awful lot of work just to scare someone they've already shot at twice today," Tim said.

"It's not really hard when you know what you're doing," Daniel said. "And maybe since they hadn't been able to kill you, they thought scaring you would make you mess up or something."

Walker let out a sigh. "Thanks, Daniel. Does this mean they are watching us?"

"Not right now. I just changed the password while you were outside. We're good for now. But they definitely know you're here."

"Yeah, we kind of figured that already," Ava said.

"So, now what?" Tim said. "We're kind of like sitting ducks here with all these windows."

Walker looked at Ava. "Any leads at all from the people who came after us?"

"Some of my people have checked on all the men from where they ran you off the road. Three of them lived alone. Nothing at their homes, but it will take a while to hack into their devices to see what we find there. Their phones were all password protected, so it will take some time to get into them."

"We don't have time," Walker said. "What about the fourth guy? You said three lived alone?"

"The fourth lived with his parents. They of course were shocked to hear he might be involved in something like this. They wouldn't let us search his room. We'll have a warrant by morning. Haven't heard anything about the mess at Arnold's house and out on the highway. I really should get over there and sift through some of it myself."

"I don't think that's a good idea," Walker said.

"Yeah, well, I don't have the luxury of picking and choosing. It's my job. I followed some leads with you, but we're dry. I need to go see if I can find some new ones."

Walker nodded. "You're right. You're the only one who can fast-track anything that is found. I'd start with the man in the car I was chasing. The one who killed the man I was about to question in Arnold's backyard."

"I'll see what I can do." Ava started for the door. "Thanks for the beer. And for, well, saving my ass back there."

"Hopefully it will all pay off," Walker said. "Be careful. They're watching."

"Comforting. You guys find something, call me. I'll do the same."

"Will do," Walker said.

Ava walked out the door and Walker turned back to Daniel and Tim. "It's getting late. Tim, you take first sleep. Get a couple hours, then relieve me and Daniel."

"What can I do?" Daniel said. "I can't sleep anyway, might as well be productive."

"Any way you or your friend Ricky can trace who hacked into the Wi-Fi? That could be a good lead."

"I can't, but I'll see if Ricky can."

"Go on then," Walker said. Then he tapped on his AR-15 that was sitting on the console table behind the couch. "You too, Tim. I got this."

"I'll set a timer for two hours," Tim said. "Then it's your turn, okay?"

Walker gave him a nod, but he knew there wouldn't be any sleep for him that night. He may not know who was behind the kidnappings, the cult, and the attempts on his life, but he damn sure wasn't going to let them sneak up on him in the dark.

Not without a fight.

30

The rest of the night had been quiet. Walker wasn't exactly surprised by this, but he was definitely relieved. Tim had come down after his two hours of sleep to take watch for Walker, and Walker had pretended to sleep his two, then took the rest of the night. Daniel had fallen asleep after an hour or two of back and forth with Ricky, but as of midnight, nothing had been accomplished. Walker wanted to sleep, but he couldn't keep the scenarios for the next day from continually running through his head.

And he hadn't heard from Ava. That he didn't like. He had called her once and texted a couple more times. He was hoping she had maybe gotten home late, then fallen asleep. But that seemed a little too easy for the way the last two days had gone. He didn't like it, but he was worried about her.

The sun was on the rise. Hot, humid, and sunny was the forecast. The coffee was in the pot, and Tim was already pouring a cup.

"You get any sleep, bud?" Tim said.

"Not really. Too much going on upstairs."

"Yeah, I was in and out all night. Find anything good swirling around in your head?"

"Nothing concrete," Walker said as he pulled a mug from the dishwasher. He walked over and followed Tim's lead by pouring a cup. "Just kept going over what we know and what the possibilities are."

"And?"

"And it's a lot of hopes and dreams really. None of the men who died trying to kill us produced anything. We had no luck with Arnold and his video. We found out that things are going down tonight and that it's happening in water, but that's like finding one certain needle in a needle stack. Daniel and his friend have yet to be able to track who hacked the Wi-Fi last night, and worst of all, I haven't heard from Ava."

"Not at all?"

"Nothing."

Tim let out a breath. "I don't like that. Sounds like we need to start there this morning."

"Yeah. I keep hoping she just passed out from exhaustion, but you already know I'm not the most positive person."

"Hard to be when we've been through so much."

Walker looked at Tim with a knowing half smile.

Tim nodded. "I hear you. That's what you were saying last night. It's all about what you've been through that shapes your view."

"It's not really something that can be helped once it's so ingrained."

"We have any idea where she lives?"

"No," Walker said as he checked his phone for what

seemed like the hundredth time. "And I have no idea who to call."

"I don't like it."

"Me either, Tim. Me either."

Tim's phone began ringing. "It's my boy. I'll be right back."

"Everything okay? It's like four in the morning in California."

"Oh yeah." Tim wore a prideful smile. "He's probably already talked to his team in China. He's got my work ethic. His mother's brains, though, thank God." Tim winked and walked away. "Whatcha up to, son?"

Walker smiled. No matter what happened with all the madness brought by his time at the lake, he knew he would walk away being glad he came. Especially if he could help Daniel's sister but, regardless, because he met Tim. Walker had never really had friends. His work didn't lend well to personal relationships. But he could definitely see what he had been missing. And he hoped that he and Tim could stay close no matter where Walker's life took him next.

However, as with most of his life, his happy thoughts were almost always followed by troubled ones. And right then, Ava not contacting him was really starting to bother him. He took a long drink of his coffee, then set the mug in the sink. He walked over to the counter and picked up his holster holding his Sig Sauer and attached it to his hip. Next, he grabbed his keys and his AR-15 and headed for the door.

"Hang on, son," Tim said. "Where you going?"

"I can't sit around and wait for Ava to reach out. She should have already by now. I have to go try to find her."

"Let me come with you."

"No. Stay here and keep Daniel safe. Make sure when he

wakes up that he's working with his friend to see if they can trace the hacker from last night. I'll call and check in when I find something out."

"All right," Tim said. "But be careful, Walker. You know they're looking for you."

Walker nodded. "Stay alert here. I'll be back soon."

The heat outside was already on the rise. When he opened the Mustang's door, a waft of hot air shot out at him. He rolled the windows down, cranked the AC, but left the music off. Unlike all his other trips in his favorite possession, this was no joyride. Walker had never been a worrier. He always knew his assignment, and he knew how to execute it. There was never anyone else to worry about in the equation. But this, like the farm in Kentucky, was totally different. His missions now were because of personal relationships, not instead of them. And he was nowhere near used to that yet.

He felt his phone buzz in his pocket. He rounded a long curve as he pulled it from his jeans. It was a message from Ava. Walker tapped the notification from her, and it took him to the message. Only, it wasn't a message. It was just a dropped pin showing a location. There was no reason to think anything bad of it, but every bone in his body told him this wasn't good.

He texted back, "Are you okay?"

Walker then hit the gas so hard his tires screeched against the pavement at thirty-five miles per hour, shooting the car forward. He tapped the phone a couple of times as he carefully navigated the winding road until the pin dropped was in his GPS. He was only five minutes away, but he was going to be there in two.

He flew out of the tree-lined road and swerved right out onto the highway, completely disregarding the red light.

Drivers honked and swerved to make sure they missed him. He only focused on the road ahead. He could feel his heart rate rising, so as he shifted to fourth gear, he started his breathing technique. A long inhale through the nose, then just before blowing the air sharply out through his mouth, he took one more quick inhale through the nose. A couple of those and he was leveled out in seconds, even as he dodged traffic.

Walker blew through a couple more lights, narrowly missed a convertible at an intersection, then yanked the steering wheel left when the GPS told him to turn. One more quick right and he was in the parking lot of a large multi-building apartment complex. It quickly set in that although he was in the right place, he had no idea which apartment was Ava's. And though he didn't know for sure that this was her apartment complex, he sensed that it was. He knew she was in trouble, and he was going to have to find her. Fast.

31

As Walker brought the Mustang to a stop, he realized as he was scanning the area that he was missing the forest for the trees. He was busy looking at the different apartment buildings as if somehow some celestially guided magic pull from the ether might lead him to the right place. But when he refocused on the parking lot, he realized that the parking spaces for each stretch of apartments were in front of each building. He just needed to find the car that was brought to them at Arnold's house last night to replace Ava's car that he used as a battering ram. Then he could work on finding Ava's apartment.

He pulled forward, looking right and left for the black Mazda sedan. He didn't know the model. He was driving in between yellow-siding apartment buildings on both sides. All of them built like an overgrown suburban home. There were a lot of black cars. This was taking entirely too long. If for some reason Ava didn't even have the strength to type a message with the pin she'd dropped and she hadn't answered his reply, she must be in trouble.

Walker had to slam on his brakes. He nearly ran right over a woman dressed for work.

"Watch where you're going, asshole!"

He gave her a wave and pulled forward. Walker then remembered that the car would have a special marking on the license plate because it was a police vehicle. So he narrowed his focus even further, until finally, he saw the back end of a black car, located the Mazda emblem, then saw a badge painted on the license plate. He pulled into the empty space beside the car. When he got out, his search started all over again. Taking time that he was nearly certain he didn't have.

Walker moved from the car into the opening in the apartments where the stairs are. Each building was three stories. One apartment in the front, and one in the back on each side. Six chances to hit or miss in finding her. He got started on the bottom level. He rushed over to the first door and began knocking. After a few rounds of beating the door, a sleepy-eyed man opened to a chain separater in the door.

"What's your problem, man?"

"Do you know which apartments Detective Ava Bailey lives in?"

"No. And if I did, I wouldn't tell some huge stranger who was just pounding on my door."

He started to close the door, but Walker got the toe of his shoe in the space before he could.

"What the hell, man?"

"I think she's in danger. Can you tell me anything?"

The man studied Walker. "Do you even have a badge?"

"I just want to help her. Someone is trying to hurt her."

"I think she lives upstairs, man. That's all I can tell you. Now, please don't—"

Walker left before the man could finish. He darted up

the first set of stairs, rounded the landing and headed for the first door he saw. Just before he brought his fist forward to knock, he heard a woman scream above him.

"Ava!" Walker shouted as he moved back to the stairs and started up. "Ava! That you?"

He ran up the last step, looked to his right, and on the landing was a tall blonde with a frightened look on her face, staring down at a pool of blood on the concrete landing. Walker rushed over and noticed that the pool of blood had streak marks going left, almost as if whoever was there had dragged themselves away. He followed the trail of blood to a door that had a bloody handprint and blood on the doorknob.

Walker looked back behind him at the blonde. "Call 9-1-1! Someone is hurt!"

The woman nodded and pulled out her phone. Walker stepped over some blood to the door and pounded four times hard. "Ava! It's Walker. You in there?"

He waited five seconds, then kicked in the door. He didn't have to search for Ava any longer; she was lying just inside the door, surrounded by blood, with her phone open to where she had sent Walker the pin and his reply asking her if she was okay. He took a knee and picked up her arm. If there was a pulse, it was as faint as a whispering wind.

"Ava, can you hear me?"

He raised the bottom of her formerly white shirt that was now soaked in blood. There was so much blood. He couldn't see any marks in her stomach to tell if the wounds were from gunshots or a knife because of all the blood. But he had to assume a knife since no one had called the police after hearing gunshots.

"Stay with me, Ava. You're going to be fine. I promise."

Walker stepped over her, searched past the living room

to the hallway. He ran there and saw a bedroom at the end of the hall. There was a bathroom inside. He went in, opened the closet door, and pulled two bath towels from the middle rack. Then he ran back out to her.

Walker put her phone in his pocket. Next, he stuffed the towels down in the top of her pants to help hold them in place. Then, like a gentle forklift, he scooped her up into his arms. He carried her outside, and the woman was just pulling her phone away from her ear. Her mouth dropped open when she saw Ava in his arms.

"Did you call 9-1-1?"

She nodded. "She's not . . ."

"Not yet," Walker said. "Please just make sure you tell them that this is Detective Bailey's apartment and that I took her to the hospital. Do you know which one is the closest?"

"Uh, yeah, uh . . . There . . . there isn't one. But CHI Memorial is in Hixson. It's like fifteen minutes."

Walker started to walk away. "Fifteen minutes is the closest hospital?"

"I know. Sorry! I hope she's okay!"

Walker hurried down the stairs. If Ava was alive, it was barely, and fifteen minutes might be enough to finish her off. He was going to have to be faster. He ran down the last set of stairs and out to his car. He opened the passenger door, laid her down gently, and put the seatbelt around her. He tried to make it where the seatbelt would help hold the towels in place, but she was still leaking heavily.

The next ten minutes were a mix of worry, adrenaline, and world-class car dodging and red-light running. But he got her safely to the hospital. He slid the car to a stop at the emergency room entrance and got out of the car shouting.

"I need help!" he said as he walked around the car and

opened her door. No one was outside to hear him, but the shouts still made him feel better somehow. "Someone, help!"

He pulled Ava out of the car and walked through both sets of automatic doors.

"Please! She's dying!"

There was a gray-haired woman in blue scrubs behind a desk beyond a few people sitting in the waiting room. As soon as she noticed Ava and Walker covered in blood, she jumped up, told her colleague to get a stretcher, and ran over.

"Dear God, what happened?"

"She's a detective. She was either stabbed or shot. I didn't want to touch anything."

"Bring her this way. We'll get her in right away."

The woman waved him forward and jogged toward the double doors leading beyond the waiting room. Walker kept pace right behind her. When the doors opened, a woman was already waiting with a stretcher.

"Get Dr. Blake to room twelve. I'll push her through," the gray-haired woman said. Then she looked back at Walker. "She's in good hands. I'll be out to talk to you in just a minute."

Walker kept following her even though she had clearly clued him to staying in the waiting room. As she pushed Ava on the rolling bed, she looked back.

"The waiting room, sir. You can't be back here. We'll take good care of her, I promise."

Walker stopped. He didn't acknowledge the woman; he just watched her pushing Ava down the bright white hallway. The florescent lights were buzzing above him, and his heart was thudding. Now all he could do was hope she would be okay.

Walker wasn't good at hope.

He was good at making people pay.

As he stood in that hallway alone, his worry turned to anger. His hands involuntarily balled up into fists. His breath became heavy. There was nothing he could do for Ava there at that hospital. All he could do was find those responsible for her being there. And just in case befriending the brother of the missing Amy Turnberry and having others trying to kill him and Tim hadn't been enough motivation, watching Ava's arm flop lifelessly over the rail of the gurney she was bleeding out on lit an even larger flame in Walker's belly.

He was going to find out who was behind all the madness. And he was going to do what he did best when he did.

Kill them all.

32

Walker left his contact information with the other woman at the front desk at the hospital. When she told him they may not be able to contact him because he isn't family, he wasn't surprised. But he did ask the woman personally, if he asked for her, Sharon, as it said on her name tag, if she would at least tell him she's all right. She winked and told him she would be there till midnight.

That made him feel better, but only marginally. He was upset with himself because he let her leave the lake house without him. He should have known she was going to be targeted next. Every sign they'd come across in the last two days had pointed to it. But he couldn't focus on what he couldn't change. That had always been one of his oldest rules. However, that didn't mean she wouldn't be weighing on his mind until he knew she would live.

Walker opened the front door, and Tim nearly dropped his glass of sweet tea when he saw all the blood on Walker's clothes.

Tim set down the glass and rushed over. "Damn, son! You all right? What happened?"

"Not my blood, but no, I don't suppose I'm all right."

"Detective Bailey?"

Walker looked disappointed as he nodded. "Found her stabbed in her apartment. Well, I think she was stabbed. There was so much blood I couldn't tell."

Daniel walked around the corner from the kitchen. "Is she . . ."

"I don't know," Walker said. "She had a faint pulse when I dropped her off at the hospital." Walker looked over at Tim. "I'm going to kill every last one of these sons of bitches," he said through gritted teeth. Then he turned and put his forearm through the wall.

"Okay, okay," Tim said. "I know you're mad. But you're no good to anybody if you're too angry to think straight. Okay?"

Walker stalked away and walked out the front door. He was on fire from the inside out, but the heat from the afternoon sun really sent him into a sweat. Tim had followed him out the door but was giving him his space by staying quiet and staying up on the front porch.

"I knew she was going to get hurt when she left," Walker was pacing. Ranting. "I should never have let her go. And they got to her. Just like I knew they would. And I let it happen." He turned back to Tim. "She's bleeding out in that hospital right now because of me!"

"Now stop it right there, damnit. You didn't have a damn thing to do with Ava getting hurt. These crazy assholes running around kidnapping children and trying to kill the people on their trail are responsible. You've got to get your mind right, Walker. Without Ava, there is no one official left to investigate this except that other detective they just hired last month."

"I shouldn't have let her go, Tim. I *knew* this was going to happen!"

"That's enough!" Tim shouted.

Walker's face morphed from angry to surprised. He was not expecting to hear Tim get angry with him.

"Now listen to me," Tim said, pointing his finger at Walker as he stepped down the stairs. "Get all this shit here out of your system right now. Do whatever it is you have to do. Kick the hell out of a tree, break a damn window, or go swim a mile in the lake. Whatever you gotta do. But then it's over. You hear me? Then you remember what it is you say you were trained to do. Did you let emotion get the best of you when you succeeded in a mission?"

Walker didn't answer.

"Did you let anger cloud your judgment?"

Again, Walker just stared into Tim's eyes.

"I asked you a question, I expect an answer."

"No! No, I didn't let emotion get in the way. I would never have succeeded. But this is different, Tim. These sick bastards are coming after little girls. They're coming after my friends. And they're coming after me!"

"Then you're right," Tim said, his voice calming a bit. "It is different. It's even more important now to keep your head. To remember and recall what you know and what you've been through. Because now is the most important time you've ever needed any of it. If you don't rely on all that you've been through right now, well then, it was all a waste. Life is never what you think it's going to be, Walker. Sometimes special people are put to tests like you have been put through that normal people like me wouldn't be able to fathom. And there's a damn reason. I haven't lived the hard life you have, Walker. That's why I'm not qualified to go and save these kids like you are. Don't you understand, son? You are the man who can help because of the man you've had to be. All that shit, the beatings, the training, the nightmarish assignments, now they all have meaning. Let them be the thing that makes you great. Not the thing that tears you down. But it's up to you. I haven't known you very long, son. But I've been around long enough to know that you're a better man than you think you are. I don't give a damn what the hell all those nasty people who raised you told you. And I don't care about all those nasty people who used you as their own personal weapon. I'm standing right here, telling you right now, that you're special. So get out of your own damn head and go be special!"

As if something unseen pushed him toward Tim Lawson, Walker surged forward and wrapped his arms around him. He didn't shed a tear, but he'd never felt emotion like the flames running through his veins in that moment. There had been plenty of people who'd told Walker how good he was at his job, but other than his foster mom, Kim, no one had ever told him that he was a good man. And he didn't know if he believed it entirely himself in that moment, but he knew it felt special to have another man, whom he respected, recognize in Walker what he'd always hoped to be.

Good.

"To hell with all those people in your past, son," Tim said as he pulled back. "They're gone. And to hell with who you think you were then too. Be the man you want to be right now, Walker. That will be good enough to move a damn mountain."

Walker took a deep breath and let it out real slow.

"You done throwing your hissy fit, now?" Tim said as he cracked a smile.

Walker couldn't help but smile too. Then he nodded. "I am. Thank you. That's twice you've pulled me out of a tailspin."

"Well, it's the last damn time. I ain't no babysitter." Tim laughed, coughed, then laughed again as he gave Walker a hard pat on the shoulder. "Now, let's go figure out our next move."

As soon as they both turned around, Daniel and his flopping blond hair came running out onto the front porch. "Ricky found him!"

"Found who?" Walker said.

"The dude who hacked your Wi-Fi! And get this, we think he's also the guy talking to BaphometsSon!"

"ConduitOfSouls, or whatever it was? How could he possibly know that?"

"It's hacker stuff, you wouldn't—"

"Dumb it down for me," Walker said.

"Basically, Ricky found the IP address—the digital signature—of the hacker. When he did, he was able to access his computer, but only for a minute or two before the guy knew and shut him out. His Discord handle—"

"Discord?"

"Sorry, just an app to communicate with friends and stuff without having to be on Facebook and what not. Anyway, his Discord handle is Souls4Me. It must be the same guy. No way it's a coincidence."

Tim looked over at Walker. Walker's blood was already pulsing. He was ready.

"Don't suppose Ricky managed to get this Souls fella's address?"

"Oh yeah. He got it."

Tim blew out a breath in excitement. "You're on, Mr. Walker."

"Let me clean this blood off, grab my spare mags, and I'll be ready to go. Oh, and you might want to grab some towels. Shelby's front seat looks a lot like my clothes."

"Not the Mustang," Tim said.

"Casualty of war."

They both started to walk toward the house when Tim stopped. "How are we supposed to know for sure this ConduitOfSouls person is who we are looking for? We go there and make a mistake, we're going to jail for a very long time."

Walker was getting ready to answer when Daniel spoke up. "I knew you were going to need to know that. I went back to ConduitOfSoul's forum post and pulled up the picture of his snake-and-cross tattoo. Look."

Tim and Walker met Daniel at the porch steps. Daniel turned the laptop screen toward them and pointed just below the tip of the tattoo on the man's forearm. Walker zeroed in on where Daniel was pointing.

"See, right there," Daniel said. "Birthmark that looks just like Florida, but without the panhandle."

"I'll be damned," Tim said. "That is exactly what that looks like."

"He has the birthmark; you have one of the SIK cult members."

"Nice work, Daniel," Walker said. "This is the best lead we've had yet." To Tim, he added, "Meet me back out here in five. Let's go get started cleaning up this mess." He turned to Daniel. "And take the first step to getting Daniel's sister back."

33

"You okay, Walker?" Tim asked.

The hum of the Mustang's engine rumbled as Walker sped down the highway. ConduitOfSouls, aka Larry Dotson, lived out in the country just on the other side of Hixson, Tennessee. That left them with about a thirty-minute drive. Walker hadn't said much. He was getting his mind right for the challenge he knew was coming.

"I'm fine, considering the circumstances. Why?"

"You've been through a lot the last two days. Normal life doesn't go the way these hours have, and not many men would be standing right now, if any. And you've had no sleep on top of that."

"I'm fine, really. I've been in worse situations . . . though, none of them quite so strange."

"How do you mean? Bad guys are bad guys, right?"

"Sure. But there are levels. These low-rent thugs they have as muscle for this cult couldn't possibly survive a guy like me. I'm used to men never seeing me coming. But if they do, they have men trained a lot more like me to play defense with. But that's not what makes it strange. It's the personal aspect. I may have been on assignment to protect thousands of lives on some of my targets, but I didn't know any of them. If I missed, there were no faces. But here, if I miss, people I've started to care about get hurt or worse."

"I'm sorry this is all on your shoulders now, son," Tim said. "I mean, I'm here with you, but I ain't no soldier. But I'm also not one to back down from a fight. Especially when my family is involved. So just know, I'm here too, and I'm not afraid of these people."

"Thanks, Tim. You've been a lifesaver this month. In a lot of ways. I really appreciate it."

"How much farther?" Tim said.

"Should be just up here on the right." Walker looked over at Tim until Tim looked back. "I'm going to ask you one time to stay in the car. But I need to know now if you're going to do as I ask. I have to know who is where in order to operate properly out here. You understand that, don't you?"

"I do. I can appreciate that. That's why I'm going to tell you that I'm not staying in the car. Count on me being your shadow. I won't get in your way."

Walker nodded as he looked back at the road. "Okay. I'd much rather you tell me like it is than tell me what I want to hear."

"Done."

Walker turned the car right on the last road the GPS had in the route. "Just a mile ahead now. I wish it was dark, but it is what it is. We'll just have to go knock on the front door."

"Maybe he'll think we're selling encyclopedias," Tim said with a laugh.

"Timmy, I would be shocked if the guy who comes to the door even knows what an encyclopedia is."

They both laughed. Seeing three cars in the driveway at Larry's house stopped that real quick.

"Shit," Tim said.

"This doesn't change anything. We stick with the plan."

"You're the boss."

As Walker pulled up, he parked out on the road instead of the driveway, just short of the house. He could see that the windows were uncovered, and he wanted to try to steal a glance of as much of the inside of the house as he could so when the front door opened, he would have a better idea of where everyone was located.

They both got out of the car, and Walker made a point to walk right through the grass to get to the front door. It was the best line of sight into the house. He could see the top of one person's head through the window on the far left side of the house. It wasn't a lot of information, but it was better than nothing.

"Keep your gun in your holster," Walker said as they started up the stairs. "No matter what. If Larry Dotson dies, our hopes of saving Amy Turnberry and your grandson's girlfriend are dead too."

"Understood."

Walker jogged up the steps and immediately banged on the door. The door opened before he could even pull his hand away. A man about the same height and same build as Walker—six feet three inches or so, 220 pounds—with a dark buzzcut and a black long-sleeved T-shirt answered the door.

"Don't you know it's not polite to walk through someone's yard there, buddy?" the man said.

There was a mirror hanging on the wall just over the man's shoulder. It showed the living room where two other men were sitting in front of a television, gaming controllers in their hands. Below the mirror was a long and skinny entry table with a stone bowl for keys and a thick cylindrical candle. Beyond the man, there was a table with a third man sitting in a chair taking a drink from a Coors Light bottle.

"Are you Larry Dotson?"

The man's face scrunched. "Who the hell is asking?"

Before Walker could speak, a woman called from another part of the house. "That the pizza man, Larry?"

Walker shot his right hand forward and caught Larry by the left wrist.

"What the hell?" Larry said as he tried to pull away. "Hey, I know you—"

Walker yanked Larry's sleeve up his arm with his left hand, revealing the snake-and-cross tattoo.

Also revealing the birthmark.

This was the man who'd shared the video of the cult and the picture of his SIK tattoo.

Walker yanked Larry toward him as he bludgeoned him with an elbow to the temple. Larry crumpled to the ground. Walker then picked up the candle and the stone bowl. He tossed the candle at Gamer 1 on the far left, who was now standing in front of the brick fireplace, hitting him somewhere around the chest. Simultaneously, he spun and hurled the bowl at the beer drinker sitting at the table. The bowl skipped off the table, missed the man, and went right through the sliding glass window behind him.

"What the hell is going on?" the woman shouted.

Walker didn't see her walk toward the table from the

kitchen, because by then Gamer 2, who was on the right side of the TV, had stood and was coming Walker's way. Walker picked up the wooden end table that sat beside an empty chair, cocked back, and busted it over the shoulder of Gamer 2. He fell back over the couch. Gamer 1 had recovered from the candle attack, pulled a wrought iron poker from the fire-tending holder, and swung at Walker's head.

Walker ducked, pounded Gamer 1 in the liver with a left hook, then snatched the poker from his hands as he went down. Walker turned just in time to smash Gamer 2 across the forehead with the poker, then toss it at Beer Man just as he rounded the table. Walker stalked over to him, turned him, then, with his left hand grabbing Beer Man's collar and his right grasping his belt, tossed him right through the unbroken side of the sliding glass doors.

That was when he got his first glance at the woman. Overweight with long curly hair, she was backing up into the kitchen like she was watching a bear tear through her home. By the time Walker turned around to make sure Gamers 1 and 2 were going to stay down, Larry was back on his feet, clearly working out exactly how he'd ended up on the ground.

"You got a lucky shot," Larry said. "Nobody gets by with that on me."

"That right?" Walker said as he began to circle to Larry's right. "Let's put that theory to the test."

Larry put up his hands. Walker could tell by the way he moved that he used to be a boxer. Rhythm is unnatural when fighting. Most have to learn it. Larry already had. And it was clear he was confident in it.

"Gold Gloves champ two years in a row," the woman said from behind Walker. "Kick his ass, baby."

"At least Mommy has faith in her little devil worshipper," Walker said, ready for Larry's advance.

Larry was in the traditional right-hand stance with his left foot forward. Walker knew if he just kept an eye on Larry's right hand that he would be fine. Larry finally bounced forward. When Walker saw Larry plant hard on his left leg, Walker kicked the inside of his thigh with his left foot, wobbling Larry.

"Fighting is about more than boxing, Larry. And Larry's mommy."

Larry didn't like that. He let his anger throw him off his game. Just like Tim had warned Walker not to do. Larry jumped forward, throwing a wild right hand. Walker stepped left to dodge the punch and kicked Larry in the stomach. When Larry doubled over, Walker brought an uppercut from the floor, punishing Larry in his forehead. It stood him up straight, and his wobbled legs had him doing the chicken dance. Walker moved in with a right hook to the kidney and a left to the liver. As Larry was going down, Walker caught him, stood him up, and hit him with a one-two that dropped Larry directly onto the table, sending him crashing to the floor.

Walker pulled his pistol from its holster and pointed it at Mom who was advancing with a butcher knife, and said, "Okay, Tim," as he froze her in place. Tim pulled his pistol and held it on Gamers 1 and 2 just in case they were feeling frisky.

"Join them," Walker said to Mom as he waved his pistol toward Gamer 1 and Gamer 2. "You too, man outside. Walk slowly back through the sliding glass door and over in front of the TV. Say yes if you don't want to get shot."

"Y-yes," the man said, then came walking through the glassless sliding door with his hands up.

Finally, Walker had made it to the point he had been trying to achieve—with someone, anyone—ever since they ran him and Tim off the road. Everyone was alive, at least one of them was involved with the cult, and no one was around to kill them before Walker was able to ask some questions.

It was time to get some answers.

34

Walker and Tim waited patiently for Larry to come around. Walker was even nice enough to get Larry, still spacey from his knockout, a glass of water. He wanted Larry to be able to be coherent. It was rather important to the next step in their difficult day.

Gamers 1 and 2 as well as Beer Man were all sitting on the couch. Larry was in the chair in the middle, and Larry's mom was standing in the corner sulking. Tim was standing by the door. Walker had his back to the TV, facing everyone, as if he were about to start an in-home sermon. The irony didn't escape him.

"Okay, Larry Dotson," Walker started, "are you back to full mental capacity?"

Larry didn't say anything.

"All right. Then let me start by saying this. I really would like the opportunity to have an excuse to hurt all of you again. So, if you don't answer me when I ask a question, I will choose someone to pay for it."

"Who the hell are you anyway?" Larry said. "We haven't

done anything. We don't know you. And we have nothing to tell you."

Walker nodded. "Okay. Noted. I'll give you one opportunity to change your attitude. Because I'm not going to sit here and play games. I know you're part of the cult. Men with that same tattoo you have there on your arm, yeah, they've been trying to kill me for two days now. They found out that's not an easy thing to do. You can, too, but as you've already seen, that will cost you. I know that you hacked the Wi-Fi and my cameras at the lake house. And what you are going to tell me next is where I can find Amy Turnberry before I bury all four of you. Are we clear?"

"I can stop you right there," Larry said. "I don't have any idea where that missing girl is."

"No? Well, let's start from the beginning, okay? Then we'll get to what you do and don't know. And as for me, I'm the man who disappears after people die. And I've been doing it for a living for more than half your life."

Everyone was quiet.

"To start"—Walker looked at the three young men on the couch—"are the three of you in the Satan Is King cult with Larry? A simple yes or no will do."

He zeroed in on Gamer 1 with his long, curly brown hair coming out from under his black beanie hat.

"No, sir," he said. "I know about it, but I'm not in it."

"Shut the hell up, Doug," Larry said.

Walker stepped around the coffee table, blocked Larry's defensive arms to the side, and took a grip around his throat that was so tight, there was no air or blood moving through to his brain.

"Larry, you're not listening. If you lie to me or try to hide the truth from me again, I won't let go. Right now you're starting to feel faint. You thrashing around beneath me is your body's automatic response to try to let you know that if you don't stop what is happening to your neck, you will die. Do you want to die right here in front of your own mother?"

Walker let go just before he passed out and just before Larry's mom made it to him. Larry gasped for air and doubled over on the chair.

"It's better if you put your hands up behind your head, Larry. Your breath will come back quicker." Then to Tim. "Can you get her in the other room? No matter how terrible of a man Larry here is, I can't make his mother watch what's about to happen next."

Larry shot a look at Walker that signaled everything had changed with that statement. He was finally frightened of what Walker might do. Walker was glad he didn't have to do worse to him to get that reaction. Larry's mom didn't fight Tim. She didn't want to see what was next either.

"Please don't hurt him," she said as she walked away. "I don't know what happened to him. He used to be such a sweet boy."

Walker didn't acknowledge her. He went back to the task at hand.

"You ready to give me what I want now, Larry?"

Larry nodded. The defiant one was no longer with us. This was a different Larry. A humbled one.

Walker looked back at Gamer 1. "You said you are not a member of Larry's cult?"

"I'm not. I swear."

"Let me see your arms."

Gamer 1 pushed up the sleeves of his sweatshirt and showed both sides of his forearms. They were tattoo free.

"Get the hell out of here," Walker said.

Gamer 1 didn't hesitate. He jumped up and ran out the front door just as Tim was getting back into the room. He pointed to the door, a gesture asking Walker if he needed to go get him. Walker shook his head.

"I'm not a member either, sir," Gamer 2 said, deciding to be proactive. He even had his arms out for Walker to see.

"Go."

He ran out just as fast as Gamer 1. Both of them drove away in their cars.

"Show me your arms," Walker said to Beer Man.

Reluctantly, he pulled up his left sleeve and there was the SIK tattoo.

"All right," Walker said, "now that we know where we all stand, let's get this over with. And I'll reiterate one last time. If I think you're not telling me everything you know, I'll kill you both."

Beer Man swallowed hard. Larry just stared down at his own hands. Maybe weighing the decisions in his life that had brought him to such a point.

"Where are Amy Turnberry and Riley Baker?"

"I told you"—Larry sat forward, using his hands for effect—"We don't know where she is. We are not high enough in the ranks to have that kind of information."

Walker turned to Beer Man. "First, what's your name?"

"Matt Stone."

"Is Larry telling me the truth?"

"He is. I swear, man."

"Okay." Walker looked back at Larry. "Tell me the name and address of the person who knows."

"Listen, man, that isn't how it works."

"You don't know the name of the leader of the cult?"

"We don't use real names," Larry said.

"It's a small town, Larry. You don't know them from around town?"

"Man, this is a lot bigger than you think. I'm a nobody in

this thing. This is the first year I have even gotten an invite to the . . ."

"It's best you finish that sentence."

"They'll . . . they will kill me if I say anything else."

"I'll snap your neck right now if you don't tell me right now. Best you worry about your present situation."

Larry looked over at Matt, then back to Walker. "This is the first year I've been invited to the Buck Moon sacrifice. People come in from all over the state for this. Some even farther."

"Okay. Good. So you know where it's going to be held?" Walker said.

"Not yet. They only give an hour's notice. Because, well, because of possible situations like this, I guess."

Walker believed him.

"This true, Matt?"

"I-I don't know. I haven't been around as long as Larry."

Walker looked at Larry. Larry nodded. "It's true, he doesn't know."

"All right. So, it sounds like in order to be invited to this prestigious ceremony, where I'm assuming real-life children are going to be sacrificed." Walker paused. He could feel the anger creeping in on him. "To be invited, you must have done something to please the cult leaders. What was that? And, Larry, be *very* specific."

"I want a lawyer," Larry said as he stood from the chair. "You have to give me one if I ask for one." Larry turned and looked at Tim. "You guys have to let me have a lawyer when I ask for one." Then he looked at Matt. "Right, man? We have rights!"

Both Matt and Larry looked back at Walker.

"You're right . . . ," Walker said, then waited.

"I knew it," Larry said. Then he looked at Matt, who stood as well, elation on both of their faces.

"You would have rights *if* I was the police. Unfortunately for you two, I'm not. And I never have been."

The elation turned to horror.

"What did you do to earn your invite, Larry?" Walker rested his hand on the grip of his pistol that sat in his hip holster. "Be careful. You only get one answer. It better be the truth."

"I-I . . . I tapped your Wi-Fi and tried to scare you away from looking into us any further. That's it, man, I swear!"

Walker pulled his pistol and shot Larry in the left thigh.

Larry's mom screamed from the back room, as Larry shrieked in pain, falling back down into the chair. Walker let him shout the pain away for a few seconds, then interrupted.

"Next one I shoot you in the balls."

Larry's eyes were wide. Walker raised his gun.

"Stop! Stop, okay. Please. Me and another member of my level killed Detective Foley. They wanted him gone before anyone wanted to talk to him about what happened last year."

"Keep going, or I'll shoot. Stream the truth right now, Larry."

"They did the same thing last year. Kidnapped a couple of people for the sacrifice. This is just the tip of the iceberg, man. They traffic kids to pay for all this shit. I'm only a part of it because my mother's boyfriend made me go along with him three years ago. It's sick, and it's evil, but I can't get out of it without them killing me."

So many things resonated with Walker in that moment that it took him a second to refocus. Walker had gotten into trouble because of a bad man who was with his foster mom when he was a kid. That led Walker into a life that he didn't want to be in, and one he wasn't allowed to leave without them killing him. A life which, just like Larry's, involved killing. Few people would give Larry the benefit of the doubt in that situation. Walker didn't really have a choice. They were too much alike, no matter how awful all of it sounded.

Walker holstered his pistol. He walked over to the small blanket lying across the love seat. Then he went over to Larry, who threw up his hands and lay back as far as he could in defence. Walker tossed him the blanket.

"Wrap this around your leg."

Walker moved past the chair and over to the front door, which he opened to have a look at the driveway. After the other two men had left in their cars, there was only one left outside. It was a silver Dodge Caravan. Just like the Amber Alert description of the car that took Riley Baker. Walker moved back to the living room.

"This is it, Larry. This question determines how our encounter ends. And whether I leave while you're still breathing or not. And I'm going to give you a little help here by telling you that I already know the answer to this question. The rest is up to you."

Larry winced as he finished wrapping the blanket around his leg. Then he nodded. "I'm done playing games with you. I'll tell you the truth."

"I know you said you don't know where Amy Turnberry and Riley Baker are right now. That still true?"

"It is. I swear."

Walker nodded. "But you were the one who took them."

Walker saw Tim's head shoot up to look at the back of Larry.

"I don't know who took Amy," Larry said. His tone was somber. "But yes, I took Riley Baker."

"You son of a bitch!" Tim yelled as he moved forward.

Tim got in a couple of really good shots before Walker got there to break it up. Tim pushed back on Walker, but Walker held his ground.

"Oh, you can shoot the son of bitch, but I can't knock his punk ass out?"

Walker moved Tim back. "I know. I know, Tim. You hit him a couple of times. He's going to get what he deserves, Tim. I swear. But we got what we needed here."

"We did?" Tim tore his arm away from Walker and straightened his glasses and his shirt. "We still don't know where the girls are, and we still don't know where this thing is going down tonight."

"We will. I promise we will."

Walker turned back to Larry. "How are they supposed to let you know the details for tonight?"

"An hour before midnight, they're supposed to text on a secure messaging app called WhatsApp. They're going to tell me where the boat is that I'm supposed to ride on to get to where the ceremony will be. That's it."

"On your cell phone?"

Larry fished inside his pocket. "Yes. Right here."

Walker stepped over and took it from him. Then he looked at Matt. "Yours too." Matt didn't hesitate and handed it over. "Larry, go get your mom."

He whipped around to look at Walker. "She'll kill me."

Walker didn't say a word.

"Right. Hang on."

Larry limped across the kitchen.

"What's the plan?" Tim asked as he followed behind Larry.

That was a good question. Walker had seen this thing going down with a lot more violence. Now that Larry had decided to cooperate, he didn't have a good next step. But he needed to figure one out fast because he and Tim had to get back to the lake house and prepare for battle—hopefully leading to a win in the war to find Amy Turnberry and Riley Baker.

35

Tim had his gun trained on Larry who was in one of the bedrooms trying to get his mom's phone. As he did that, he leaned back so he could see Walker. "Got that plan yet?"

"I'm working on it," Walker said.

Walker knew this was where they really needed Ava's help. But he didn't even know if she was still breathing. His trainer at Maxwell Solutions, John Sparks, would have told him to kill them all. That it was the only way to ensure, without a doubt, that Walker could right their wrongs and save the girls. But he couldn't do that. Not without them endangering him in that moment.

The only other option was to lock them up. But where? Then he remembered a month ago in Kentucky when he'd been locked in the basement of the farmhouse. Sure, Walker had managed to get out, but that was because they'd made a mistake in the way they tied him up. He wasn't going to make that mistake.

"You see a door to a basement?" Walker said to Tim as he kept an eye on Matt.

Walker stepped around so he could see Tim. Tim checked the only door left that was closed. It was locked at the knob when he tried to turn it.

"Hey, what are you doing?" Larry said as he turned around and limped back into the hallway.

"Finding the basement so we can lock you in there for the night."

"You . . . you can't go down there. We've got . . . family heirlooms and things."

Tim looked over his shoulder at Walker. Walker knew what he was thinking. There was a lot more than just "family heirlooms" down there that was making Larry react so harshly.

"Tim, get Larry's mom's phone. And get it now!"

Tim started to walk that way, and Larry shuffled over to block him. Tim didn't wait for Walker to step in; instead, he raised his right foot and kicked down, right on Larry's gunshot wound. Tim gave him a forearm to the throat, shoving him up against the wall, then walking in to get the phone.

"You can't take that! Give it back!" Larry's mom shouted.

Tim walked back into the hallway, phone in hand. Walker could see how nervous Larry was getting. That made Walker sick to his stomach. He knew bad news was coming. Tim was looking at the screen, shaking his head. He handed the phone to Walker.

"We may have just blown it," Tim said.

Walker took the phone and could see the WhatsApp logo at the top of the screen. One message sent below it: "The man from the lake has Larry's phone."

Walker felt the life force being sucked out of him. He knew that meant they weren't going to send the location of the ceremony to Larry's phone. They'd just lost the only hope they'd found since this entire mess started.

Walker looked up at Larry. Judging by Larry's frightened reaction, he could see the anger in Walker's eyes.

"Listen, man," Larry said as he held up his hands. "I told her not to send it. I swear."

"Larry, you little ungrateful shit!" his mother said from the bedroom.

"Just hear me out," Larry went on. "I'll help you find them. I promise."

"Your word means nothing to me," Walker said. "Now before I change my mind and decide to shoot you right here, right now, unlock the door to the basement."

"What? I told you—you can't go down there. What's down there is none of your business. If you're going to lock us up, do it right in here somewhere."

Walker's patience had run out. He stepped over and kicked the locked door so hard that it flew off the hinges and crashed down on the landing.

"Stop!"

Larry limped quickly over toward Walker. Before Walker could move, Tim smacked Larry with the butt of his pistol, sending him to the ground. Watching Larry protest so much against going in the basement really made Walker nervous. Something bad was down there, that much was obvious. Now it was just a matter of how bad it was going to be.

"Don't let any of them out of your sight," Walker told Tim.

"Be careful down there," Tim said. "Hard telling what these bunch of crazies might have down there."

Walker stepped toward the stairs and hit the light switch that was just inside the demolished doorway. He thought he heard something downstairs when the light came on, but his couple-second pause before taking another step didn't produce any sounds at all. He took his pistol from its holster as he moved down. At the landing where the broken door was now lying, the stairs went left, so Walker couldn't see anything down below.

Walker stepped lightly, then maneuvered around the broken door to the first step that then finished at the floor of the basement. He paused there as well. He could see the right side of the basement, but not the left because of the way the wall came down beside him. There was nothing but boxes on the right. Walker would be relieved if Larry had been telling the truth about family heirlooms, but he knew that wasn't going to be the case. Every fiber of his being said so.

Even though he was confident in that, nothing could have prepared him for what he saw when he stepped the rest of the way down. If his jaw had been long enough, it would have bounced off the floor. He stood, holding his pistol toward the floor, his mouth wide open, and his eyes full of shock. He'd seen more terrible things than most would see in five lifetimes. This topped them all.

On the left side of the basement there was a row, wall to wall, of seven cubes. All clear, thick glass that stretched high to just below the ceiling. The roof and back of each cube was made of the same glass, and also those glass walls were separating each cube. There were hoses coming into each cube, going outside through the glass panel and to the cement wall behind them. The only air coming in and out of those cubes. But none of that was the shocking part. The part that took Walker's breath away was something that for as long as he lived, he would never forget. It would be burned into his memory forever.

Inside each cube was a girl. All were around the same age as Amy Turnberry. And all seven of them were pounding against the glass wall in front of them. Their faces were red as beets and soaked with tears. They were wailing, it was obvious to see, but there wasn't a single sound coming from the cubes.

Nothing.

It was the most surreal moment Walker had ever experienced. He was caught so off guard that he couldn't move. It took hearing them shout his name for the third time for him to snap out of it. Then a gun went off.

Walker knew it wouldn't mean anything to those poor girls trapped in that basement, but it was almost like a reflex for him to hold up his index finger, trying to let them know he would be back in just a minute. Then he tore up the stairs. As soon as he was able to see into the kitchen, he saw Matt, Larry, and Larry's mom, all on top of Tim. It was as if a bolt of lightning crackled through Walker's veins. And everything went red.

The first thing he grabbed was the closest thing to him, and it was a handful of Larry's mom's hair. He pulled her back so hard he nearly pulled it all out. Then he reached for the back collar of Matt's hooded sweatshirt. He yanked him backward, then grabbed a handful of the chest of his sweater and a handful of his crotch. He power-lifted him up to his chest, then on up over his head. Matt was screaming at the top of his lungs, but Walker could only hear the beating of his own heart.

When Walker got about six feet from the red brick fireplace, he spun once to get some momentum, then twisted his hips as hard as he could to throw Matt headfirst into the bricks. Walker thought he heard his neck snap, but he wasn't about to make the same mistake two times in one day and let them get the best of him. All he could hear other than his own heartbeat was John Sparks shouting at him, "I told you so!"

Walker then reached behind him to pick up the poker. Now all he saw instead of Matt's face were those girls who were probably still screaming their lungs out right below them.

"What kind of sick bastard buys and sells little kids? And then keeps them separated by soundproof glass?"

Both questions were rhetorical, because Matt was in no position to answer questions. But Walker didn't see him that way. He saw him as a monster. And the only way to get rid of monsters is to kill them. That's when he brought the wrought iron fire poker straight down and slammed it into Matt's throat. Then he turned around to find Larry.

What Walker found was that without Matt, and Larry's mom's help, Tim had turned the tide in the fight and was on top of Larry in the kitchen. Walker would have felt happy knowing Tim hadn't been shot by the gunshot he'd heard from the basement, but he was too focused on putting an end to this part of the trafficking ring the best way he knew how.

Walker stalked toward the kitchen. When he got to Tim, he lifted him up by his armpits and sat him off to the side. When Larry saw Walker standing over him, he saw the very thing he'd been worshipping for the last three years. If Walker believed in the devil, he would've described that moment standing over Larry as being possessed by Satan himself. Because there was zero regard for the life of a man who could do that to innocent girls. The thing that would mess with Walker later was the fact that maybe he was actually possessed by another spirit altogether. One who tries to always do good. But to him, in that moment, it felt anything but holy.

Walker reached down and pulled Larry up to where they were eye to eye. He looked deep in the man's eyes because he wanted to know if you could determine whether a man was that evil just by looking at him. But all he saw was a coward. Ready to beg for his life. And that was the last thing Walker was going to wait for.

Walker wrapped his right hand around Larry's throat. If Walker would have looked down, he'd have seen the man's feet were off the ground. What he did see were his eyes bulging. He was trying desperately to speak, but Larry Dotson, human trafficker, had already spoken his last words.

Walker held his grip as he dragged Larry outside. He slammed him down so hard on the concrete porch that Larry went unconscious. Walker let up on his grip just enough so Larry would come back around. While he waited, he fished his phone from his pocket. He went to his search engine and typed in "Amy Turnberry, Soddy Daisy." The picture that started him on the path to saving her came up. Same picture of a girl with blond curls and blue eyed that was in the paper he'd been reading on the dock while he was eating his steak a couple of evenings ago. The one that reminded him of his first kiss, Kelly Clark.

Larry began regaining consciousness, and when Walker saw that his eyes could focus again, he clamped back down on Larry's neck with his right hand. As Larry's eyes bulged once again, Walker brought his phone up in front of him to where the screen was facing Larry. The full screen picture of Amy. Smiling. Happy. The way a little girl is supposed to be.

"Amy Turnberry," Walker said. "Twelve years old.

Happy." Walker took a breath. His adrenaline was at an all-time high. "You're going to look at her face until you draw your last breath. You're going to take her image with you as you meet your Maker. Then I hope your Maker sends you to the evil thing that you did all of this in the name of. There you'll get what you really deserve."

Walker held both Larry and his phone perfectly still. Larry started to gurgle. Walker moved the phone even closer to his face. Larry closed his eyes, but he was still moving beneath Walker.

"Look at her!" Walker shouted. His voice echoed off the trees and a murder of crows fled some branches they were watching on from. Finally, Larry stopped moving. Walker put away his phone but held the choke for another ten seconds. Just to make sure.

Walker didn't know much about the things people called heaven and hell. But if there was such a thing, Walker knew that there were some dark souls dragging Larry Dotson to a fiery depth.

Where Walker hoped he burned for all of eternity.

36

Walker fell back onto his ass. He was winded. His right arm was on fire from holding the choke for so long, and he was mentally exhausted. Tim walked over, looked at Larry, then slowly took a seat on the concrete beside Walker.

"I tied Mom up in her bedroom," Tim said.

Walker wouldn't have been able to say a word, even if he'd wanted to. He felt Tim put his arm around him.

"You okay, son?"

Walker wasn't sure what it was exactly, whether it was people trying to kill him for two days, finding Ava half dead on her living room floor, covered in blood, or if it was seeing the nightmare of those girls being held captive in such an inhumane way down in that basement, or if it was finally having a man in his life who gave a shit about him, the way an actual dad would, one that he never had. Either way, Walker lost it right there in Tim's arms. He had a full mental break. The tears came so fast that there was no way to wipe them away, so he let them run like a faucet from his eyes.

"It's okay, son," Tim said. "I've got you."

Walker, out of some asinine male instinct, tried for a moment to push Tim away. But Tim held fast.

"You need to let it out. It's just me and you here right now. It's been a tough day, but we're all right."

Walker let the tears flow. It felt like a river made up of decades of pent-up emotions, heartache, loneliness, and pain flowing from his body. They must have sat there for ten minutes or more. Tim never wavering, patient, as Walker slowly pulled himself out of his own despair. He never realized he was this broken.

"What did you see down in that basement?" Tim said.

That sobered Walker immediately, and he whipped his head up, looking Tim dead in his eyes. "Don't go down those stairs, Tim. You hear me?"

Tim pulled away. Walker used his shirt to dry his face.

"What is it, Walker? Do I need to help somebody?"

Walker beat Tim to his feet. "I said don't go down there, no matter what. You will never be the same if you do, and I won't let that happen to you."

Tim looked like he'd seen a ghost. It was as if he knew.

"Call the police. And as you do, find the keys to the minivan out front. Don't do anything else."

Tim nodded. "Okay. I'll get the van ready."

The two of them walked back inside. Walker could hear Larry's mom struggling, grunting, and moaning. She was probably trying to get free of whatever Tim had tied her to. That was the least of Walker's concerns. He walked through the kitchen and found the mirror in the hallway. He smoothed back his hair, took some deep breaths, and tried to wave some air into his bloodshot eyes. The last thing he wanted to do when he went back to the basement was let the girls see him emotional. They'd been through enough. They need the Tom Walker that looked like he could bend an oak tree. Not the tear-filled, broken man of a few moments ago.

He took a couple more deep breaths on his way down the stairs. He'd seen the horror once, and he'd let it get to him. This time he was going to act like they were just waiting for a ride home. Which was essentially what they were doing at that moment; they just didn't know yet that they were all going to be okay.

Walker turned the corner and stepped down into the basement. The girls in their prisons came into view. Walker forced a smile. They all stood and faced front to get a look at him. He could tell they didn't know what to think as they saw him smile. It was the one time in his life he wished he had a badge. He knew it probably would have given them comfort even sooner.

Walker approached the glass cube on the far left. He mouthed the words, "It's okay. You're safe," to the little brown-haired girl who was staring up at him. She mouthed the word "Really?" Walker smiled again and nodded. "You're okay."

She began sobbing. Not like the first time he'd seen her a few minutes ago. This was relief. And Walker had to do everything in his power not to shed tears right along with her. As Walker noticed the standard padlock that was keeping the girl locked in, she turned to the girl beside her, and Walker was able to see her mouth the words "We're saved."

All the girls began cheering and crying. Walker couldn't hear them yet. The soundproof glass was that good. And now that he was up close, he saw that it was triple paned. He also saw in their faces that they never thought this moment would come for them.

Walker stepped back and looked around. There was a

small toolbox at the far corner of the basement. He walked over, opened it up, and found a hammer. When he turned back around and the girls saw it, they were jumping up and down. Finally, smiles on their faces.

A lot of things were going on in Walker's mind at that moment. All the torments of the last two days, the torments in Kentucky, and the torments of his thirty-three-year existence. All of them seemed to be crashing down on him all at once. Probably because he, as much as anyone, could understand something in one's childhood affecting them forever. And he was just now finding out exactly how much more about that than he realized.

But even with this newfound recognition of the impact of his past—knowing just how broken he was by those things—he understood in that moment what it was all for. That no matter how sick and twisted, his past had a purpose. All that he had suffered had made him strong enough to be the man who could help when no one else could. And the biggest realization of all, the one that would set him free, that was standing in front of him seven times over, was that growing up without a family of his own, the beatings, the training to be the best at taking human lives— it wasn't all for nothing.

In fact, it was worth it.

Walker moved back over to the first cube, and with one swing of the hammer, the deadbolt broke free. He opened the glass door and heard the girl breathing so hard that she was about to hyperventilate. She threw her arms around his waist. He took a knee in front of her.

"What's your name?" he said.

"Emma."

"You're safe now, Emma. Let me get the rest of them free so they can feel the same way you do right now, okay?"

Emma smiled and nodded. "Thank you." She threw her arms around his neck for one more safe embrace. Walker had never felt anything like it. It was transcendent.

He continued down the line until every girl was free. Katie, Haley, Anna, Taylor, Sadie, and last but not least, Savannah. Every single one of them was just as elated as Emma was to be set free.

"You girls ready to get home?"

They all shouted "Yeah!" and cheered. Walker was exhausted from the roller coaster of emotions, but it was in that moment that his heart broke all over again. It broke because he realized that none of these seven girls were named Riley Baker or Amy Turnberry.

He didn't let the girls see his disappointment, but it was moving all through his soul. He knew he was running out of daylight, and as good as saving these girls from the monsters of the world was, it would never feel like it was enough if he didn't finish the job and get Riley and Amy back too.

He ushered the girls up the stairs. He made sure to shield them from Matt's dead body in the living room. As he walked outside with them, he had never seen a happier face on a man before. Tim looked at the girls coming out as if they were daughters of his own. He needed no explanation; he just fell into the fatherly role that he was born to play. Walker was proud of what they'd been able to accomplish. He didn't get that feeling too often in his life, so he was a little unsure of what to do with it.

The girls piled into the minivan. Tim had the AC running already—taking care of them before he ever even knew about them. He closed the van's sliding door and turned to Walker.

"You see what I told you—you were meant for this."

Walker nodded. "I do. But none of them are Riley and Amy."

Tim nodded. "I saw that. But there are seven families that will be just as happy to see their girls home as Riley's and Amy's families will be when we find them tonight."

Walker gave Tim a smack on the shoulder. "Don't think I didn't see how you were whoopin' Larry's ass before I came over and interrupted. I'm impressed."

"Yeah? Well, this old dog has quite a bit of fight left in him."

Walker's demeanor went serious. "We're going to need every bit of that fight if we want to find Amy and Riley tonight. *If* you're still with me."

Tim smiled. "Just you try to get rid of me now."

Walker smiled in return. "I don't think I will." Then he handed Tim the keys to the Mustang. "I'm going to drop the girls off at the police station. Meet me back at the lake house with the boat?"

"I'll be there. And if I beat you there, I'll make sure Daniel is okay too."

"Oh, any word from your nephew who was supposed to watch that piece of land for us where they had the preparation ritual? I meant to ask earlier, but it's been a hell of a day."

"Yep. He texted a bit ago. No sign of anyone as of an hour ago. It's been hard to communicate with him. Cell service is terrible out here around the lake."

"I've noticed. Wi-Fi is the only way I can really get texts."

"Yeah, but he said he found a spot to text from. He just has to come down from his tree to do it."

"All right, let me know if he texts. Be safe. I'll see you back at the lake house, old man."

Tim laughed. "Will do."

Walker gave him a pat on the shoulder. Tim gave him a couple of taps on the jaw.

In the realm of possibility, Walker would never have seen any of this coming when he accepted Alison Brookins's invite to stay at her friend's lake house for the summer. But the last thing he could ever have imagined is if something like this did go down, that a retired family man like Tim Lawson would be the one to make it possible for Walker to have a chance to make it all right. And quite possibly, all things considered, that Tim would be tougher than the man who killed killers.

Walker knew the euphoric feeling he had as he drove the girls to safety would be short-lived. And even though he was tired of fighting, he'd never been more ready to fight for the two girls who were still right smack dab in the middle of harm's way.

37

Walker drove back into the lake house driveway in the enemy's minivan. The sun had said its good-byes, and now it was the Buck Moon's turn to shine. A term Walker wished he had never heard. Dropping off the girls at the sheriff's department wasn't easy. He felt responsible for them, and letting them go without first seeing them in their parents' care wasn't easy.

Walker had never been much of an energy-drink sort of guy, but on the way home, he had to make a special stop at the gas station by the highway. Two 5-hour ENERGYs and a tall can of Red Bull later, and he was checking to see if he actually had wings or not.

Before he went inside, he had one last thing he had to do. Detective Ava Bailey hadn't been far from his mind since the moment he left her at the hospital. And that was saying a lot considering the day he'd had. So he dialed CHI Memorial, and when a woman answered the phone, he asked for Sharon.

"This is she. How can I help you?"

Walker realized he'd never given her his name. "This is

. . . the big guy who dropped off the detective earlier today. I was hoping you'd give me an update on how she's doing."

"Mr. Walker," Sharon said. Her smile was detectable even through the phone. "I've been waiting for you to call. It was really touch-and-go for the better part of the day. But now I can't get Ava to stop asking for you."

Walker smiled. Ava had made it. A weight he didn't realize had been there lifted from his shoulders. "Now, that's the best news I've heard all day."

"She tried to get a hold of you, but her phone was ruined by all the blood. I checked on her just a few minutes ago. She's getting some much-needed rest."

"That's great news, Sharon. Thank you."

"You saved her life, you know. She knows it too."

"I'm just glad I was able to get her to the hospital in time. If she wakes before your shift ends, would you just tell her we're making progress? She'll know what I mean."

"I sure will, hon."

"And tell her I'll come visit in the morning."

"She'll be glad to hear it. Have a nice night."

"You too."

Walker ended the call as he got out of the car and walked into the lake house. He was happy to see that Tim had already arrived. He was looking over Daniel's shoulder at his computer when Walker came through the door.

"Walker!" Daniel stood from his bar stool. "You're a legend!"

Walker walked over to him shaking his head. "Sounds like Tim's been filling your ears with fantasy."

"Whatever, man. Saving all those girls, even if one of them wasn't Amy, is amazing."

Walker appreciated Daniel's praise but wanted to shift

the focus. "Amy and Riley are next. We'll get them back. We just have to get moving."

"Speaking of *legends*, as Daniel puts it," Tim said, "he might just be one himself. Albeit in an entirely different way."

"You find something out?" Walker said.

"I don't understand it," Tim said. "But I gave the kid Larry's phone, and he was able to, well, I'll let the kid explain it. It's over my head."

"The number that Larry's mom messaged on Whats-App, so they wouldn't accidentally give you any more clues about the location tonight, was obviously encrypted."

"Obviously," Walker said. Then he looked at Tim and shrugged.

"So I sent it to Ricky. He's the one who really knows this shi—stuff. Anyway, he was able to find the alternate numbers allocated to the one Larry messaged."

"Layman's terms, kid," Walker said.

"I know where they are doing the Buck Moon sacrifice. I read it right in the text they sent out that excluded Larry. But we have to hurry. They are moving the ceremony from midnight to ten thirty."

Walker checked his phone. It was already nine thirty. Then he looked at Tim. "Shit, it's late. Do you know how to get to where they are doing it?"

"I do. We have time, that's why I wasn't in a rush as soon as you walked in. But I already got the boat prepped. We're ready to roll out right now. I got all your toys down there with mine."

"Plenty of spare ammunition?"

"We're good."

"You think we can get in unseen?" Walker said.

"That's why I waited up here for you. Take a look at

this." Tim stepped over to the bar at the edge of the kitchen. "I keep this map in my boat in case I ever get turned around out on the water." Tim pointed at a tiny green spot in the middle of the blue that was surrounded by the land around the lake. "This is where they're doing it. It's an island, I guess you'd call it. About half a football field long. As you can see here, it's situated back in a cove. Definitely the most remote part of the lake. There are some bald eagles that live in the trees behind it, so it's been designated a conservation area, I think they call it. Can't build anywhere near it, so at night it's pitch black and no one around. Perfect spot for some nut jobs to host a séance, or whatever they're calling it."

"So how will we get to it without being noticed?" Walker said.

"That, my friend, is more your area of expertise."

"Yeah, if I have time to scout it. I've never even seen this place before. And when we get there, it will be dark, right?"

"Unless they do a fire or something, there won't be a single light. But I imagine if the skies stay clear, it's going to be pretty well lit with that full moon. Probably how they like it."

"This is so messed up," Daniel said. "I can't believe this kind of stuff happens and no one knows it goes on. Right under their noses."

"You have no idea," Walker said. "But yeah, I agree."

"I'll get us close on the boat. I've been by this cove a few times over the years. The last house before it goes off limits is probably too far to see, but I can dock there. Hopefully, they won't be using it. I do have to say, though, the one flaw I see in what they are doing is not taking into account how sound travels over water. If they're making very much noise at all, they'll be able to be heard. Maybe no one out around there or awake at that time, but it's a risk."

"That means they'll probably have guards of some sort," Walker said.

"Yeah, but probably nothing more than someone like Larry."

"Never underestimate your enemy. Assassination 101. We'll go in expecting military-grade security. Anything less will be a nice surprise."

"Sounds like a plan," Tim said. "But we'd better get going. Being late isn't an option."

Daniel started packing up his stuff.

"Where do you think you're going?" Walker said.

"I'm going with you guys, okay. This is my sister. I'm—"

"You're not going, and I don't have time to argue with you."

"Come on, man!"

Walker looked at Tim. "You ready?"

"Ready as I'll ever be."

Tim walked toward the basement stairs to go out the sliding doors leading to the dock. Walker was about to follow when his phone began vibrating. He pulled it from his pocket. It was a 423 number, which he recognized as a number local to Soddy Daisy. He was about to ignore the call when he remembered that Ava's cell phone was ruined.

"Hello?"

"Walker. Hey, it's Ava."

It sounded like Ava, but a very weak version.

"Ava, how did you remember my number without your phone."

"I have a numbers thing. I don't forget them even if I've only seen them once."

"That's helpful. You doing okay?"

"Thanks to you, I'm breathing. Sharon told me you were quite worried about me when you brought me in."

"Oh yeah? Nah, I just didn't want carrying you around and you bleeding all over my car's interior to be for nothing."

Ava laughed, but it was followed by a groan of pain. "Don't make me laugh. Doctor's orders."

"A personality like mine can't be tamed."

She laughed again. And groaned again.

"All right, I'll stop. But you're okay?"

"I'm going to make it. The reason I'm calling is because a deputy was in checking on me just a minute ago. Said there was a group of girls dropped off anonymously at the station. You wouldn't happen to know anything about that, would you?"

"It's been a long day."

"Yeah, but it's over now, right?"

Apparently, the deputy hadn't known whether or not Amy and Riley were among the girls Walker had found.

"Amy and Riley are still missing."

"Wait, what? How?"

"They weren't there. The guy holding them made mention that the cult is much bigger than just satanic worship. It's also a pedophilia ring trafficking kids."

"Oh my god. I have to get out of here. You need my help."

"We know where Riley and Amy are being taken. I'm going to get them back. But right now, I have to go. I'm glad you're okay, Ava."

"I—okay. Be careful. And call me as soon as you can."

"I will."

Walker ended the call just as Tim came running back

up the stairs. The color had drained from his face. Walker braced himself.

"My nephew texted," Tim was out of breath. And he was panicked. "He's been trying to text for a half hour, but he couldn't get down from the tree stand to go send it."

"What is it?"

"They've been where we were last night for that long. He said they're all set up. He couldn't get out of the tree because they didn't stop in the field where we saw the fire pit last night. They walked on down past where he was. Down to the creek. They're going to do it there, Walker. Or they may already be finished."

Walker reached behind him and grabbed the keys.

"The guns are all down on the boat!"

"We don't have time," Walker said as he ran past Tim toward the front door. "Call the police, Tim. Get them over to that field right now!"

"Wait! I'm coming—"

Walker slammed the door behind him and ran out to his car. He was inside and in reverse before Tim made it outside to protest. He saw Tim smack the stair rail in anger. It was better this way. Walker didn't have time to worry about anyone else.

He only had time to worry about saving those girls.

38

As soon as Walker made it over to the flagpole that overlooked the land the cult was using to carry out their ceremonies, he understood why Tim's nephew might have been a little caught off guard. He'd expected to see a bunch of cars, but there were none. He wasn't sure how many people were attending, but he imagined, as his car slid to a stop in the gravel, that they must have all come together in some sort of bus and found a way to hide it. He put the car in park, took his spare pistol from the glove box, and jumped out of the car.

Walker raced up the hill, then down over the other side, nearly falling as he went. It wasn't as dark as he thought it might be. As he stayed close to the trees, he looked over his shoulder, and nature's nightlight was shining bright enough to light his path. There were no signs that anyone was around, even as he ran past the field where they'd held their previous meeting. He continued running, heading straight for the trees in front of him.

Walker had no idea how far the creek was from the field. It could have been half a mile. And he didn't know how long ago they had started, but there was a good chance he was already too late. That meant there would be no covert operation to the extraction, only a smash and grab. Which went heavily against how he would normally operate, but he could only play the hand he was dealt.

As he dashed into the trees, he was thinking about how the head of the Satan Is King cult had made a good move using the WhatsApp messenger to throw Walker off. They knew he would attempt to hack their number on the app, and they played it well by trying to get him to go to a different location. And it would have worked if not for Ava's suggestion to put someone on watch. Walker figured the cult must have had a contingency plan in place—a different line of communication—in case something like Walker finding a member's phone happened.

That also led Walker to believe that they would then be smart enough to have at least a couple of shooters at their party. But that didn't really matter to Walker. He was just going to have to wing it once he ran up on their little get-together. If someone pulled a gun on him, he would deal with it then. His only focus was to locate the girls. The rest would just have to be a test of his ability to survive.

As he dashed through the woods, dodging trees and fallen branches, his heart rate was steady. He tuned his ears, trying to find a clue as to which direction to go, but the noise he was making didn't allow him to detect any. He slowed his pace. As much as it pained him, it was necessary. He pulled up to a stop and leaned his shoulder against a tree. Every second he wasted could be the difference between life and death. But a truth he learned long ago is that slow is smooth and smooth is fast.

He listened.

A breeze rustled the leaves above him. Something small

was moving in the grass to his left. Just below that frequency, he heard a hum. He could almost feel its vibration. He tuned out the sounds of nature and pulled in a vibe that was wafting with the wind. It sounded like a group of people. He made out a chant. And it was off to his left.

Walker bolted from the tree. He didn't care if he made noise. In fact, a part of him thought it might interrupt anything they were about to do. He was getting closer. He knew it because now he heard the chant over the noise under his feet. Finally, he saw the first signs of the people he was hunting. Through a break in the trees ahead he saw a red-orange flame flickering, casting light on people standing around it. He was almost there.

Then he heard the sirens.

Walker had asked Tim to call the police. As he ran with all he had to get to Riley and Amy on time, he knew he'd made a mistake.

Walker was at the edge of the trees when he heard one of the people around the fire shout, "The police are coming. We have to leave!"

Walker sprinted into the clearing.

A woman's voice followed, "No! We must continue! Do it now!"

Walker pulled his gun as he ran up on the nightmare. Between the fire and the moon, he could discern a woman standing at the water's edge wearing antlers on her head. Her hands were covered in blood. As he came to a stop and raised his gun, he could see that the fifteen or so people surrounding the fire, looking toward the water, were covered in blood as well.

"Do it, let's finish this!" the woman cried.

Walker looked left of her. He saw the back of someone bent over in the water where the members at the fire were staring; then he saw feet kicking just on the other side of that person in the water.

"Pull her out of the water or I'll shoot!" Walker said as he continued moving toward the fire. The woman with the antlers and the person in the water were only about twenty yards away.

At the sound of Walker's voice, everyone turned to look at the same time. It was like something out of a horror movie that his foster mom, Kim, would sometimes sneak and watch after Jim had passed out in bed. But Walker had to look past them, because the man who was drowning a girl in the creek had turned to look at Walker as well, then swiveled his head to the woman as if seeking her instruction.

"Don't stop! The sacrifice must be made!" The woman turned to the people staring at Walker. "Don't let him interrupt this sacred moment!"

The people moved in unison. They grouped together and blocked Walker's view of the man in the water. His first reaction was to just start shooting. But then his gut chimed in and told him that it would be quicker just to run right through them. So he holstered his gun.

Walker pushed off his back foot and dug forward on the balls of his feet like a sprinter waiting to hear the starting gun. He lowered his shoulder, found the smallest woman he could pick out, then trucked forward with the force of a raging bull. He plowed through the woman, then bounced off the man standing behind her. It kicked him sideways, but he was able to keep his balance and continue moving forward.

The man holding the girl underwater looked back just as Walker dove. There was nowhere for the man to go. Walker connected at his shoulders, wrapped his arms around the man's chest, and took him for a ride as they both slammed into the cold water of the creek. Walker's momentum forced him to let go of the man so he could roll when he hit the water. He popped back up as the man was sitting up. The water was chest high on him. But what Walker really cared about was that the person being held underwater began sitting up. He could hear her gasping for air.

"No! We must finish this!" the lady shouted.

The sirens were close now, but not close enough to help.

As Walker stood, the light from the fire showed that the girl in the water was blindfolded. Walker imagined she was beyond terrified. This made him angry. When he saw the people around the fire move toward her, he was scared for her. The people were just about to enter the water. They were going to kill her. He was just going to have to fire every round he had and then fight whoever was left until the girl could get away. Walker pulled his gun, and just as he raised it to fire, a shotgun blasted and echoed through the trees. The mob stopped when they heard it.

Then he heard Tim Lawson's voice. "Anyone who lays a finger on that girl is getting shot. Now, back away!"

"And I'll shoot from this side," Walker said. "We'll kill you all if we have to."

The antlered woman turned toward Walker. For the first time, he could see her face. And he couldn't believe it when he realized that he knew who she was.

Emily Turnberry.

Amy and Daniel Turnberry's mother.

Walker couldn't believe it. She seemed so worried about Amy when she was at the lake house looking for Daniel. But she knew where Amy was the entire time. Walker didn't see Amy and Daniel's dad at this horror show, so maybe she was putting on an act for him so he would think she had nothing to do with it. What in the hell was happening? Walker was still stunned, but he couldn't let it affect him right then. And before all of it could sink in, Emily ripped the antlers from her head, shouted something Walker didn't understand, and ran into the water toward the girl.

Walker had no choice.

He fired his gun three times, and Emily fell into the water. The man who'd been sitting in the water awaiting instructions jumped up and ran at Walker. Walker hit him so hard in the forehead that it knocked him out instantly, and he face-planted into the creek. Walker grabbed the man by the back of the black robe-like garment he was wearing and began dragging him toward the crowd of people standing at the water's edge.

"Amy, is that you?" Walker said. Her hair was wet, and it was dark, so he couldn't tell for sure if her hair was blond or not.

The girl was sobbing. And shivering. All they had her in was a white dress. She had managed to wiggle the gag out of her mouth. "Yes," she managed.

"You're safe now, okay? No one is going to hurt you."

Walker could see blue and red lights flashing through the trees. He threw the man he'd knocked out onto the ground and looked at everyone staring at him.

"If one of you tries to make a run for it, before the police get here, I'll kill you."

No one said a word. He walked over to Amy. She was sitting up awkwardly because they had her hands tied behind her back. Tim walked up.

"Keep your eye on them, please," Walker said.

Tim nodded and raised his shotgun. "You people make

me sick," he said. His nephew was with him now. He, too, was holding a gun on the crowd.

Walker made it over to Amy. "Amy?" he said. She jumped when she heard his voice so close. "You're okay now. I'm going to pick you up and carry you out of here. Is that all right?"

She was crying again. She nodded. Walker bent down and scooped her up. He could feel her shivering in his arms.

"Are you hurt?"

"No," she sobbed.

"All right. You're okay. Is it okay if I leave your blindfold on? I don't want you to see what I see. I don't want you to have that memory."

Amy nodded; then she threw her arms around his neck.

"Go get her warm, Walker," Tim said. "We've got this."

Walker gave him a nod and plodded out of the creek. He walked right by Amy's mom, facedown in the water, blood running into the creek. He knew that Amy knew it was her mother. A child knows her mother's voice, so he knew that was adding to Amy's sorrow. He was just glad she agreed to keep the blindfold on. He did not want that to be her last memory of her.

As Walker moved around the people, he held her in front of the fire for just a moment. Amy took her hand from Walker's neck and held it out for warmth.

"I need to ask you just one question, Amy. Then I'll let you be. Is that okay?"

She nodded.

"Do you know where Riley Baker is?"

Amy began sobbing again, and she put her arms back around Walker's neck. His stomach dropped.

"I do," she said with a sob. "They hurt her real bad. There was blood everywhere."

Walker's mind flashed to the blood on everyone's hands when they were standing around the fire.

"Is she alive, Amy?"

"I don't know," she said, crying even harder.

"Okay. All right. Will you tell the police where she is when I get you to them."

Amy nodded.

Just then, men in uniform came running down the hill. "Nobody move!"

One man came running directly to him. "Are you David Walker?"

That caught Walker off guard. He wasn't used to hearing himself being called David, and he didn't have any idea why the officer would know who he was.

"I am. This is Amy Turnberry."

"Oh God. That's good news. Detective Bailey said you would be the one with the girl if one was found. Guess she was right."

More officers went running by. All with their guns drawn.

"I just want to get her warm," Walker said. "Can I go?"

"Of course! I'll walk you up. We can take my car to the hospital."

"There's another girl who is hurt. Amy, can you tell him where?"

Amy raised up with a nod. "The basement of Crossroads Ministries Church."

Walker couldn't believe his ears. It made him truly disgusted, and that wasn't easy to do.

The officer spoke into his shoulder radio, telling dispatch to send any available units to the church. Walker nodded forward so the officer would begin leading them out.

Walker patted Amy on the back as he carried her. "I've been working with someone who has been *very* worried about you, Amy."

Amy raised up. She was still crying, but she wanted to hear.

"Your brother, Daniel. He is the reason we found you. He didn't stop until we knew where you were."

Amy sniffled, then a small smile appeared. He would never forget that moment as long as he lived. All the pain and suffering that little girl had been through, and just one mention of someone she loves, fighting for her, and she found joy. Even if it was only for a moment.

Walker vowed to himself, as he carried Amy Turnberry to safety, that he was going to do his best to try to help as many people like Amy as he could. No matter how far he had to go to help them.

That was just what he was born to do.

39

The sun was high in the sky on a hot Saturday afternoon in Soddy Daisy, Tennessee. Lake Chickamauga was buzzing with boats, skiers, jet skis, and every other sort of watercraft lake goers could get in the water. A few days had passed since the night Walker carried Amy Turnberry seemingly out of the clutches of hell itself. It took every one of those days to sift through all the stories, evidence, and he-said-she-said of those violent couple of days.

Soddy Daisy PD was getting a lot of assistance from Chattanooga, and they even brought a couple of experts up from Atlanta to help them sift through all the mess. And it was a huge mess. If it wasn't for Ava going to bat for Walker, and, well, Walker actually saving Amy Turnberry, he might be enjoying his Saturday in a cell instead of lying on his back, on a float, tethered to a dock.

They found out a lot of disturbing things about SIK and its members. Nothing more disturbing than the fact that the mayor's wife, and the mother of the victim, Amy Turnberry, had been running the cult ever since her own father left the business of it to her a decade ago. All that time, her husband and Daniel and Amy had no idea. They just knew there had always been something off about her. Crazy what can go on right in front of you and you never know it.

The best news of the week was that as of yesterday morning, Riley Baker was in stable condition and other than a few scars would make a full physical recovery. Recovering mentally, Walker knew, was going to be a completely different story.

Apparently, after they cut her up and used her blood as part of a ritual, they all boarded a wacko bus and drove over to where Walker found them trying to drown Amy in the creek. That's the reason Tim had been able to find them so quickly. His nephew had messaged where they'd hidden the bus. They ran in to help Walker save the day from there.

The story, of course, due to its wildly sinister nature, made national news. Walker was able to keep his name out of it. Daniel and Tim got most of the recognition along with Detective Ava Bailey, who was recovering quite nicely—and even looked good in her short shorts as she sat on the dock, feet dangling into the water below.

"I'm surprised your toes can even reach the water, Ava," Walker laughed from his float.

"Hardy-har-har, Walker. You don't think by now that I've heard all the short jokes?" Ava said.

"Probably, but you haven't heard them from me."

Tim stepped down on the dock, two ice-cold bourbon and sweet teas in his hand. He reached down and handed one to Walker.

"Have I mentioned just how much I like you, Mr. Lawson?"

Tim grinned as he lit a cigarette. "I'd like me, too, if I kept handing me bourbon." He laughed with a wheeze.

"Only one thing I don't like about you," Walker said.

"Yeah, I know. Save it. I get enough shit from my kids. Speaking of, Abby, Gauge, and Knox should be here in just a bit. They're bringing barbecue."

"Yum," Ava said.

"Ah shit," Tim said. "Sorry, hon. I forgot you can't really eat much yet."

"Oh no. Don't you be sorry. This is getting me back to my high school weight."

They all laughed.

"Has Gauge said how Riley's doing?" Walker said.

"That's where they're coming from. Last night he said she was keeping food down. I hate that for the poor girl. Gauge, he's a good one, though. Likes being there to take care of her."

"Must take after his PopPop," Walker said.

"Nah, he's more like his GiGi, Abby's mother."

"Speaking of Abby's mother," Walker said. "I'm officially homeless come Monday. Chuck and Tammy will be back from their travels then."

"Yeah, I talked to them," Tim said as he took a drink. "Tammy's been worried sick since Abby told her about all of it. I'm leaving for a bit on Monday too. Gonna stay with my boy in Laguna for a couple of weeks."

Walker took a drink. The sweetness tasted good against the salty sweat on his lips. "That's great news."

"What are you going to do, Walker?" Ava said. "Go back to Kentucky?"

"Nah. Not ready to go back there. Not sure what I'm going to do yet."

"Hell, I know what you should do," Tim turned toward him. "My buddy's got a condo in St. Pete Beach on the gulf in Florida. Got a boat there too. Not a bad place to figure out your next move. He's got to be in Knoxville for a while with his mother. She's not doing so good. I know he won't mind if you go down there and look after the place. Throwing him a few bucks worth of rent."

Walker laughed. "Yeah, because house-sitting worked out so well for me this time?"

The three of them laughed.

"Well, that's why I say rent it," Tim said. "Maybe that will change your luck, you freeloader." Tim laughed so hard at his own joke he had a coughing fit.

"Maybe if you promise to come down and show me how to work the boat when you get done at your son's house, I'll think about it."

"Hell yeah, consider it done." Tim said. "I'll find me a snowbird sugar momma at one of those rum shacks on the beach."

Walker laughed picturing Tim hitting on old ladies by asking to bum a lighter.

"I'm gonna run up and help Abby with the food," Tim said. "I'll be right back."

Walker started to paddle over to the dock. "Let me get out here and help you."

"No, no. We got it. Gauge and Knox will do all the lifting."

"You sure?"

Tim waved him off as he walked away.

"If I take Tim's offer, you should come down," Walker said to Ava. "How long you on leave?"

"Forever," Ava said.

"What do you mean?"

"I mean, I don't think I can go back to that job. I'm not cut out for it."

Walker scoffed. "Bullshit. Let me tell you something, no one is cut out for what you went through last week."

"You are."

"Yeah, maybe. But that's because I've been in fires like that since I was fifteen years old. You're good, Ava. If you like it, you should stick with it. They'd be lucky to have you."

"That's kind of you, but I'm just not sure. I like helping people but . . ." Ava trailed off.

"I'm going to go change this bandage," Ava said. "Want another drink?"

"I don't turn down drinks from pretty ladies on sunny days. It's one of my rules."

"Oh, that's one of your rules, is it?"

"No, but it sounded good."

Ava smiled. "Be right back."

That left Walker to himself. The lake water was lapping up against the dock. The first break without a boat going by for a while was happening, so the water below his foam float was nice and calm. Walker laid his head back and let the sun beat down on his face. His right hand was dangling in the cool water. He took a deep breath and enjoyed the warm breeze blowing over him.

He was in a good place.

A few days ago, he would have called someone a liar if they told him he'd be able to enjoy himself again so quickly after such tragic and menacing things just went down. He supposed it was because he had been able to help save some good people. That lessened the burden he'd otherwise be carrying. Hearing that Riley was recovering and Amy was doing well didn't hurt either.

Walker had heard a country song once by Thomas Rhett that said something about when you're in a world full of hate, be a light. He hoped that's what he was to the people he'd come across in Soddy Daisy. Because he really was just repaying a debt to Tim, who had certainly been a light to him. He was hoping that would be the case for many years to come. Walker never would have a father, or really know what it was like to have one, but he imagined that the way Tim made him feel when he talked to him was as close to having a dad as he would ever experience.

Walker couldn't help but smile. Despite all the darkness he'd come across, all he could think of was the light he'd found in Tim.

Walker wanted to be that for someone himself. Maybe he was for Amy and Daniel Turnberry. And maybe if he went down to St. Pete Beach, he could find someone to help there too.

Walker took another drink, hummed the song that gave him his next goal, and floated blissfully on the water as he waited for his friends to come back down to the water.

For the moment . . . life was good.

Pre-order
BLIND PASS
Book 3 in the Tom Walker series
TODAY!

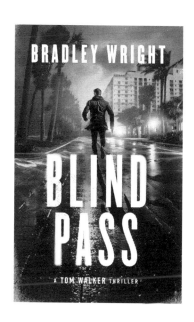

Blind Pass
by
Bradley Wright
Pre-order book three in the
Tom Walker series today!
Coming September 30th

ACKNOWLEDGMENTS

First and foremost, I want to thank you, the reader. I love what I do, and no matter how many people help me along the way, none of it would be possible if you weren't turning the pages.

Thank you to my editor, Deb Hall. You make me look good with the way you turn my inconsistent writing into a legible piece of reading material. I'm forever grateful.

To my family and friends. Thank you for always being there with mountains of support. You all make it easy to dream, and those dreams are what make it into these books. Without you, no fun would be had, much less novels be written.

To my advanced reader team. You continue to help make everything I do better. You all have become friends, and I thank you for catching those last few sneaky typos, and always letting me know when something isn't good enough. Tom Walker appreciates you, and so do I.

About the Author

Bradley Wright is the international bestselling author of espionage and mystery thrillers. HOLY WATER is his twentieth novel. Bradley lives with his family in Lexington, Kentucky. He has always been a fan of great stories, whether it be a song, a movie, a novel, or a binge-worthy television series. Bradley loves interacting with readers on Facebook, Twitter, and via email.

Join the online family:
www.bradleywrightauthor.com
info@bradleywrightauthor.com

Printed in Great Britain
by Amazon